SEPARATE WAYS

ISBN: 978-0-9993861-0-1 (print)

ISBN: 978-0-9993861-1-8 (e-book)

Visit the author's website at www.joshuasrobinson.com

Edited by Debra Burge.

Cover design and back cover photo by Anna Robinson.

SEPARATE WAYS

JOSHUA S. ROBINSON

For Anna

who never let me stop believing
in true love, this story, or myself.

I started looking for you, not knowing
how blind that was.
Lovers don't finally meet somewhere,
they're in each other all along.

Rumi

one

Chloe Sullivan found herself surrounded by water and chaos. She stepped out of the elevator onto a concrete stoop that, for now, remained a foot or so above the flood that covered the basement level of her Brooklyn apartment building. The super and several other men carrying toolboxes splashed past her and shouted at each other in a language Chloe didn't understand.

She stepped down into the icy, ankle-deep water and shivered, wishing she'd thought to remove her shoes or roll up her pant legs, which were now soaked and heavy. When her roommate Madge had called to tell her the basement was flooding, Chloe rushed to the elevator without a thought as to whether or not she was prepared to handle the situation. She took a deep breath to compose herself, then slogged toward the room they used as an art studio.

Madge had commandeered a large work cart and was stacking supplies and paintings onto it as fast as she could. Crimson curls flew about her head as she turned her tall, lanky frame from the shelving unit to the cart and back.

Madge panted, her freckled face twisted with anxiety and exhaustion. "I got all the stuff off the bottom shelves, but I'm worried there's not enough room on the cart for those." She pointed to the far side of the room, where a short rack held at least twenty canvases.

Chloe took mental stock and determined that she had brought several of those paintings with her when she moved to New York. Most of them had adorned the walls of her apartment at one time, and though other pieces had taken their places, she couldn't stand the idea of losing them to the flood. She trudged toward the rack as quickly as she could without splashing water everywhere.

"If you help me," Chloe called to Madge, "I think we can lift the whole thing at once."

Madge joined her, but even together they struggled to carry the rack. The rising water slowed their progress as they tried not to splash the canvases.

"Mondays suck," Madge complained.

"Could be worse," Chloe said between labored breaths. "If you hadn't come down to get something for class, we might not have heard about the leak until it was too late, you know?"

Madge blew a damp piece of hair out of her face. "I guess, but it still sucks."

"Better to get the inevitable disaster out of the way early in the week." The days leading up to an art show opening at Lumina Gallery were always stressful, and while Chloe loved her position as gallery manager, it came with a lot of responsibility. As one of the most respected art dealers in the country, Frederick Lumina commanded high-profile clientele who expected nothing short of exacting professionalism from the gallery staff and dazzling opening galas. Each event took a lot of hard work, but Chloe had been through the process enough times to feel sure things would be perfectly set up for Friday night's opening.

As they neared the door the super came running through, his hair, face, and shirt completely saturated. "You girls need to get out of here," he shouted in a thick accent.

"But I have more paintings in there," Chloe argued. "And supplies, and—"

"I need you out of the way so we can get the heavy sump pump in here." He shooed them toward the elevator. Madge reached for the cart and the super helped Chloe carry the rack. When they reached the stoop, he said, "We'll try to save what we can. Take this to the lobby."

"Can't we put it in our apartment temporarily?" Chloe asked.

The super shook his head. "That wet cart will soak the carpet, and building policy is no paint or chemicals in apartments. I don't need more complaining right now. Leave it in the lobby or get it out of the building. You choose." He shoved the rack into the elevator with Chloe, Madge, and the work cart, then pushed the button for the lobby level and pulled his arm back.

The doors closed and the car began moving upward. Madge and Chloe leaned back against the wall, both of them panting, soaked from the bottom with water and the top from sweat.

"What do we do now?" Madge asked. "I don't want to leave our stuff in the lobby."

"We could just leave the supplies and carry the paintings up a few at a time," Chloe thought out loud.

"That'll take forever, Mrs. S," Madge whined. Despite the fact they'd been living together more than two years and had gotten to be pretty good friends, Madge still refused to call Chloe by her first name. It was an almost constant reminder of the seventeen-year age difference between them, but Madge's endearing "Mrs. S" had grown on Chloe over time. Even though she had declared David legally deceased two years ago and technically he wasn't her husband anymore, Chloe still preferred to be called Mrs. Sullivan, rather than Miss or Ms.

Chloe closed her eyes tightly and threw her head back in frustration. She didn't have time for this. Friday's opening was to feature art by Richard Harlin, who hated unexpected issues and schedule changes. Since he and Chloe had been seeing each other for a little over a year, she hoped Richard would forgive her tardiness. She should have been on her way to the gallery by now to meet the box truck and pick up Richard's artwork from his personal studio. Her eyes shot open at the thought.

"I have an idea." She pulled out her cell phone. "I'll call the truck that was supposed to meet me at the gallery. Hopefully Fred won't mind if we leave our things there for a few days." Fred had never taken issue with personal favors in the year and a half she'd worked for him, but Chloe still hated to ask.

"Think you can drop me at school on the way?" Madge asked. "I need to take a few of these to class anyway."

"I don't see why not." Chloe mentally mapped a route to the Upper East Side that would take them past the art school Madge attended. "I can handle unloading the rest at the gallery." She dialed the driver's number and held the phone to her ear.

Chloe unloaded the last of her paintings from the box truck and carried it into the Lumina Gallery's storage room. All the canvases she and Madge had rescued miraculously escaped damage, and Chloe didn't worry much about the ones she left behind. Most of those were attempts at expanding her subject matter or techniques, experiments prompted by Richard that Chloe acknowledged were valuable experience but nowhere near the quality or importance of her landscapes.

She set the painting down and stared into it while she caught her breath. Chloe was especially glad they'd saved it and the other scenes piled on the rack from the back of the studio, paintings she had done in the years between David's disappearance and coming to New York. On this particular canvas, a rushing stream, swollen from the spring thaw, cascaded over smooth stones between still-bare trees, casting both a fine mist and steady roar into crisp air that still smelled of snow.

Chloe remembered her focus then, her determination to push herself through the loneliness and despair, to paint herself whole again. Pride swelled in her even as she wondered, as she did from time to time, if this painting would have been the same or even existed had David not vanished. After searching for him nearly three and a half years and accumulating staggering debts, she had sold their house in Morgantown, West Virginia, and moved back in with her parents in Stroudsburg, Pennsylvania. On weekends, she hiked around the Pocono

Mountains and painted some of her favorite places. When the terrain precluded carrying an easel, she took photographs or sketched with colored pencils, then recreated the scenes on canvas later. Her creativity reawakened, sparking a fire from the ashes of her life with David to illuminate the path forward.

She didn't think about him as much as she used to, though the late October chill and shortening days reminded her that the anniversary of David's disappearance was close. October twenty-seventh had also been their wedding anniversary, and this year it happened to fall on Friday, the same day as Richard's opening.

She took a deep breath and let the thought go, replacing it with the mental list of what she needed to accomplish that morning. Her little disaster had already delayed picking up Richard's work, though not by more than an hour. Before she left to do that, Chloe needed to check the gallery space to ensure the temporary partition walls were put in place over the weekend, and that the room had been properly cleaned up.

Chloe jumped when Fred called to her from the entrance to the storage area. She didn't expect to see him, as his Monday mornings were typically filled with meetings at his other ventures. His long, confident strides covered the gap between them quickly. Fit, handsome, and radiating charisma, Fred almost always dressed in a tailored designer suit, though this morning his top button was undone, the necktie lost somewhere. He had the bright smile and well-styled blond hair of a man in his late twenties, though his laugh lines and a few small creases near his eyes gave away that he was actually three decades older.

"I'm sorry about what happened this morning," Fred said. "You know, I probably could find some better studio space for you and your roommate. Why didn't you ever ask me?"

Chloe looked away. Fred was well-connected and dealt in real estate all over Manhattan, mostly places far beyond what Chloe and Madge could afford. While he would almost certainly cut her a deal, Chloe couldn't bring herself to accept such generosity. It had been hard enough to ask about storing her paintings at the gallery. "You know I don't like asking for favors—"

"Yes, yes," he said, waving her off. "I wouldn't want to damage your pride. Just know that the offer's always on the table. So, did you get everything out of there?"

"Almost everything, yeah," Chloe said. "Sorry again for the chaos. I promise this won't put us too far behind..."

She trailed off as Fred brushed past her, apparently more interested in the painting Chloe had just brought in than her apology. He picked up the canvas and examined it. "This is your work?"

"Yeah." Chloe inhaled sharply and braced herself for criticism. She had always doubted her work would be anything but pedestrian to Fred, whose gallery regularly featured some of the world's best artists. Based on the exhibits Chloe had managed, he seemed to prefer more avant-garde work like Richard's, bold mixed media full of social commentary that awed as much as it disturbed. She awaited the verdict, unable to tell if he was enthralled by the rushing Pocono stream or stalling to find the most polite way to let her down.

After what felt like an eternity, Fred grinned at Chloe over his shoulder. "This is incredible. I love it!"

Chloe blinked, unsure whether or not to trust what she'd just heard. "What? Really?"

"You've got just the perfect level of detail here, not too realistic but not too abstract, either." He turned back to the canvas. "I feel the scene more than I see it, and that's a rare gift. There's loneliness but hope, like you were trying to move on from a painful memory when you painted this."

Chloe's heart pounded. She couldn't believe Frederick Lumina identified so clearly with the emotion in her work. Her parents had said her paintings were good, Madge had praised them, and even Richard, who guarded his emotions and rejected sentimentality, had noted there was more to them than the scenery they depicted. She stood flabbergasted as Fred studied canvas after canvas, growing more excited with each piece.

"Why on Earth haven't you shown these to me before?" Fred turned back toward Chloe with an astonished look on his face. "This is some of the finest work I've seen in years. You've been holding out on me!"

"I didn't think they were your style," Chloe said. "They're just landscapes."

"Just landscapes?" Fred cocked an eyebrow at her. "You're too modest for your own good. You know as well as I do these are more than 'just landscapes.' They're stories, powerful moments in time, your memoir told through brush strokes." He sighed. "I've met artists like you before, though. You're smart, you recognize other talent, and you know the business, but you don't see the same value in your own work."

Chloe blushed. Fred had a tendency to get worked up about pieces or artists that struck him, but she never thought she'd be one of them.

"Have you shown these anywhere?" he asked. "Have you sold any or made prints? Shopped them to other galleries or collectors?"

Chloe took a deep breath in an effort to control her excitement and disbelief. She had heard him ask those same questions to other artists he scouted for the gallery. "No, I haven't done any shows or sold anything from that series." Saying the words out loud made her wonder why she hadn't. The only pieces she'd shopped around were painted after she moved to New York, and they hadn't been received very well.

Fred broke into a wide grin. "Excellent. We're going to show them here, as soon as possible."

"Really?" Chloe's heart raced and her breath caught in her throat. "I mean, of course! I'd love to do a show for you."

"Do you have more?"

Chloe hesitated, thinking. She'd rescued the best pieces from the basement, and a few still hung in her apartment. Most of her past work was still at her parents' house, stacked floor to ceiling in her bedroom closet, leaning against her dresser, and covering the walls. As she pictured the space, one painting jumped to the forefront. It hung above the headboard of her bed and depicted an old brick building on the windy autumn day she'd first met David. Chloe winced and fought against the flood of memories.

"What is it?" Fred asked.

"Sorry, it's been a rough morning," she answered, dodging the real subject. "I have lots more paintings, but they're all over the place thematically. There are maybe five or six more from that series."

Fred frowned. "That's not quite enough to fill the gallery, but I don't want to wait. We've been without a landscape artist of your talent for over a decade and I want to get a jump on this." He paced back and forth for a moment, then asked, "What about the east wing? How long until it's ready?"

Chloe had been supervising the remodel of an adjacent space that Fred intended to use for smaller exhibits. Between her father's talk about his construction business and the DIY shows she watched, she practically considered herself an expert even though she'd only occasionally picked up a tool. "We paused work on the expansion to get ready for Richard's show," Chloe said. "If we build according to plan, there's another month or so of construction and finishing work left."

"And if we cut corners?"

Chloe took a deep breath and thought out loud, "We could lay a manufactured floor over the hardwood instead of refinishing it. That would probably save a week. The electrical's roughed in, but still needs to be inspected. If we could get that done, the perimeter walls could be finished with paint in a few days. The reconfigurable walls for the interior of the space are backordered and aren't due for another three weeks, but we could probably repurpose some of the main gallery partitions in a pinch."

Fred grinned. "So, what you're saying is that it could be done by this Friday."

Chloe wasn't sure she had said *that*, but he didn't give her time to object.

"Good. Get a crew in here today, as soon as possible. Work them overtime, whatever it takes." Fred put his hands on Chloe's shoulders and beamed at her. "You are going to have your debut this Friday. Richard will draw a huge crowd, so it will be the perfect time for the east wing's grand opening. It's too late to properly market you, but I'll call a few collectors I know who would love your work."

Fred continued talking as he walked past her, but Chloe tuned him out as she tried to wrap her mind around what had just happened. She was going to debut her art, paintings she had made with her own hands, during a grand opening gala at the internationally recognized Lumina Gallery. Tears welled in her eyes. Her lifelong dream was finally within reach.

"Hey, Chloe," Fred called. "Come on, there's lots to do!"

She wiped her eyes and turned to follow Fred out of the storage room. Nothing in the world could stop her now.

two

Chloe rode in the passenger seat of the box truck as it pulled up to Richard's studio, which occupied the entire ground floor of an old four-story brick building in Hell's Kitchen. Her adrenaline was still racing from Fred's praise of her paintings, even though she had negotiated with contractors all the way there, tablet computer in her lap, making lists and notes and cost calculations. Despite the fact that her workload for the week had multiplied, Chloe eagerly accepted each task as one step closer to something she had wanted since she was very, very young.

It would have been far easier to let the driver handle loading Richard's pieces so Chloe could stay at the gallery and ramp up the construction work, but Fred insisted that his gallery manager supervise all pickups personally. If it had been anyone but Richard, she might have tried harder to convince her employer to make an exception.

He was waiting outside when the truck came to a stop. Richard leaned against the building, arms crossed, wearing dark skinny jeans, sandals, and a sleeveless shirt despite the chilly late October weather. His face showed no expression, his chestnut eyes stared blankly, and his mouth made a flat line behind his well-trimmed goatee.

Chloe got out of the truck and greeted him with a kiss. "Aren't you cold?"

Richard shrugged. "It's a meditation exercise. I had to fill my time with something productive since you changed the schedule on me. You know I don't like that."

"I know," she said, blowing off his complaint. "I have a surprise for you, though." A gust of wind cut through Chloe and she shivered, though Richard remained stoic. "Let's go inside," she suggested.

Richard led Chloe into the studio, a much larger and well-maintained space than Chloe and Madge's basement. It even had a storefront that sold prints, art books, and recreations of Richard's sculptures. Beyond that was a large open space where he did most of his work. Paint and plaster had left the concrete floor stained and uneven, and his supplies filled several cabinets. A few small, wheeled carts were piled with supplies, too, but they were pushed to the side since Richard wasn't working on a piece at the moment.

He showed the truck driver to a side room where his pieces for the opening were packed and ready for transport. Chloe double-checked the list and scanned over the parcels, then instructed the driver to begin loading. She and Richard stepped back out into the studio, where she told him about the water leak and having to take her own work to the gallery, Fred's excitement over her paintings, and his idea of doing a double opening.

"It will be a lot of work," Chloe said, "but can you believe we'll finally get to do a show together?"

Richard didn't react right away, and Chloe feared he might be upset about having this dropped on him at the last minute. He hated surprises, especially the week before an opening, but this was such good news she figured he'd make an exception.

"So Lumina liked your older work?" Richard asked. "Personally, I think your newer paintings show a lot more promise. What did he say about those?"

Chloe hesitated. She didn't care as much for her most recent work, and she didn't want to tell him that most of those hadn't made it out of the basement. "Well, there weren't as many of those. Between what I have here and at my parents' house, there are enough of the Pocono landscapes to fill the east wing."

Richard squinted at her, and Chloe couldn't tell if he'd seen though her excuse. "Don't let Lumina pressure you into debuting in the east wing. If you want to wait and create more pieces so you can use the main gallery space, you should do that."

Chloe crossed her arms. "Are you trying to talk me out of this?"

"No, of course not." Richard rolled his eyes. "I just don't want you to get so overeager that you jump into this without considering all the options. Your first opening can have a huge impact on your career."

Chloe took a deep breath. While she wished he were happier for her, Richard did have a point. "Even if it is the east wing, it's still Lumina Gallery, you know? Plus, there will be some big collectors there for your show and getting my work in front of them could be huge. I think it's the right call."

Richard stared at her a moment before a smile finally broke across his face. "All right then, let's do it. But first, I have another painting you need to see."

Richard led Chloe back to the apartment beyond the studio, where he stayed when work consumed him. There was little in the way of furniture, giving the space more of a hotel room vibe. A king-sized bed and armoire occupied one side of the space, separated by a folding curtain. A black leather couch, the matching recliner, and a coffee table provided a basic seating area. Along the back wall, a small wet bar served as a kitchenette, including a coffee maker and microwave. An easel stood beside the couch, a sheet covering it.

"This is a very special piece," Richard said. "I want to show it Friday, and given the circumstances it might even be a centerpiece."

Chloe cocked an eyebrow at him jokingly. "We'll see about that."

Richard grinned and pulled the cover off the easel to reveal a canvas covered in swaths of color that swirled in a way that felt incredibly familiar yet unknown, like a photograph of a favorite landmark blurred by fog on the lens. Darks and lights came together in unexpected ways, and there seemed to be a story to it if she followed the lines just right. She was overcome by memories of home, of David, of the empty years looking for him, of moving to the city, of meeting Fred, of her relationship with Richard. It took her breath away.

"I call it *Chloe's Journey*," Richard said proudly. "Did you notice the canvas? It's the same kind you use. I tried to emulate your brush patterns and duplicate your palette, too."

"It's incredible." Chloe could barely breathe the words. Somehow, he had captured in abstract the same style as her landscapes, weaving together tones and techniques from those paintings to evoke stories from her past. While others wouldn't see the same memories, the piece spun a tale of love, loss, and redemption that gave it a universal beauty. It embodied Chloe's favorite themes, ones Richard tended to shy away from.

Richard put his arms around her. "I wanted to capture the essence of how you created a new life for yourself. I remembered it was around this time last year you were dwelling on the past, and this was the best way I could show you that I believe you have a bright future." He chuckled and added, "I guess Lumina beat me to the punchline though. Oh well, that might increase the asking price a little."

Chloe pulled out of his embrace and turned to him. "You're going to sell it?"

Richard shrugged. "Of course. Why wouldn't I?"

Chloe's face flushed as the bliss the painting had brought her fell away into disappointment. "I assumed it was a gift."

"Oh." He seemed genuinely surprised at Chloe's assumption. "Well, I suppose you can have it if you want, but you know I don't like my own work hanging in my apartment."

Chloe cocked her head to the side. "Why would I hang it in your apartment and not mine?"

"Well, I was hoping you would consider making my apartment your apartment."

"Are you trying to sell me your apartment?" Chloe asked, confused.

Richard laughed. "No, I want you to move in with me. I know I'm not the best at this relationship stuff, but we've been together more than a year now and I think I'm ready to take the next step."

"I don't know what to say." Chloe had never considered moving in with Richard as a possibility. Before they started seeing each other, he had developed a reputation for being a playboy. He didn't believe in marriage and she wasn't sure she could be a wife again anyway.

"At least think about it," Richard said. "You obviously need new studio space, too, and there's plenty here to share. There's no rush, though. We can talk more about it after the opening, but I want you to know I'm serious about this. And if you don't want me to sell the painting, I can hold off on that, too."

Chloe appreciated that he didn't want an immediate answer, as it had already been an eventful day and it wasn't even noon. She was about to kiss Richard when her phone rang. Thinking it could be Fred or one of the contractors, she pulled it from her purse and looked at the caller ID. Emma Rogers.

Chloe rolled her eyes and held her phone so Richard could see the screen. She did need to talk to Emma, but now wasn't the time. Chloe declined the call.

"That's the lawyer, right?" Richard asked. "Your ex's best friend or something?"

Chloe nodded. "She's probably just calling to check in. Terrible timing, as usual."

As soon as she said that, her phone rang. Emma again. Chloe intended to decline this call as well, but Richard advised that she take it. "If I remember your stories about Emma right, she won't stop calling until you talk to her. It might even be important."

Chloe kissed him and answered the phone. "Hello?"

"Good morning," came the response in Emma's trademark measured tone. "So nice of you to take my call."

Chloe already regretted doing so. "I'm in the middle of something right now. Can I call you back later?"

Emma sighed. "I apologize for the inconvenience, but I assure you that what I need to discuss is, in all likelihood, far more important than anything I may have interrupted."

The gravity in Emma's voice pulled Chloe in. A twinge of fear shot from her stomach outward to her hands, feet, and head. She swallowed. "I'm listening."

"Are you sitting down?"

The fact that Emma had asked such a question was enough to make Chloe's knees feel weak. She sat on the sofa while her mind spun, trying in vain to enumerate the possibilities of what Emma might say. "Go ahead," Chloe said, her voice cracking.

Emma took a deep breath. "I found David."

three

Emma's words danced around Chloe's brain. They teased her and kept their full weight hidden for a split second before pummeling her right in the chest. Her vision blurred and her head spun and her whole body felt like it was about to buckle. Chloe leaned against the back of the sofa, panting, her heart racing.

Emma found David. Had she heard it correctly? Chloe attempted to speak, but her parched throat wouldn't allow it.

"Chloe? Are you all right? Chloe?" Emma's voice sounded distant and hollow, like she was speaking through a tunnel.

Chloe stammered a few unintelligible syllables, but couldn't pull her disparate thoughts into words.

"What's happening? What's wrong?" Richard stared at her, but she couldn't make out his expression. His hand passed back and forth before her, and a cool breeze licked at her face.

Chloe waved her hand in front of her throat and tried to ask for water, but her voice was barely audible. She tried to swallow but that only irritated her throat more.

"Do you need something to drink?" Richard asked.

She managed a nod.

"Are you still there, Chloe?" Emma asked. "I'm not hanging up. Stop trying to speak and take a moment to recover from the shock. Focus on breathing, nice and slow."

Richard pulled Chloe's phone from her trembling hand, which immediately dropped to her side. The sudden motion jarred her enough that she regained a little control over herself.

She blinked hard several times and tried to breathe more slowly. Her vision cleared and she watched Richard walk to the sink, fill a glass, and carry it back to her.

He pressed the cool glass gently against her bottom lip. "Here, take a sip."

Chloe sucked in a small amount of water, not nearly enough to alleviate the dryness in her throat. She tried to drink more but Richard pulled the glass away.

"Easy, easy," he said. "Just a little at a time."

Chloe nodded, then took another sip of water. Her mind cleared enough to return her thoughts to Emma's unbelievable news, and a sudden sense of urgency gripped her.

"Emma?" She looked around. "Where's my phone?"

"I've got it." Richard held the phone out and Chloe carefully grasped it and pressed it against her ear.

"Where is he?" Chloe asked.

Emma chuckled. "I told you to sit down. Are you sure you're all right?"

Chloe took a deep breath. "Yeah, I mean, as all right as I can be."

"Well, don't be embarrassed. I had nearly the same reaction when he called me this morning," Emma said.

"What happened? Is he okay? Where was he? Is he with you?"

"Chloe, slow down. First of all, I believe David is fine for the most part. He seems to be suffering from some sort of partial amnesia, but as far as I can determine he is physically unharmed."

Chloe let the words replay in her mind, attempting to pick out the important parts from Emma's awkward and overly proper wording. "Amnesia?"

"He can't recall anything from the time he's been missing," Emma explained. "He remembers everything prior to that, up until he went outside to investigate a strange noise in the early morning hours of your fifth wedding anniversary."

Chloe thought back to the morning she'd woken up without him, ten years ago. She had searched and called everyone she knew trying to find her husband. Her breathing quickened at the memory. Richard sat next to her and rubbed her leg, but it did little to comfort her.

"He awoke on the front lawn of your old house this morning," Emma continued. "He claims to have no idea how he arrived there. The new owners of the house called the police, and because my number was the first listed on his file, they called me. I..." Emma's voice became softer. "I'm embarrassed to admit I didn't even recognize his voice."

Chloe sympathized with Emma and wondered if she would know David's voice if he called her on the phone. She tried to imagine the sound of it, but couldn't focus. "Where is he now? Can I talk to him?"

"We're at my apartment. David is in the shower. I bought him some clothes and made him an appointment with a neurologist this afternoon. I'm no expert, but I don't think the two of you should talk until we further assess David's mental state."

"You can't be serious," Chloe said.

"It's merely a temporary precaution," Emma said. "Once the doctor clears him, I'm certain you'll be the first person he wants to speak with. I assured him that you are well, and I told him you live in New York, but nothing further."

"I want to talk to him now," Chloe protested.

"I told you, he's in the shower."

"Then get him out of the shower!" Chloe stood, a rush of adrenaline coursing through her. "Damn it, Emma, you can't just tell me that you found David and he's with you and then not let me talk to him!"

"Did you say she found David?" Richard stood beside her.

Emma's voice remained steady. "I understand that you're upset, but—"

"But nothing! I want to talk to David, now." Tears welled in Chloe's eyes even as her irritation with Emma grew. "Please don't do this to me."

"Hey." Richard grasped Chloe's shoulder. "What is going

on? Did you say—?"

Chloe raised her free hand to silence him, then wiped her eyes. It wasn't fair. She needed to hear his voice, to know he hadn't forgotten her, and, more importantly, to know she hadn't forgotten him.

Emma sighed heavily. "I'm sorry, Chloe, but we have to consider what's best for David's well-being right now. You of all people should remember his anxiety issues."

The fire in Chloe's chest cooled a little as memories of David's past episodes returned to her. He'd had difficulty with occasional panic attacks as long as she'd known him, some of them quite severe. Given the shocking nature of the situation, Chloe reluctantly conceded that Emma was probably right. Still, it hurt so much to know that David was right there, within reach, within speaking distance for the first time in a decade, and yet she remained cut off from him.

As if sensing her pain, Emma spoke up. "Hold on, I have an idea." Chloe heard some movement followed by a barely perceptible click. Emma whispered, "I've opened the bathroom door just enough to hold the end of my phone inside. He won't be able to hear you, but you can listen."

Chloe strained her hearing and tried to visualize Emma's condo, a place she'd visited several times before but now struggled to recall any and every detail she possibly could. The sound of running water came through the earpiece, and then, starting muffled and growing louder, a man's voice echoed around the tiled bathroom.

He was singing. It only took Chloe a second to recognize David's voice, singing without music The Pretenders' "I'll Stand by You," one of their favorites. He'd sung it to her over the phone when she returned home during the summer between their freshman and sophomore years of college. They'd played it at their wedding and engraved the title inside the rings they exchanged that day. Chloe wanted to sing along with him, but her voice caught in her throat. She covered her mouth with her hand and tears flowed freely from her eyes.

It was really him.

David's voice faded and Emma came back on the phone. "How was that?"

"I can't believe it," Chloe sobbed. "He's really back." Suddenly an intense urge to act flowed through her. "I have to get down there. I need to see him."

"Get down where? You can't go anywhere right now," Richard said. Chloe continued to ignore him, too focused on her conversation with Emma.

"Of course," Emma said. "But do take your time. I've no idea how long we'll be at the hospital, so finish whatever it is you're busy doing."

Emma's words gave Chloe pause. What was she busy doing again? She looked toward Richard, who seemed agitated, and it all came rushing back to her. She had to prepare for his show. She had to supervise the completion of the east wing. She was supposed to have her own opening.

As happy as she was that David had been found, Chloe felt torn between her obligation to him and her opportunity to finally have a real art career. Giving up her debut simply wasn't an option, but she couldn't ignore the situation with David, either. Somehow, she would have to find a way to do both.

"I'll be there as soon as I can," Chloe said.

"Let me know your travel plans as soon as you have them established," Emma said.

Chloe agreed and hung up the phone. Richard grabbed her upper arm and gave it a gentle shake to get her attention.

"Okay, what the hell is happening?" Anger creased Richard's face. "What did you say about David and going someplace?"

Chloe blinked and tried to focus on Richard, her face frozen in disbelief. "He's alive." Her mind spun, trying to reconcile what had just happened with everything she needed to accomplish, and she gave voice to the only clear thought. "I have to go."

"Chloe, hang on," Richard's tone carried a slight edge,

though his expression had returned to neutral. He took her hand in both of his and stared into her eyes. "Take a breath, then back up and tell me what happened."

Chloe's mind raced through memories of David, fragments fitfully arranging themselves into a presence, a feeling that a hole in her world had suddenly been filled. She took a deep breath and focused on the words as she said, "Emma found David. He woke up this morning in Morgantown, in front of the house where we used to live."

"In Virginia?"

"West Virginia," Chloe corrected. "That's where he and Emma are originally from, and where I went to college."

Richard crossed his arms. "How did he end up there?"

Chloe shook her head. "He doesn't know. Emma said he couldn't remember anything since he disappeared."

"Like some kind of selective amnesia?" Richard har-rumphed. "How convenient."

"I have to go see him," Chloe insisted. She began mentally shifting her schedule, wondering how soon she could get a flight. Morgantown had a small airport, but Chloe guessed she'd be better off to fly into Pittsburgh, then rent a car and make the ninety-minute drive south.

A twitch of irritation broke through Richard's stoic expression. "You can't go anywhere right now. You have to finish setting up my show. Plus, you have your own big opportunity, remember? You can't just throw that away."

"I know," she said. "I'm not. But I have to deal with this. He was my husband, you know?"

"I can't let you do this." Richard took her hands in his. "You've worked too hard and endured too much to be pulled away by a guy who left you." Chloe started to protest, but Richard kept going. "I know you think something terrible happened to him, that he didn't just walk away, but listen to reason. He was gone all this time, and now suddenly he reappears and can't remember anything?" He squeezed her hand. "You deserve better. You have better. Let Emma deal with David.

Don't let them take you away from the life you've built here."

Chloe shook her head. "It isn't that simple. I was only able to move on because I accepted that I'd probably never see David again. I mean, I still hoped I would, but I accepted that chances were slim, you know? But I just heard his voice; I know he's out there." Her lip trembled and her eyes misted. "How could I live with myself if I just ignored him after all this time?"

"So, what, all this is just over?" Richard looked away, incredulous. "Your job at the gallery, your art, us...this guy shows up and suddenly none of that matters?"

Chloe put her hand on his cheek and turned him back to her. "No, of course not." She kissed him softly and stared into his eyes. "This is my life now. I'm sure I'll always love David in some way, but I promise I'm not going to drop everything and get back together with him. I just need some closure. I need to know what happened to him and I need to make sure he's okay."

Richard didn't look convinced. "That's all nice to hear, but do you have to go right now, with so much happening here? Would you really risk your debut? It isn't fair."

Chloe shrugged. "Life isn't fair," she said, borrowing one of her father's favorite lines. She turned so she could see Richard's painting, wondering what colors and strokes could possibly represent that morning's events in *Chloe's Journey*. She was still on that journey, still standing in the face of everything, still chasing her dream, still moving forward. Conviction rose in her, pushing aside the doubt, confusion, and stress. Not even something as huge as David's reappearance could get in her way now.

She turned back to Richard with a confident smile. "I can do this. I can go check on David and be back in time for the opening. I can leave detailed instructions and coordinate things over the phone."

Richard stared at her, his face neutral. He looked at her the way he looked at people in public, studying, distant. "This is a lot to take on. I still don't think you should go. You don't have to do everything yourself."

"I have to go," Chloe said, resolute and calm even as her heart raced. "I will find a way to make this happen. And this," she indicated the painting, "is going at the east wing entrance, right between our two shows."

Richard broke his stoicism and embraced her. "Lumina isn't going to be happy about this." He kissed her on the forehead, his beard bristling against her skin. "I'm not happy about it, either."

Chloe sighed. "Look, I know it's outside of your comfort zone and you hate dealing with surprises, but this is something I have to do." She leaned away from Richard so she could look him in the eyes. "I need you to trust me. I need to know you're on my side."

Richard held her gaze for a long moment. "I still think this is a mistake, but I trust you. I'll do what I can to help while you're gone."

Chloe giggled. It was a flimsy commitment, but at least he was trying. "See? You're not so bad at this relationship stuff," she teased, then gave him a firm kiss on the mouth.

They held each other in a tight squeeze, then Richard pulled away. He turned and picked up *Chloe's Journey*. "I'd better get this packed up," he said, then carried the painting out of the apartment toward the main workspace.

Chloe hesitated a moment before following, trying to read Richard's reaction. She feared she had hurt or scared him, and she wished he would talk with her about how he felt instead of distancing himself and making unhelpful comments. He only seemed to release those emotions when he created, loosing an intense flurry into his art that had brought him fame and success. It was just how he operated, and Chloe resigned herself to the fact that she had gotten as much support from him as she was going to.

She took a deep breath and shook off those thoughts. Richard would be fine. Chloe worried more about how she was going to explain to Fred that she had to leave town as soon as possible.

four

Chloe stood in the gallery office and watched Fred pace. "I don't like this," he said. "I'm sympathetic, I am, but I also have a major event this Friday and I don't feel comfortable letting my gallery manager leave town."

"The timing couldn't be worse." Chloe's heart pounded and she tried to steady her breathing. The confidence she'd mustered before leaving Richard's had dissipated in her employer's presence.

Fred stopped pacing and gave her an intense stare. "He's been missing how long again?"

"It will be ten years Friday."

"Ten years," Fred repeated. "What's another week?"

It was a fair question, but Chloe was ready for it. "I'm worried about him. I'm afraid I won't be able to focus until I take care of this."

Fred shook his head and sighed. "That's understandable, I suppose, but what do you suggest we do? Leave Conner in charge of setting up the opening?"

Chloe bit her lip. Conner, the only other full-time staff at the gallery, was just an associate. Though competent, he had little experience with anything other than sales and occasionally assisting Chloe with shipping and inventory. "I can leave him very detailed instructions, and I'll only be a phone call away."

"If we were just setting up a single exhibition, I would have no reservations about that," Fred said. "But you said yourself that getting the east wing finished is going to be a huge effort. I can't see how it will get done without you here."

"I can handle it," Chloe said, even as she began to doubt it herself.

"There are thousands of artists in this city. Any one of them would trade everything they had for an opportunity like the one I'm giving you. Look at this." Fred picked up a paper from his desk. "I've already wasted an hour putting this press release together."

Chloe shook her head, confused. "How is that wasted—?"

"Because I'm not going to make a fool of myself promising a dual opening and failing to deliver." He slammed the page back onto the desk.

"I'm going to get it done," Chloe insisted.

"I believe you will work as hard as you possibly can, but I can't risk my reputation on that." Fred rubbed at his temples. "I had complete confidence in the idea earlier, but if this release goes out, there's no going back. Any number of things could happen, Chloe. Your return flight could be delayed, or you could have a medical emergency, or you could see this long-lost husband of yours and decide not to come back at all."

"No, Fred, I promise—"

He held up his hand to stop her. "Did this man know about your ambitions? Did he support your creativity?"

Chloe nodded. "Yes, of course he did." David supported her in everything except living in New York, she amended internally, but tried to push those thoughts away.

"Then wouldn't he understand that you have the opportunity of a lifetime here?" Fred asked. "Wouldn't he want you to succeed?"

Chloe felt like a deer in headlights under Fred's intense stare. He was right, leaving town and introducing any more risk to the situation was crazy. Her rational mind clashed with specters of the years following David's disappearance, when she had searched and worried and followed every lead clutching desperately to the smallest shard of hope. That version of her demanded answers.

"He isn't making me go," Chloe said. "I am. I can't concentrate knowing he's back, after everything I went through trying to find him."

Fred crossed his arms. "That's your decision then?"

Chloe took a deep breath. "Yes. I have to do this."

"And what about the opening? I'm not going to submit that press release unless you stay."

Chloe thought a moment. "That's okay. Richard's going to draw a crowd anyway, and while some of them are fans of his particular style, most of the guests are coming to socialize or because they just like art in general. So demographically, I'm not worried about it."

An idea formed in her head, and Chloe played to Fred's sense of showmanship. "What we could do is have a big surprise reveal. No press release. Put a curtain in front of the east wing entrance and drop it just before the show starts. We could even make it a drop cloth or something, so people would think it was still under construction when they arrived. That way all the risk is on me. If I don't get the expansion done, I don't get my co-opening with Richard, but you haven't promised anything. But when I do get it done, we'll be able to make it a major event that people will really talk about."

Fred rubbed his chin. "A surprise like that would certainly increase post-opening talk, and might draw more people to later events. You may not make as many sales opening night, but could sell out soon after. Okay, I like it. I may even extend some invitations to collectors who might be interested in your work but not Richard's, and if they show up we'll have to give them something if the east wing isn't done. Would you mind having a private, informal viewing for those people?"

"Not at all," Chloe said. "I don't think we'll need to, but I'm more than willing to accommodate."

"As you should be." Fred smiled at her. "Nice pitch. I knew I hired you for a reason."

Chloe sat in a daze the entire ride from Manhattan to Brooklyn, staring out the window as the city moved past and around her, shadows soft beneath an overcast, grey sky. It had taken her years to move past David's disappearance and get here, and she had wondered before if she could only have this life because he wasn't in it. This time, the guilt that crept into her stomach was a little bit harder to bear.

The cold October wind slapped at Chloe's face as she stepped out of the taxi in front of her apartment building, her physical discomfort stealing focus from the questions and worries taking root in her mind. While she rode the elevator upward, memories of Richard's concern and Fred's doubts crept back into her thoughts to chip away at her confidence.

Madge hurried into the room as Chloe stepped into the apartment, nearly knocking her over. "Oh, Mrs. S! I wasn't expecting you back so soon. Is something wrong?"

"Well, um," Chloe stammered. Her conversation with Emma seemed like weeks ago, and her mind had been so lost elsewhere that she hardly knew where to begin. "Sorry, I need a minute."

Madge's freckled face took on a concerned expression. "Are you okay, Mrs. S?"

"Yeah, fine," Chloe replied, smiling a little to try and reassure her. "I've just got a lot on my mind, that's all." She shook her head and tried to change the subject. "How was everything at school this morning?"

Madge shrugged. "My professor liked a lot of the stuff we brought from the basement, and I have a little exhibition tonight. But then I got assigned this group mixed-media project, and I have no idea what to do for that. The other people in the group are really talented but I'm afraid it's going to be hard to work together."

Chloe chuckled, remembering how much she hated group projects in college. "I'm sure you'll do fine."

"I don't know, Mrs. S," Madge said. "Our first meeting went really bad. I was so stressed I had to come back here to take a break, instead of getting things ready for the show to-night."

"I could probably stop by your school on the way to the airport, if you need a little help with your layout." Chloe made the offer without thinking, then winced internally as rational thought caught up with her automatic desire to lend a hand.

Madge blinked. "The airport? You're leaving?"

Chloe closed her eyes and sighed. "Yeah, sorry, it's been a weird day."

"Weird how?" Madge asked. "What happened after you dropped me off?"

Chloe mentally rewound the day's events so she could tell Madge the whole story. The energetic redhead shrieked with joy when Chloe told her about Fred's offer to show her paintings.

"OMG, Mrs. S! This is it! You finally got your big break!" Madge jumped up and down, then threw her arms around Chloe and squeezed. Before Chloe could hug her back, Madge pulled away, the giddiness abruptly dissipated. "Wait a sec. If you're supposed to do a show Friday, why are you leaving?"

"I need to go back to West Virginia for a couple days. There's been a, um..." Chloe struggled for the right word, and finally settled on, "development."

Madge tilted her head to the side, and long, curly red locks tumbled across her shoulder. "A development? Mrs. S, you aren't making any sense."

"I got a call from an old friend this morning, right as I was meeting with Richard." Chloe took a deep breath, still coming to grips with the reality of what she was about to say. "She found David."

Madge didn't react for a moment, then her eyes grew wide. "Wait, David? As in, your long-lost Mr. S?"

Chloe nodded. "I didn't believe it at first, but then I heard his voice." The memory of David singing brought tears to her eyes. "He's back. He's really back."

Madge's face lit up, then she squealed and pulled Chloe into another tight hug. "OMG, Mrs. S! This is awesome!"

Chloe wiped her eyes as she pulled out of Madge's embrace. "It is, I mean, it's unbelievable. I just wish everything wasn't happening at once, you know?"

Madge grinned. "That's kind of how a best day ever works."

"Best day ever, huh?" Chloe chuckled, considering Madge's assessment. She had let herself get so wrapped up in the logistics of how to handle her responsibilities that she forgot to acknowledge how wonderful it felt to know David was alive and safe.

Suddenly overjoyed, Chloe laughed out loud. "I guess it is, isn't it? Thanks, Madge." Confidence surged through her. "I'd better go pack. Do you care to help me out with selecting pieces and setting a layout for the opening?"

"It's under control, Mrs. S. Anything I can do to help you get ready?"

Chloe made a quick mental list of things to do before she left. "Can you look up flights for me? Find the first manageable departure for Pittsburgh."

"You got it." Madge turned to their cluttered desk and started moving papers aside in an effort to uncover her laptop. She freed it and opened the lid.

"Make sure there's enough time for us to stop by the art school and look over your work before I go," Chloe added.

Madge looked up from the screen. "It's okay, Mrs. S, don't worry about that."

"But—"

Madge emphatically shooed her away with both arms. "Go pack."

Chloe thanked Madge and hurried down the hall to her bedroom. She tossed a few clothes out of her closet onto the bed, then freed her luggage from behind a pile of shoeboxes. Some dust had settled on top and she brushed off what she could, revealing a light pink trim along the edges of the dark brown suitcase. A swirling design of lines, hearts, and flowers was stitched into the largest sides in the same shade pink, and a smaller version adorned the tag holder hanging from the handle. Chloe unzipped the suitcase and pulled the matching carry-on from inside.

She paused a moment to remember the day she bought her luggage set, three weeks before her wedding to David. Chloe had needed a new suitcase to pack for their honeymoon, and though she adored the cute brown and pink set, she worried she was too old for it. David's winsome smile had cut through her insecurity then, and now she looked forward to those kind eyes of his, the way he could put her soul at ease. Chloe sighed, the mixture of nostalgia and anticipation bringing joy to her heart and a smile to her lips.

Chloe set the luggage aside and pulled a small plastic box from the shelf in the top of the closet. She removed the lid and sifted through the mementos of the nine years she'd spent with David, including photos, notes he'd written her, trinkets and tchotchkes from trips they'd taken together, his wallet, and the wedding ring he'd given her fifteen years ago.

She picked up the traditional, plain gold band, and remembered how strangely incomplete she had felt when she stopped wearing it, even though it had been years after David's disappearance. Chloe held the ring close to her face and studied the inscription inside: "I'll Stand By You 10-27-2002." The words reminded her of David's voice on the phone, and her heart leapt. In only a matter of hours, she'd finally see him again.

Her cell phone rang, and Chloe snapped out of her reverie. The sudden jolt back to reality disoriented her, and her heart raced as she fumbled through her purse. A lump of guilt formed in her stomach when the screen showed Richard as the caller. She cleared her throat and answered the phone with a forced, "Hey, babe."

"I just got off the phone with Lumina," he said. "He's pretty worked up. If he didn't trust you as much as he does, you'd probably be out of a job."

Chloe's confidence evaporated, and doubt crept into her

mind again. Could she really pull this off?

"Why couldn't David just come to New York?" Richard asked.

Chloe winced at the flash of memory that struck her, a collage of the trip she and David had taken to the city years ago, his debilitating panic attack, and the difficult conversation that followed. She had neither the time nor desire to get into any of that with Richard now. "I don't know," she said. "I assume if that was an option, Emma would have suggested it."

"Maybe *you* should suggest it," Richard said.

"I have no idea what he's been through," Chloe said, idly fingering her mementos. "He might not be able to travel at all." She caught herself making excuses for David, and reminded herself that Richard was her boyfriend now. "I know you're worried, but I'll be fine. We'll be fine."

"You're going to be on the phone constantly," Richard said. "Lumina isn't going to let Conner handle this on his own."

"I know, but I have to go." Chloe closed her eyes and rubbed at her forehead with her free hand. "Did you need anything else?"

"No, I just wanted to try one last time to talk you out of leaving," Richard said. "Since that's obviously not going to happen, I'll let you get ready for your trip." He paused a moment, then asked, "You're not taking that brown and pink suitcase you used when we went upstate, are you?"

Chloe rolled her eyes. "Don't make fun."

Richard laughed. "I meant to ask back then, did you get that in high school or something?"

"I like it," Chloe said, pouting.

"Look, it's all right," Richard said. "There's nothing wrong with holding onto childhood memories, but I think it's time you got some new luggage. How can you travel with that thing at your age? It's embarrassing."

The insecurities David had melted away all those years ago returned in a rush. They mocked her, and Chloe's face flushed.

She wanted to lash out at Richard, but the part of her that had rejected the cute suitcase before won out, and she said nothing.

five

Chloe's plane touched down in Pittsburgh well after dark. The airport lights flashed past in a blur as the aircraft slowed and turned onto the taxiway. Chloe clutched her purse and tried to steady her breathing. She was closer to David than she'd been in ten years, a fact that scared as much as it excited her. Chloe had tried to relax during her flight, but couldn't stop fretting over what it would be like to finally see David again. Would he even recognize her? Would she recognize him? Had he changed? What did he expect from her?

Chloe turned her phone back on as soon as she was able, unleashing a series of dings and alarms and flashes announcing the mountain of messages that had come in during the flight. Most were from Fred and Conner, but she read the one from Emma first. It stated that she and David were on their way to meet Chloe at the airport.

Her breath caught when she read it. Chloe had thought she'd have the ninety-minute drive to Morgantown to prepare for seeing David again. Emma's message didn't say anything about what had happened at the doctor's office, either. She fretted over the change in plans, and distracted herself by sending Fred, Conner, and Richard text messages to let them know she had landed.

Her phone rang almost immediately. Fred told Chloe that Conner had sent the drywall crew away, and they complained about canceling another job to get to the gallery on such short notice. She tried to calm him and said she'd get to the bottom of it, hung up, and called Conner. Conner said the inspector told him something about a wiring issue, and the electrician couldn't come until the evening. Chloe explained that the drywall contractors could have been staging the job while he waited. He whined about not understanding any of this and suggested they hire a general contractor to take over.

Chloe rolled her eyes. "Just stay at the gallery and make sure the electrician finishes everything tonight. Don't let him leave until he does."

"How do I know if he's finished everything?" Conner asked.

"I gave you a list, remember? And concept sketches?"

"But what do the sketches have to do with the electrician?"

Chloe squeezed the bridge of her nose. "Are you looking at the sketches now?"

She heard a shuffling of papers. "Yes."

"See where there are lights on the walls?"

"Yes."

"Okay." She spoke slowly, trying to control her frustration. "Everywhere there's a light, there should be an electrical box. All the sconces should be on dimmers, and the overhead track lighting needs to be wired so that half the fixtures can be turned on at a time."

Chloe heard Conner fumbling with something. "Slow down," he said. "I'm trying to take notes."

"I already gave you all these notes," Chloe said. "Look, I need to call the drywall guys back. You just tell the electrician to get started when he gets there. Call me and I'll go over everything with him, got it?"

"Yeah, I think so," Conner said.

Fred called as soon as Chloe hung up with Conner. "My friend at the building inspector's office wasn't very happy to come in after hours for an incomplete job," he said.

Chloe sighed. "I know. I'm working on it, I promise."

She felt a tap on her shoulder. A young male flight attendant gave her a fake smile. "Miss? You need to leave the plane now."

Chloe looked around and saw that everyone else had disembarked. She apologized, slung her purse over her shoulder, grabbed her carry-on, and rushed up the breezeway, still trying to convince Fred that things were under control. She settled him and called the inspector while she walked the long concourse, past other gates, shops, and restaurants. She apologized for his inconvenience and asked for an explanation of the wiring issue.

"There were two overloaded junction boxes," the inspector said. "Look, I know Lumina doesn't hire hacks, so it was probably just a rush job. Get your guy in there and have him e-mail me pictures of the finished repair, and I'll push your paperwork through first thing in the morning."

Relieved, Chloe thanked him and verified that he would send his e-mail address via text message. She reached the end of her concourse, where it met with three others at a central shopping hub. The airport wasn't very crowded, so Chloe decided to take a lap around the large, mall-like area, anxious to see David but wanting to have as much of her work done as possible before she did. She called the drywall contractor and pleaded with him to bring a crew in that evening to get started. Conner called to tell her the electrician had arrived, and she passed along the instructions from the inspector. The electrician said it should take less than an hour to complete the necessary repair.

Convinced things were under control for the time being, Chloe took a deep breath, used the restroom, and walked across the concourse toward the escalator that would take her down to the tram that connected the terminals with the airport entrance. Before she got there, though, the flooring supplier called to say that the style she'd requested was unavailable for six weeks. Chloe asked the sales representative to e-mail her a list of alternatives that could be installed this week, but the rep said she wouldn't have it to her until morning. Chloe tried to persuade her to expedite the process, but the manufacturer apparently left their offices promptly at the end of the day and nothing could be done about it.

Chloe let out a frustrated sigh and stepped onto the escalator, already doubting her decision to leave New York. She closed her eyes and tried to push the stress from her mind, replacing it with thoughts of what David might look like and what she would say to him. Part way down, she opened them only to stare into the gaping jaws of a Tyrannosaurus Rex skeleton, its teeth almost close enough to touch. Chloe jumped, having forgotten about the cultural displays on the small mezzanine before the final descent to the train. She rushed past statues of George Washington and Franco Harris, regretting that she never seemed to have time to stop and study them.

She reached the tram platform and waited with several dozen other passengers, some chattering on cell phones, others trying to corral their children. Two young men in fatigues stood nearby in detached silence. A young couple grinned and gazed into each other's eyes, their hands locked together. They may have just returned from their honeymoon based on how affectionate they were with one another, and Chloe smiled, remembering the bittersweet bliss of returning from romantic trips with David.

Chloe drifted on her nostalgia and allowed the scene to speak to her. Instead of people, she saw brush strokes, places where light, shadow, color, and contrast brought out the love in the young couple's eyes, the wonder in the children, and the stoicism of the soldiers. She pulled the tablet computer from her purse, opened a drawing application, and made quick swipes with her finger to place the major elements, outlining the story told by this eclectic group of people.

She captured as much detail as she could before the train arrived and took a deep breath as she boarded, feeling charged, electric. Chloe couldn't remember the last time she'd been so awash in inspiration, and she wanted nothing more than to transform her visual notes into a painting right then and there. It would have to wait, though. First, she had to take care of

David, and the current calm in the gallery expansion wouldn't last forever. But for now, she savored the adrenaline and let the creative fire burn through her veins.

She stepped out of the train and into the current of people moving around the security checkpoint toward the airport exit. Chloe realized that Emma's message didn't indicate exactly where they would meet her, so she reached down to pull her phone from her purse.

Then she saw him, and stopped dead in her tracks.

They locked eyes, and the rest of the world melted into a silent, slow motion blur. David stood mere yards ahead of her, and recognition flashed in his eyes. That easy smile she remembered so clearly lit up his face, revealing more lines than the last time she'd seen it. He was trim, clean-shaven, and handsome, and though he had obviously aged, he looked as familiar to Chloe as her own reflection.

The shudder started in her chest and made its way to her lips. Breath came in desperate pants, and tears welled in her eyes. He mouthed her name and took a step toward her. Instinct drove Chloe to move, all conscious thought lost to oblivion as she strode toward David. She braced herself to crash into him, her free hand already outstretched to wrap around his back and pull him in. She anticipated the embrace with every pounding, racing heartbeat.

But David stopped short, his eyes wide, a haunted look on his face as he drew in a sharp breath. Chloe came to a halt in front of him and took hold of his shoulder. "David? Are you okay?"

David stammered through labored breaths. "They th...they thought..."

"Hey, just take it easy." Chloe blinked back tears, fearful that something terrible had happened to him. "It's all right, David. It's me, it's Chloe."

David's face twitched and tears ran down his face. He tried to smile, but was still trembling and panting. "They thought..."

Chloe shushed him. "It's okay, just calm down." She led

him to a nearby bench and helped him sit. She settled in beside him, rubbed his back, and tried to soothe him even as panic took hold in her own mind.

"Hello, Chloe." Emma smiled as she approached with a large bottle of water. Her smile faded when she saw David. "What happened?"

"I'm not sure," Chloe said. "He just started freaking out."

Emma knelt in front of David and guided his head so he was facing her. "Take a deep breath," she instructed. David complied, and Emma uncapped the water bottle and handed it to him. "Just a sip."

David took a drink and handed the bottle back to Emma. He closed his eyes and took a few breaths, then turned to Chloe. "Sorry," he said with a weak smile.

"It's okay," Chloe said. "Just relax. Just breathe." She continued rubbing his back.

"He's been getting flashes of memories this afternoon," Emma said. "Each one seems to exacerbate his anxiety, and he had a severe panic attack at the hospital. The neurologist indicated that David is fine physically, and expressed the opinion that his amnesia—in addition to these strange memories he's having—may be psychological."

Chloe nodded, unsure what the diagnosis meant but concerned that Emma called his memories strange. She slid herself over on the bench so she could squeeze him against her. "I'm just glad you're here," she said. Tears formed anew. "After all this time, I can't believe this is actually happening."

David wrapped an arm around Chloe's back and returned her embrace. "I...missed you." He said it with a hint of uncertainty in his voice.

"I missed you too," Chloe said. "So much."

Emma took a seat on the other side of David and pulled a notepad from her purse. "What did you remember just now?"

David stared intently at Chloe and took a deep breath. "They thought I murdered you."

Chloe flinched and pulled away from him. "What?"

"I've been getting these little pieces of memories," David said. "The first one was at Emma's, when I saw the application to file for my death certificate."

Chloe flushed with guilt. "Emma said it would be easy to reverse—"

"I know." David looked toward Emma. "We've already been over that. I'm not upset about it." He turned back to Chloe and took her hand. "She told me things were hard for you."

Chloe swallowed as memories of those first years without David flooded her mind, the days of working with the police, searching missing persons websites, and contacting every single lead she could find. She had spent nearly every moment and dollar trying to find him, but David didn't need to hear that now, especially considering his fragile mental state. "It was a little rough at times, but it doesn't matter now."

"What I'm trying to say is, I think I know a little about that," David said. "The way I remember it, you disappeared and I was left looking for you."

It took Chloe a moment to process this piece of information. Confused, she looked to Emma. "How is that possible?"

Emma shrugged. "I have been trying to deduce that myself all afternoon."

"When I first saw you coming out of the terminal, I remembered something else. I went to the police for help finding you, and when no leads turned up they assumed you'd been murdered." He took a deep breath. "I didn't even think you were dead, and I tried to convince them to keep searching, but they thought I'd killed you."

Chloe scrunched her face and David looked away. She leaned into him and put her arm across his shoulders. "That's terrible." She paused and then added, "I know you would never do that."

The absurdity of what she had said hit Chloe and David simultaneously, and they began to giggle together. Their laughter grew, and Chloe saw in David's bright eyes and mischievous smile the same man she had fallen in love with back in college. The levity of the moment cut through the ten-year wall between them, and in those fleeting few heartbeats it was as if they had only been apart for a weekend. Chloe's chest felt lighter, the pit in her stomach filled in, and her smile came easily and eagerly. She had no doubt that she and David could figure out how to deal with this situation together.

"You look good," David said, still chuckling. "How long have you worn your hair short like that? And what happened to your glasses?"

Chloe blushed. "I switched to contacts, and I've had my hair like this a few years now."

"I like it. It's different, but still somehow..." David rolled his hand through the air, hunting for a word. "You. As different as you look now, I still recognized you as soon as I saw you."

Chloe lost herself in his eyes for a moment, a loving gaze that sent a wave of warmth through her. "I just assumed Emma had shown you pictures."

David recoiled, then he and Chloe turned toward Emma. She groaned and shook her head in frustration. "How did I fail to think of that?"

The three of them laughed together, and Chloe's heart leaped. In spite of everything, David still knew her.

As their laughter petered out, Emma pulled the conversation back to David's memories. "Let's return to this murder accusation business. What evidence did the police have to suggest foul play?"

David shook his head. "None that I can remember. It's still pretty fuzzy, but I think the lead detective tried to claim that the lack of evidence was proof I had cleaned up after myself."

Emma scowled and crossed her arms. "That is simply preposterous. I would have destroyed such a feeble attempt at prosecution."

David smiled. "You did."

Chloe blinked. "So, wait, you remember Emma being wherever you were, but I wasn't?"

David nodded. "From what I've been able to piece together, it was like you disappeared from my life instead of the other way around. So yes, Emma was there, and she defended me."

"How is that even possible?" Chloe asked. "Where would these thoughts and memories come from?"

"I know it sounds crazy," David said, "but it doesn't feel like a dream or hallucination to me. It feels like a memory, just like the memories I had before any of this happened."

Chloe had a sinking suspicion that the situation would only get more complicated from here, and feared how it might impact her obligations at home. "So, is there anything we can do besides wait for your memories to come back?" She asked, looking first to David, then to Emma.

"I would have preferred that approach," Emma said. "David, however, insisted on a more proactive investigation."

"Of course he did." Chloe arched an eyebrow at him. "You haven't changed a bit, have you?"

"I wish I knew." David hesitated a moment, then pulled something from his pocket. "I'm not absolutely sure about this, but I think I got remarried. And I think I have a daughter, too." He opened his hand to reveal a gold ring. "I was wearing this when I woke up this morning. When I saw the death certificate application in Emma's files, I remembered filling out the same form, but for you. I also remembered talking to Emma about a woman named Madison and our daughter Candice. Then at the hospital, I remembered being in Adam's office with Candice."

"Adam?" Chloe asked. "As in, Amy and Adam? From college?" While Chloe didn't talk to them as often as she used to, she knew Adam Greene had opened his own pediatrics practice a few years earlier. If David had been there—especially with another woman's child—Adam would have told her.

David nodded. "They still live here in Pittsburgh, right? That's why I wanted to meet you up here, so we could go talk to them tomorrow."

Chloe couldn't believe it. She picked up the wedding band and studied it, noting it was a little fancier than the traditional, plain gold ring she had given him almost fifteen years earlier. Smooth yellow gold lined the edges, flanking a brushed inlay, and it felt heavier than she expected. The inscription inside read, "David and Madison, June 15." Who the hell was Madison? How could David have run off and married somebody else, while she was struggling and beside herself worried about him?

"This is, it's..." She couldn't find the words. Disappointment, anger, and confusion mingled together in a muddled mess of half thoughts and ambiguous emotions. Her phone rang and she jumped, then fumbled frantically through her purse to retrieve it. She hesitated a moment before declining the call from Fred.

"You can take that if it's important," David said. He took the ring from Chloe and put it back in his pocket.

"It's fine," Chloe said, wondering if it truly was. "Just a work thing."

"What do you do now?" David asked. "Emma told me you live in New York."

Chloe nodded. "I do, yeah. I've lived there a couple years now. I work at an art gallery. I manage it, actually."

David beamed and excitement danced in his eyes. "That's awesome! Do you get to sell your own paintings there?"

"Actually, I have my first show coming up this Friday." Chloe wondered how much detail she should tell him. She didn't want to add to his stress.

"Wait, your own show like, it's all your paintings?" David hugged her close. "Wow! How did this happen? I mean, I always knew you were good and I know how you always wanted to have a show in New York. Obviously, I missed a lot."

"Congratulations," Emma said. "That is quite a significant accomplishment."

"Thank you." Chloe's cheeks burned. "I don't even know where to start."

"Start from the beginning," David said. "What happened when I disappeared?"

Chloe's excitement faded, and she took a deep breath to steel herself against the sadness that would surely come with the story. "The beginning. Okay. I woke up on the morning of our anniversary..."

She trailed off as she remembered waking up to David's alarm blaring, the strange sensation of rolling over to the empty half of the bed where he should have been lying, and the panic that grew with each step as she frantically searched the house. She wiped away fresh tears. "It was awful. I woke up and you were just...gone."

David took Chloe's hand in his own and squeezed it, offering a comforting smile.

"I looked and looked for you, but all I found was the necklace you had bought me." Chloe pulled on the chain around her neck and freed the silver heart-shaped pendant from inside her shirt.

"It looks beautiful on you," David said.

Chloe tucked the necklace back into her shirt. "I always wear it inside my clothes. I used to wear it outside but too many people asked about it, and it was too hard to talk about, you know? Plus, I like feeling it against my skin so I always know it's there."

David smiled. "I'm glad you like it."

"I love it." Chloe smiled, took a deep breath to collect herself, and continued her story. "I stayed in Morgantown for a few years, until I couldn't afford to live in our house by myself anymore. Plus, it was just too painful sometimes, you know? So, I moved back to Stroudsburg and lived with my parents for a while. I worked there until I got my debt under control. That's when I switched to contacts, actually."

"I was wondering," David said. "You always told me you were grossed out by the idea of touching your eyes."

Chloe shrugged. "I got over it, I guess. My dad found me a job at a cabinet factory, and I had to wear safety glasses on the shop floor. Contacts made it a lot easier."

"You look great," David said. "It's different, but good."

"Thanks." Chloe smiled and let her gaze linger on David's face a moment. "So anyway, two years ago I finally took the plunge and moved to Brooklyn. I got a retail job near an art school, found an apartment, and I have a roommate. Her name is Madge and she's an art student. She's so young, too, but we get along really well."

"How young?" David asked.

"She's only twenty," Chloe answered. "But Madge is great. She's really sweet, and just bursting with energy. It's weird though, she paints these strange, dark scenes that are the complete opposite of her personality. They're amazing, though. She has a ton of talent."

David grinned and nudged her with his elbow. "Just like someone else I know."

Chloe blushed and Emma rolled her eyes. "It's as if no time has passed at all. You two still behave just as I remember."

Chloe and David grinned at each other, and a familiar comfort settled over her. Part of her wished so badly that it was true, that the last ten years had simply been a dream. Another part, though, wondered what she would have missed out on.

"So what happened next? How did you go from working retail to managing a gallery?" David asked. He was still smiling but Chloe thought she saw a little sadness in his eyes, like maybe he'd been wondering the same thing.

"That first spring we lived together, Madge and I decided one day we'd treat ourselves to an afternoon in Manhattan," Chloe said. "We got dressed up and went to a fancy restaurant for lunch, then we went to the Lumina Gallery."

"You know, I never did manage to go there," Emma said. "It opened when I was in law school, and several of my colleagues at Columbia raved about it, yet I never found the opportunity to visit."

"Must be a pretty great place," David said.

Emma gave David a pitying look. "Lumina Gallery is one of the most famous—not to mention, most exclusive—in the country, and possibly the world."

"Oh." David pursed his lips, obviously embarrassed.

Chloe patted his hand until his smile returned. "Anyway, Madge and I were only in the gallery for a few minutes when I noticed something didn't feel right. The arrangement of the pieces was weird, so the whole space felt disconnected and choppy."

"That doesn't sound like something you'd expect from such a famous gallery," David said.

"Not at all, and we were both a little shocked," Chloe said. "We were talking about it and I was showing Madge how I thought the paintings should be arranged, when this guy in a suit came over and started asking me questions. I thought he was the gallery manager and I was a little embarrassed, but he was friendly and I told him what I thought was wrong. And it turns out he wasn't the manager but the owner, Frederick Lumina himself."

Emma turned to David. "I'm a little ashamed to admit that the first time Chloe told me this story, I was quite jealous. Mr. Lumina is a fascinating man, though in this situation I shudder to think how intimidating he must have been."

Chloe chuckled. "It was pretty nerve-wracking, yeah. He said he'd recently lost his longtime gallery manager and was struggling to find a replacement. He started asking about my qualifications and was really surprised when I said I didn't go to art school, but I told him about how Mom and I would go to museums and galleries in the city when I was young and how I always loved and appreciated art. Apparently that was good enough, because he hired me on the spot. By the end of the day I'd rearranged the current show, and before I knew it I was planning the next opening."

David smiled and squeezed her hand. "I bet it looked amazing."

"Well, Fred said it was, but I was a mess," Chloe said. "I had no idea how hard it was to plan and coordinate everything for a gallery show. Not only did I have to manage the contractors who came in to rearrange the space, coordinate with the artist, and send out marketing material, I also had to plan the opening gala."

"Wait a second." David shifted in his seat so his shoulders were turned toward her. "Is your opening, the one this Friday, at the gallery you manage?"

Chloe nodded. "Yeah, but don't worry about that. I've got things under control."

David shook his head, looking concerned. "You probably should have taken that call."

"No, it's fine," Chloe said. "I can call him back."

"You are on a first name basis with Frederick Lumina, and you feel comfortable enough to ignore his calls and return them at your convenience?" Emma arched an eyebrow at her. "I knew you were doing well, Chloe, but I had no idea you ran in such exclusive circles."

"Wow." David shook his head and looked away, obviously troubled.

"What?" Chloe asked.

"It's really weird," David said. "I have these memories of being worried about you, missing you, thinking you were out there somewhere, hoping you were safe. And yet here you are, doing just fine. Better than fine, actually."

Chloe didn't know how to react. Was he upset at her for

moving on with her life? "It's not like things were easy," she said, trying not to sound defensive.

"I know," David said. "I'm not saying it was. It's just a messed up situation and I don't know what to think. I'm really happy for you, but I feel bad that I can't explain where I've been or why you had to go through what you did."

"I don't need an explanation." Chloe sighed and squeezed his hand, trying to ignore her growing anxiety. An explanation might make things easier, but she had little hope of finding one anytime soon. "Not right now, anyway. I'm just glad you're back."

David smiled. "Me too. And I promise, we're going to figure this thing out."

<h1 style="text-align:center">seven</h1>

Chloe called Fred back while she followed David and Emma to the short-term parking garage. He was less flustered than before, but still concerned. By the time they reached Emma's car, Chloe felt stressed about work again and wanted to talk about something else.

"What did you want to talk to Amy and Adam about?" Chloe asked. She rode up front with Emma while David sat in the back.

"Madison, the woman I remember being married to, is a friend of theirs," David said.

The name did sound familiar, though Chloe couldn't quite place it. "And you think if you meet her, it might bring back some more memories?"

"That's the idea," David said.

"Won't that be weird?" Chloe asked. "You might remember being married to her, but she's never met you. If someone approached me with that story, I'd think they were a little strange, you know?"

"Thank you, Chloe," Emma said. "You see, David? I'm not the only voice of reason here."

"I can't just wait around for my memory to come back," David said. "Who knows how long that would take? I'm tired of getting all weird and panicky every time I remember something. I want to know what happened to me. Don't you?"

"We should at least run it by Amy and Adam before we do anything else. I mean, we don't really know anything about this woman." Chloe bit her lip, partially nervous about David's plan, partially guilty about not staying in better contact with Amy and Adam. "And it would be nice to see them anyway. I've only been back to visit a couple times since the wedding."

When David said nothing, Chloe turned around to see him staring off into the distance, like he had been in the airport. "Are you remembering something else?"

David blinked and turned to her. "Amy and Adam's wedding. I was there. That's where I met Madison. She was the maid of honor."

"If that's true, then I definitely would have met her," Chloe thought out loud. "I was a bridesmaid. So let's see, Madison..." She tried to picture the rest of the bridal party. "A little shorter than Amy, kind of skinny, straight blond hair? Really protective of Amy?"

"That's her," David said. "I remember feeling really sad at the wedding. I missed you a lot."

Chloe offered a commiserating smile. "I felt the same way."

David continued, "It got so bad I had to get out of there at one point. I just knew I was going to break down and I had to get some air. I rushed out of the reception room, down the hallway, and I ran right into her. She was coming out of the bathroom and I didn't see her. I made sure she was all right and then hurried on to the door to get outside. Well, she followed me out. She remembered my being uncomfortable the whole day and wanted to know what my problem was."

"You make it sound like she was mad at you."

"She was. I guess she was just looking out for her friend, didn't want some crazy downer ruining Amy's wedding. Anyway, I apologized again and told her I was just feeling emotional and needed some air. And then she offered to take a walk with me. Turns out she had just been through a breakup and was having some drama in her life, too. So I told her about you and she was very kind, and we eventually went back inside."

Chloe's muscles tensed, and she paused to remind herself

that what David said was impossible. She couldn't completely hide her irritation as she asked, "And then you supposedly started a relationship with this woman?"

"I don't remember exactly how it started," David said.

Chloe leaned back in her seat and crossed her arms. When David had first disappeared, more than a few people suggested he had run off with another woman. Chloe never believed that, and David's memory had to be wrong, but she still felt a little betrayed.

"So, um," David started. After a moment's hesitation he asked, "Are you seeing anyone?"

She had been a little torn about how much to discuss regarding her relationship, but David seemed completely open about his alleged second marriage. Chloe turned her head to speak over her shoulder, but didn't make eye contact with him. "Yeah, for almost a year and a half. His name is Richard. He's an artist."

"Oh, okay. Good. I'm glad you found someone." David stared out the window.

They rode in awkward silence the rest of the way to downtown Pittsburgh. Emma had booked two rooms at a hotel where she got a nice discount, and insisted that David stay with either her or Chloe due to his panic attacks.

"I'd probably better stay with Emma," David said to Chloe. "I wouldn't want to mess anything up with your new boyfriend."

Chloe forced a smile and nodded her agreement, and the three of them rode the elevator upward. They started down the hall and reached Chloe's room first. Emma said good night, handed David his key, and proceeded toward her room.

"Hey," David said, touching his hand to Chloe's upper arm. "I really am glad you're seeing somebody."

Chloe sighed. "Thanks." She smiled and added, "I'm really glad you're back, though."

"Listen, you don't have to stay," David said. "I know you have a lot going on right now, and it's such a huge opportunity for you to do an art show in New York. Change your flight. Go back early. I'll be okay."

"No, I couldn't do that," Chloe said. In truth, she was less concerned with hurting his feelings than with getting the closure she needed to focus on her work at the gallery.

"I promise I'll be fine," David said. "This is too big for you to pass up."

"I just got here," Chloe said. "And I haven't seen you for ten years! I'm not just turning around and going home."

David laughed. "Nobody said you have to leave right this minute." Turning serious, he added, "I know if you let this opportunity pass you by, you'll regret it. Plus, I'll feel guilty too. It's bad enough I couldn't give you New York before—"

"David, no—"

He held up a hand to stop her protest. "—and I am not going to keep you from it now."

"It will be fine," Chloe said. "I've got things under control. It's a lot of work and yes, it's a bit harder without being there, but I'll be fine."

David shook his head. "I'm not going to drop this. You need to—"

"You don't get to tell me what I need to do," Chloe snapped. "You weren't here. You don't know how hard I worked to get where I am, so you don't get a say in how I handle this situation." She realized she'd raised her voice and looked away, ashamed. "Sorry," she said quietly.

David said nothing for a moment. Chloe continued to look away from him, hoping she hadn't hurt his feelings. Whatever had happened wasn't his fault, and she really didn't blame him for not being able to move to New York after college, either.

David's fingers weaved into hers. It startled her a little at first, but the touch of his hand, the way he held hers, felt immediately comfortable and familiar. She turned back to him, and David smiled.

"I'm not going to let you say no," he said. "It doesn't matter how long it's been since we've seen each other. I still believe in you, and you deserve this."

Chloe's heart raced as the incredible conviction in David's face filled her with confidence. She paused just enough for her rational side to catch up. "Let's see how things look tomorrow. I'll change flights if I absolutely need to, but for now I think leaving first thing Wednesday morning will be fine."

"Okay," David said. "But no more missing calls on my account, all right?"

Chloe nodded. "Okay."

They embraced and held each other for a long moment, then David kissed her gently on the cheek. "Good night, Chloe."

She said good night in return, and watched him walk away until he disappeared around a corner. Chloe took a deep breath, trying to quiet the barrage of questions assailing her mind. How could David think he had some obligation to another woman, especially one he's never met? Was he really the same man she had known all those years ago? Did feeling comfortable around David mean that she was betraying Richard? As she stepped into her room, one feeling rose above the emotional turmoil.

She missed David already.

eight

Chloe's ringing cell phone woke her early Tuesday morning, the too-bright glow of its screen illuminating much of the otherwise dark hotel room. As she rolled over and rubbed her eyes, one of her grainy contact lenses slid out of place. She adjusted it, fumbled for her phone, and answered it groggily.

"Chloe? Are you all right?" It was Fred.

"I didn't sleep well." Chloe recalled falling asleep on the chair with the TV on, making her way to the bed sometime in the middle of the night, then tossing and turning for hours.

"I'm sorry to hear that." Fred sounded less concerned than being polite. "Conner tells me the drywall contractor made a real mess of things overnight. I'm on my way to the gallery now to assess the situation and decide if this project is still worth doing."

"Didn't he stay and supervise?" Chloe came more awake at the edge in Fred's voice. She turned on the bedside lamp and squinted against the sudden flood of light.

"He apparently stayed in the office, then locked up when they were finished and left without looking things over." The irritation and frustration in Fred's voice were palpable. "I've let him know that is not acceptable."

Fred's ominous tone started Chloe's heart racing. "I'll tell him to send me some pictures, then I'll call the contractor when I see what we're working with."

"Okay." Fred paused. "I hope things are going well there."

"I'm still planning to fly back first thing tomorrow morning," Chloe said, understanding it was what he really wanted to know. She wondered if she should start looking for a flight that afternoon, instead.

"You'd better hope Conner can keep this project moving until then," Fred said. "As you can probably guess, my confidence isn't exactly high at this point."

"He can handle it." Chloe tried to hide the doubt in her voice. "I'm going to call him right now and get things back on track."

"Is Conner also handling the remaining preparations for Richard's exhibit and the opening gala?" Fred asked.

"I was planning to make some calls this morning and finalize the catering and sound contracts," Chloe answered. "I might need him to run an errand or two, but the rest should be fine until I get back."

"I doubt I need to remind you that Richard draws a large and well-connected crowd," Fred said. "While I would love to see you debut on Friday, his show has to be your top priority. Understood?"

Chloe tried and failed to swallow the lump in her throat. "Of course."

Fred hung up and Chloe immediately called Conner to demand that he send her pictures of the drywall as soon as possible. When she hung up, she fell back onto the bed and closed her eyes. Despite her exhaustion, she was much too worked up to sleep any more. Being so far away from everything, so out of control, only made a difficult opening week worse. Why did David have to reappear now?

She hadn't even begun to process her feelings about David coming back. Chloe tried to convince herself she was happy, elated even, just to know he was alive and safe. She had no idea what to think about his weird memories, and wasn't sure what could possibly be accomplished by meeting Madison. David had seemed so confused and anxious the night before, and Chloe couldn't turn her back on him.

But she couldn't just lie around, either. If she really wanted to make the opening happen, Chloe would have to step up and push herself to get things done. She rose from the bed and went to the bathroom, then started collecting her things to take a shower. She was about to remove her pajamas when someone knocked on the door.

Chloe started, as she wasn't expecting anyone. She approached the door, looked through the peephole, and almost didn't recognize the long haired, bearded man standing there in his loose clothes, medallions hanging from his neck.

He knocked again. "Chloe? Is this the right room? I'm looking for Chloe Sullivan."

She unlatched the lock and opened the door to greet her younger brother. "Tommy? What are you doing here?"

Tommy embraced her, then continued into the room. "Good to see you, sis. Where's David?"

"How did you know about David?" Chloe closed and locked the door behind them.

"I sensed something." Before Chloe could ask for more of an explanation, he added, "Also, Mom called me."

"What? When?" Chloe had only spoken briefly with her mother before she boarded her plane for Pittsburgh, and sent a quick message after settling into her room last night. "I can't believe Mom has your number. I haven't known how to get ahold of you for years. I didn't even think you were in the country."

Tommy shrugged. "Well, I wasn't. I only came back a couple months ago. I've been traveling up and down the East Coast, and I stay with Mom and Dad whenever I pass through there. They asked for my number and I gave it to them."

Chloe put her hands on her hips. "And nobody bothered to tell me this because...?"

"You were busy. Plus, I don't think Mom and Dad wanted to get into it with us again."

Chloe sighed. "Did you ask them for money?"

Tommy frowned. "No. See, that's why they didn't tell you."

"Did you come to ask me for money? Did you think there

was something to gain from what I'm going through with David?" She stomped past him, trying to pace off her frustration. "I can't believe they sent you to check up on me."

"Calm down," Tommy said. "Believe it or not, I'm here to help."

"This should be good." Chloe sat on the bed and leaned forward in a mock attentive position. "Do go on."

Tommy sat down and put his arm around her shoulders. "Hey, I know you haven't agreed with some of my choices, but I'm serious this time. You could be in some real trouble."

Chloe rolled her eyes. "I'm guessing you aren't talking about how stressed I am trying to get this gallery opening set up."

Tommy looked at Chloe intently. "We think David coming back might have catastrophic consequences."

"We?"

"For the last several years, I've been involved with a brotherhood—"

"Oh God!" Chloe threw her hands in the air in exasperation. "You joined a cult?"

"The Brotherhood of the Sacred Phi is not a cult." Tommy crossed his arms and took an exasperated tone, and Chloe gathered this wasn't the first time he'd been asked that question. "We are a group dedicated to studying the elemental and fundamental powers that comprise our world."

"I take it there's no commune, since you had to crash with Mom and Dad," Chloe said, still refusing to take her brother seriously. "Did you give up all your worldly possessions to join?"

"No," Tommy said. "Not that I have much to give up. You know I like to travel light."

She looked him up and down, noting the loose-fitting, poncho-like top and baggy cargo pants he wore. While they didn't give him the neatest appearance, the clothes appeared to be durable and well-made. "Do you all dress like that? And what's with all the weird medallions?" She took one in her hand, half-expecting it to be plastic. On the contrary, the cool, smooth disk felt heavy enough to be real gold, and was inset with what appeared to be small but authentic gemstones. It could have come from a jewelry store, except for the glyphs that had obviously been hand-carved into it.

"These are just my traveling clothes." Tommy took the medallion from Chloe's hand and let it fall back against his chest with the others. "Would you please take this seriously?"

Chloe sighed. "Fine, let's hear it."

"I first encountered the Brotherhood when I was trading in Asia," Tommy started.

Chloe scoffed. "Trading? You mean smuggling?" From what little information she and her parents could gather about Tommy's whereabouts and activities at the time, it had seemed like he was involved in some less-than-ethical dealings.

Tommy rolled his eyes. "It wasn't smuggling. Anyway, the Brotherhood reached out and asked me to help with a business deal that didn't seem very lucrative at all, but they promised to compensate me in full even if things went south. Turns out, that deal facilitated a land exchange that led to further business development and brought a lot of public works to the area, too. I was impressed by how well they'd orchestrated everything and decided to get further involved."

"Wait," Chloe said, confused. "Is this a cult or an investment firm?"

"It's not a cult. Investments and business dealings are just one way to affect the world energies." Tommy's expression grew intense. "We've tapped into some of the most primitive forces that ebb and flow through this world and everything in it. There are powerful energies dedicated to both creation and destruction, and they must be kept in balance or, well, boom."

Chloe cocked an eyebrow at him. "Boom?"

"Well not 'boom' exactly. Basically, everything goes to shit. Natural disasters, breakdown of society, people die. It's not good. While these forces are raging around unchecked, the world they are contained in suffers." He puffed out his chest a little. "We have sworn to protect the balance."

Chloe shook her head, frustrated by her brother's idiotic fantasy. "I really don't have time for this." She stood but Tommy put his hand on her shoulder.

"Please, just hear me out." Chloe sat back down, and he continued. "Now, you might think creative and destructive forces would just cancel each other out, but they don't. There are also binding forces, things that keep one side or the other from gaining an upper hand. One of those binding forces is true love."

It only took Chloe a moment to speculate that the conversation was about to include David. "You can't be serious."

Tommy ignored her. "We think, and I personally have always believed, that you and David might be soul mates."

Chloe took a long breath. "I'm really glad David is back, but I'm in another relationship—"

"This isn't about your relationship! This is about destiny." Tommy paused and regained his composure. "I'm not talking about 'soul mates' the way people tend to throw that term around. Real soul mates are truly two halves of the same whole, a binary energy created not just for each other but because of each other."

He put his hands on Chloe's shoulders. "You and David might be part of the binding force that keeps the world energies in check. If someone or something interfered and sent David away for a long time so that you both moved on, it could upset the balance of nature itself."

Chloe shook her head and squinted at Tommy. "Do you know how crazy you sound? Look, I don't know what happened to David and he doesn't seem to know, either. We'll figure it out. But right now, I have important things to do."

"This really can't wait," Tommy said.

Chloe closed her eyes and grit her teeth. She didn't want to ask the question, but convinced herself it might make Tommy go away faster if she did. "Why not?"

"Don't you think it's interesting that your big art show just happens to fall on the same day as your wedding anniversary, which just happens to be the day David disappeared?"

Chloe rolled her eyes. "It's a coincidence."

"Maybe, maybe not," Tommy said. "I don't know for sure, obviously, but my instinct tells me it's a tipping point. A grave imbalance may be imminent."

Chloe scoffed. "It's been ten years. This imbalance or whatever could have happened multiple times by now."

"Things have changed," Tommy said. "Your feelings for each other waned during your separation, but that fire is suddenly burning bright again. An abrupt change like that can drastically shift the world energies. I can't say for sure what will happen, but if you and David got back together, things would probably work themselves out."

Chloe stormed away from him. "Oh, is that all? Well I tell you what then, I'll just break things off with Richard, quit my job at the gallery, and move back in with David. We'll just pick things up right where we left off as if the last decade didn't happen. How does that sound?"

Tommy tilted his head. "Is it really that hard to imagine you and David together again?"

Chloe hesitated. Since David disappeared, she'd worked hard to move on and build a new life. Despite the happiness she'd found in New York, seeing him again left her pining for the years they'd spent together. She wasn't about to leave her job or Richard, though, and hadn't yet thought about how David fit in her present situation, if at all. They'd have to talk about it eventually, maybe after David put all these strange memories—including this Madison woman—behind him.

Chloe locked eyes with her brother and spoke slowly, deliberately. "He and I will figure it out, but right now I have work to do. I don't have time to worry about where David and I stand."

Tommy closed his eyes and took a long, deep breath, as if he were trying to meditate. "Has he told you anything about what happened while he was missing?"

She sighed and sat back down on the bed. "David doesn't remember much. He's been getting these flashes, little snippets of memories, I guess, and they seem to freak him out even though they don't make any sense at all. So far all he remembers is that I was missing and that he got remarried." The last word caught in Chloe's throat.

Tommy crossed his arms. "Interesting. Has he tried to contact this woman?"

Chloe shook her head. "That's on today's agenda." Her phone buzzed with an incoming message from Conner. "Along with a million other things."

"Okay, this is good," Tommy said. "If we can get to the bottom of why David has these memories, we might be able to figure out why he was missing."

Chloe stood. "There is no 'we' in this. You're not coming."

"I am trying to help you." Tommy stood and faced her.

"David is having enough anxiety issues as it is, and I don't want you throwing this mystical bullshit into the mix," Chloe said.

"I could just observe from a distance," Tommy offered.

"No."

"I really need to get a feel for his energy field if we're going to resolve this," Tommy said.

"No." Chloe put her phone back onto the nightstand and walked toward the door of the room. "Would you just go? I need to get in the shower."

Tommy threw up his hands in frustration. "Fine, but I'll be around. Keep me in the loop."

"I don't have your number," Chloe reminded him. She opened the door and motioned him out.

"I'll send you a text," Tommy said as he brushed past her. "Please take this seriously. Something really weird is happening here, and I don't want you to get hurt."

Chloe scoffed. "Funny how you've never seemed to care about that until now."

"Hey, that's not fair," Tommy said. "I have tried—"

"I don't want to hear it," Chloe said. "Just get the hell out of here."

"Are you going to be mad at me forever?" Tommy asked. Chloe thought she heard a hint of sadness in his voice, but she could never tell with him whether it was genuine.

"What does my energy field tell you?" she mocked.

"You're confused, scared, and stressed, and it's clouding your judgment," Tommy said flatly. "You're trying so hard to keep everything together that you aren't following your heart."

Chloe's face flushed as the truth in his words burrowed into her chest. She shook the feeling off, unwilling to be distracted by her brother's supposed insight. "Goodbye, Tommy." She let the door close in his face.

<h1 style="text-align:center">nine</h1>

Chloe showered and dressed, then sent a text message to Amy to see if she was available to meet for lunch. An ecstatic Amy called back immediately, and her excitement only grew when Chloe told her about David's reappearance. Amy suggested a restaurant near Adam's office and a time that coincided with his lunch break.

"Okay, that sounds good," Chloe said. "We'll meet you there."

Amy squealed. "Can't wait!"

Chloe ended the call and sighed. She hadn't talked to Amy and Adam much in the last few years, and wished they were getting together under different circumstances. She hadn't been as comfortable around them since David went missing. They'd met in college as couples, and usually spent time together as a foursome. Sometimes David and Adam would play golf together, and Amy invited Chloe out with the girls occasionally, but those had been the exceptions rather than the rule.

She feared it would be an awkward reunion, but it had to be done. Maybe it would help David, and maybe it wouldn't, but he wouldn't be satisfied until they had at least tried it. David always needed an explanation for things. Life and circumstances were puzzles to be solved, complex combinations of cascading causes and effects that David built and connected and studied until he reached a conclusion or the stress of it all overwhelmed him.

Chloe remembered that aspect of David's personality as the

main reason he never understood art. He always wanted to analyze it, rather than just let himself feel. That reminded her of Tommy's words, and she tried to convince herself her brother was wrong about her. She still followed her heart, but sometimes that required a little planning and problem solving.

She looked down at the hotel note pad she'd been doodling on during her conversation with Amy, which very closely resembled the painting Richard had made for her. Strokes swirled around and shot off in various directions, and the lines were thicker and better defined in places, but there was a shape to it, a purpose. She took that as proof that she still could allow her intuition to guide her, even if it was just an absent-minded doodle. Chloe tore the page off the pad, folded it, and stuck it in her purse.

Chloe sent Emma a message indicating where and when they were to meet up with Amy and Adam, then buried herself in her work, filling several more pages of the note pad with doodles. She made a few phone calls and had just finished talking with the caterer when there was a knock at the door. It wasn't yet time to meet up with David and Emma, so she assumed it was Tommy again. Chloe sat still, hoping that if she ignored him, he would go away.

The knock came again. "Chloe?" It was David's voice.

She exhaled, relieved. "I'm coming," she called. Chloe opened the door and let David in. He wore workout shorts and a tee shirt that had obviously never been washed, as she could still see the creases where it had been folded.

"Good morning," David said, smiling. "Are you busy?"

"A little, but it's okay. Come on in." She waved him past, locked the deadbolt, then sat back down in the desk chair while David sat on the bed.

"You're wearing your glasses," David said.

"Yeah, I accidentally slept in my contacts last night, so they're all dry and weird." She stuck out her tongue at the thought of the disgusting, grainy lenses, then quickly changed the subject. "So how are you feeling today?"

David shrugged. "I didn't wake up outside, so it's an improvement over yesterday. I think the lawn was softer than that couch, though."

"You slept on the couch?" Chloe asked. "Didn't Emma ask for a room with two beds?"

"She did *ask* for a room with two beds. She did not *receive* a room with two beds." He rolled his eyes. "She called the front desk and argued for a while, but apparently all the rooms with two beds were taken."

Chloe grinned. "I always thought you and Emma were close enough that you could share a bed without it being weird."

David laughed. "Sure, but the problem is that Emma's a sprawler. Once she falls asleep those long arms and legs of hers go everywhere." He leaned back and waved his arms around wildly in a mock demonstration.

They laughed together a moment before Chloe's phone dinged. She turned to check it and found a message from the caterer saying the final menu and contract would be e-mailed to her shortly. While she typed a reply, David picked up the note pad from the desk.

"I see you still doodle while you're on the phone," he said, still smiling. He squinted, scrutinizing the pad for a moment. "This one, it just kind of looks like random swirls but it isn't, is it? There's something really familiar about it."

Chloe leaned toward David and he held the pad so he could point to the doodle, but she already knew which one he was talking about. It was yet another rough recreation of *Chloe's Journey*. After the way things had gotten awkward the previous night, she hadn't wanted to bring up the subject of her current relationship, but now it seemed she had to.

"My boyfriend, Richard, did a painting for me, an abstract kind of like this." She paused to check David's reaction. He smiled at her, so she continued. "Of course his looks better than mine, it's nicely textured and really colorful. He showed it to me yesterday, right before I talked to Emma, and I guess I've been a little obsessed."

"It's really interesting," David said. He set the pad down and patted Chloe's leg. "I'm sorry if I was weird last night. I really am happy that you're seeing someone." He beamed at her. "So tell me about this guy. How did you two meet?"

Chloe started to speak, then burst into laughter. "I'm sorry, this is really weird, you know?"

David's face lit up with a big, stupid grin. "What's so weird about it?"

"Oh, I don't know," Chloe teased. "Maybe it's because the last time we saw each other, you were my husband. Now you're sitting here asking about my boyfriend."

David made a dismissive gesture. "People do this all the time."

"Uh-huh. Sure they do." Chloe shook her head and sighed. "Do you really want to talk about this?"

"Of course," David said. "I know it's a little weird, but I want to know what's been going on with you while I've been...wherever."

"Okay," Chloe said. David didn't seem as anxious this morning, and she didn't want to stress him further, but since he insisted she started telling the story. "I hadn't been working at the gallery very long, and Richard was either the first or second opening I managed on my own. He was really difficult. Sometimes he can be a real diva when it comes to his shows, plus he knew I was relatively new at the job and didn't have a lot of confidence in my ability to understand his work. Luckily Fred backed me up the whole time, and it turned out to be a sellout opening."

"How much does a ticket to an opening run?" David asked.

Chloe giggled. "We don't sell tickets. By 'sellout opening' I meant all of Richard's pieces got sold the first night of the show. That doesn't happen very often. Usually people come to the opening gala to browse the collection and decide which pieces they're interested in. A few things, usually statement pieces, are bought that night, but most of the time it's at least a few days before everything is sold."

"Oh," David said, obviously embarrassed at his misinterpretation. "So Richard is pretty famous, then?"

"In fine art circles, he's very famous," Chloe said. "Not so much mainstream, though. By the time I met him he was already famous enough to get invited to exclusive parties and date lingerie models. I didn't see him that way and I think it threw him off a little, you know?"

"So he respected you, then? After his opening was so successful, I mean."

Chloe rolled her eyes. "It took a little longer than that. The week after the opening he insisted that we have lunch together, and that's when I told him I was an artist myself. And he mocked me!"

David's eyes went wide in disbelief. "You're kidding!"

"No," Chloe said, aware of her own exasperation at the story. "He said, 'Everybody thinks they're an artist. Just because you work in a gallery and know how to arrange a show, that doesn't make you a real artist.' Or something like that."

"And then you punched him in his stupid face, right?" David asked. He was smiling, but Chloe thought she saw a hint of hurt in his eyes, as if he were offended on her behalf. She found it strange how the conversation seemed to be bringing her and David closer, even though she was telling him about how she met the man she was currently seeing.

Chloe laughed. "I didn't punch him, but I did walk out on him. Later he called to apologize and said that made him respect me more."

David recoiled. "Sheesh. Sounds like this guy can't take a hint."

"Well, the kind of women he was used to seeing just liked the idea of being with a celebrity artist without really caring about his art. Either that, or they were aspiring artists looking to use him for a break."

David shrugged. "Yeah, okay, I get that, I guess."

Chloe paused a moment to judge David's reaction. She

surmised that Richard wasn't coming across very well thus far in her story, so she pressed on to when things got better. "Anyway, Richard and I started talking a little and occasionally he'd stop by the gallery. One night he called while I was painting and wanted to meet for drinks, and I told him I'd rather keep working but he could come see my work if he wanted."

David smiled. "And that's when he really knew, right? That you weren't just some hack but an incredible artist?"

Chloe blushed at David's pride in her work. "Yeah, I think so."

He continued smiling, though David's gaze drifted and he seemed to be far away. "I always loved your paintings." He sighed and returned his focus to Chloe. "And as far as I know, I'm still pretty clueless about art. If I loved them, I can't even imagine what a famous artist like Richard must have thought. He must have been totally blown away by your awesomeness, right?"

Chloe chuckled. David was being completely naive, thinking her paintings were somehow above criticism. But then, that's the way he'd always been, and even though Chloe knew that Richard's careful, studied reaction the first time he saw her work was normal, she found herself missing David's childlike enthusiasm.

"Well, our styles are very different," Chloe said. "Richard is all about shocking people, about social commentary and making bold statements, and I'm sure you remember that my paintings are a lot more subtle. But it did get us talking seriously artist to artist, and we discussed techniques and trends and the little rituals we each follow. I know now that his tantrums are all an act, but I think this is the first actual relationship he's been in for a long time."

Chloe turned away. Even though David had been gone, they hadn't broken up. Now that he was sitting here with her again, talking about seeing another man felt like crossing some kind of line.

David took hold of her hand, and she turned back to face

him. He smiled at her, not a trace of agitation or jealousy on his face. "He's a lucky guy. Not only are you amazing, you're also about to have your big debut. He'll get to be the arm candy for a change."

She laughed at the thought of Richard being paraded around like some kind of trophy, even though he'd never tolerate that. "Actually, Richard and I are doing a joint show." Chloe told him about the flood the previous morning that forced her to take her paintings to the gallery, which resulted in Fred wanting to show her work at Richard's opening. "So we're kind of rushing the construction, you know? That would be fine except it's impossible to find a reliable contractor, even on the Upper East Side."

"What about your dad?" David asked. "Could he help?"

"I wish. He's busy with a big job right now, plus he's not licensed in New York." Chloe grabbed her tablet from the desk and spun her chair so she could show David the screen. "Look at what these jokers did last night."

She turned on the device and put in her security code, and the screen showed the list of flights departing Pittsburgh that day. Chloe winced and hit the button to return to her home screen as fast as she could, but there was no way David couldn't have seen. She fumbled with the controls and pulled up a picture of the sloppy drywall work.

"I mean, just look at this." Chloe stammered as she pointed out the uneven seams and places where the drywall compound wasn't applied properly, frantically hoping he wouldn't say anything about the flights.

David cut her off. "You need to go home."

She switched off the tablet and set it back on the desk. "I'm sorry," Chloe said. "When I saw those pictures this morning I panicked a little, but I think things are under control now." They weren't, but David didn't need to know that.

He squeezed her leg. "I told you last night, I don't want to be in the way of this. If you need to go, go."

Chloe pushed her glasses up and rubbed her eyes, partly out

of stress, partly to cut off the tears that were forming. She shook her head, then turned to face David's concerned expression and forced a smile. "It's fine," she said. "It's just stressful because apparently I'm alone in this. Conner, the guy who's supposed to be helping me, is clueless and Richard is busy getting ready for his own show."

She closed her eyes and took a deep breath to collect herself. "But it's all right, I can handle this," Chloe said, more to convince herself than David. "I'll get it all taken care of."

David stood and paced. "I wish I knew what happened to me. If I could offer you some kind of explanation, some kind of closure on this, maybe you could focus more on your work." His breathing quickened and his hands trembled.

Chloe got up and went to him, wrapped an arm around his shoulders, and guided him back to the bed to sit. "It's okay," she said. "We'll figure it out."

David nodded and took a few deep breaths. "I'm really glad you're here, but you don't have to stay."

"I want to." Chloe sighed, unsure if she was helping or not. Despite how much she wanted to be back in New York, she found herself increasingly willing to stay by David's side. "Unless something changes, I'm still planning to fly back tomorrow morning."

"I hope we figure all this out before then," David said. "You definitely shouldn't stay any longer than that. I know how important this opening is to you, and it should be. It's a huge opportunity."

"Maybe seeing Amy and Adam will help," Chloe said. "And if it does, then maybe I'll look into an earlier flight. But let's just see how it goes."

ten

Emma was on a work call during the entire twenty-minute drive from the hotel to the restaurant where they had arranged to meet Amy and Adam, so Chloe and David rode in silence to keep from distracting her. Chloe occasionally glanced over her shoulder to look at David, who seemed content to stare out the window. She wondered what, if anything, he was remembering as they drove through the neighborhoods of Pittsburgh.

Emma parked the car and continued her call while David and Chloe got out and walked toward the restaurant. Amy stood outside waiting for them. Short and full figured with close-cropped hair and a beaming smile, she waved wildly with both arms as they approached. Chloe smiled when she saw her. Even though they didn't talk as often as they used to, Chloe still considered Amy one of her best friends.

"Hey, Chloe!" Amy squealed, then pulled Chloe into a tight hug. "It's so good to see you! It's been way too long."

Chloe returned her embrace. "It's great to see you, too!"

Amy turned to David and looked him up and down, shaking her head. "I can't believe it's really you! I thought I'd never see you again!" She threw her arms around him and squeezed.

David patted Amy's back and chuckled nervously. "That seems to be the norm."

Amy released David, then punched him lightly in the shoulder. "Don't be such a downer. I'm so glad you're okay, and that you're both here. So, you really have no idea what happened to you?"

"It's kind of complicated," David started.

Amy shivered. "Well, we can talk about it inside, once this straggler catches up." She laughed. "How have you been, Emma?"

Emma walked briskly to join the group, then extended her hand to shake. Amy ignored the gesture and wrapped her up in a hug, too. "I'm well, Amy, thank you."

Amy released Emma. "Adam got us a table," she said, and led them into the restaurant. Most of the tables sat empty, as they had beat the lunch rush. Chloe kept her phone on vibrate but in her hand, anxious that it would go off at any second.

Adam stood and smiled as they approached the table. "I still don't believe it." He shook David's hand, then pulled him in for a hug. "You don't seem any worse for wear, so that's good."

David stepped back and shrugged. "I guess I'm doing okay, considering."

Adam turned and greeted Chloe, as well. He had larger bags under his eyes and less hair than the last time Chloe had seen him. Pediatrics had apparently been very stressful, though his calm, soft-spoken demeanor remained unchanged.

Three chairs lined each side of the long, rectangular table. David sat in the middle seat on one side, between Chloe and Emma. Amy took the end seat across from Chloe, and Adam sat beside her, across from David.

"I'd offer a celebratory drink," Adam said, "but I'm going back to work after this."

Amy elbowed him. "Sorry, we don't get out without Beth much these days."

Chloe flushed, embarrassed she had forgotten to ask about their daughter. She'd seen a few pictures on social media lately, and Beth had inherited her father's broad shoulders and her mother's laughing eyes. "How old is she now?"

"Four and a half." Amy looked toward David. "I guess we have a lot of catching up to do!" She held out her left hand, showing her wedding ring. "I don't know how much Chloe told you already, but Adam and I finally got married. That was almost six years ago, and we have a daughter, Beth."

Adam pulled his cell phone from his pocket and held it across the table so David could see the screen. Chloe leaned over so she could also look at the photo of Beth. The little girl sat on a carpeted floor, surrounded by dolls, looking at the camera with a gleeful, laughing smile.

David smiled. "That's wonderful." He fidgeted and was quick to spot the approaching waiter, who filled their water glasses and left a basket of bread. David took a slice and spread butter on it, digging the knife into the soft bread.

Chloe sensed his discomfort and decided to jump right into the issue at hand. "David actually remembers being at your wedding."

Amy looked toward David, confused. "But how can that be? Nobody saw you there."

"What'd you do, sneak in for some free food and then leave without even saying hello?" Adam joked.

Amy laughed. "Yeah, you could have at least left a gift."

David chuckled nervously. "I got you a rice cooker." He took a bite of his bread.

Chloe turned to him, shocked. "You didn't tell me that part."

Amy and Adam shared a look. "Whoa, this is getting weird," Adam said.

David washed his bread down with a drink of water. "It didn't seem important."

"Well, it isn't really," Chloe said. "It's just that I got them a rice cooker."

"I picked it out because I thought it was what you would want to get them," David said.

Amy alternated staring wide-eyed at David and Chloe, her smile tinged with confusion and concern. "What is happening here?"

Emma interrupted the exchange to explain about David's sparse memories of the past decade. "Those recollections seem to indicate that David was experiencing a scenario in which Chloe disappeared, which we all know to be impossible."

"So, wait." Adam pointed at David. "You actually remember going to our wedding, but Chloe wasn't there?"

David nodded. "You asked me to be a groomsman."

"That is so bizarre," Amy said. "It's like some kind of freaky parallel dimension. Were we any different?"

David laughed. "Not one bit. Which is kind of strange, now that I think about it. You guys are the same, Emma's the same." He pursed his lips a moment, then added, "I wonder if Madison is the same."

Amy was about to bite into a piece of bread, but stopped short. "Madison? As in, Madison Bennett, my friend from high school?"

Chloe took a long drink of water, but it wouldn't wash down the lump that had formed in her throat.

"I met her at your wedding," David said. "Sometime after that, we got married and had a baby together. A little girl. We named her Candice."

Amy and Adam looked at each other in shock. "What the hell are you talking about?" Adam asked. "Madison never got married, and Candice's father is some deadbeat."

Amy rolled her eyes. "Ugh, Lyle. What a turd." She shook her head. "But that's another story. How in the world could you know about Candice?"

"Because I remember being there when she was born." David swallowed hard and his hands started to shake. Chloe took one in her own to try and soothe him, even as she reeled from his revelation.

"I don't recall you sharing that before," Emma said.

"I don't either," Chloe said. "When did you remember that?"

David took a deep breath. "Last night. I wasn't sleeping well, and the memory just kind of hit me." He looked at Chloe apologetically. "I was going to tell you this morning, but then you were busy and it was so nice just talking like we used to."

Chloe squeezed his hand and smiled. She too had enjoyed their earlier conversation, and was a little glad they didn't talk about his latest memory. "It's okay."

"This is..." Adam shook his head. "Well, it's very unusual, that's for sure. Have you seen a psychiatrist?"

Emma answered for David. "Not yet, despite my urging him to do so. The neurologist he saw yesterday suggested it, as well."

"I'm not crazy," David said with a slight edge to his voice. "I can't explain what's happening, but I'm not crazy."

"No one's saying you're crazy," Chloe said. She wiggled her hand to try and coax David into loosening his tight grip without giving him the impression she was pulling away. "We're all just worried. Regardless of what you remember, to us you've been missing for ten years."

"Chloe's point is well taken, David," Emma said. "Please try to understand that we can only speak to our own experiences, not yours."

David still looked distressed, even though Chloe could tell he was trying to make sense of the situation. She wanted to comfort him, but had no idea what to say. Instead, she worked her hand free and massaged the area between his shoulder blades, something she remembered working to calm him when they were married.

David took a few deep breaths while everyone else at the table fell silent. "You're right," he finally said. "I'm sorry. I guess I thought if we met up with you guys it might help me remember something else, something that could explain what's going on. Maybe seeing Madison will—"

"Wait," Amy said. "Did you talk to Madison?"

"Well, no, not yet," David said. "I wanted to, but they"— he indicated Emma and Chloe—"thought it might be better to talk to you two first."

Amy and Adam again shared a look, but this time it was worrisome. "Madison went through a pretty rough patch after Candice was born," Amy explained. "Lyle made it very clear that he wasn't going to stick around or pay any child support. She started having these recurring dreams about a guy living with her and helping raise Candice, and I thought it might have been postpartum depression."

"We took her to a specialist who decided it wasn't, though," Adam said. "Madison did start seeing a therapist, and we did what we could to help her, but for a year or so she was in bad shape. She's doing better now, but I don't know if a stranger telling her he remembers being married to her and raising Candice with her would be healthy."

David fidgeted and looked down at his bread plate. "I just want to talk to her," he said quietly. "I'm not trying to force my way into her life or anything."

"Except that you are," Amy said. "Look, I know this is a messed up situation and you're only trying to make sense of it. I trust that you're not trying to hurt anybody. But Madison's been through a lot and I don't want to risk putting her in a bad place again."

David's already frustrated expression intensified, and Chloe pitied him. "There must be something we can do." Turning to him, she asked, "What would you want to ask her? Maybe Amy and Adam could—"

"I need to talk to her myself," David snapped. "Pictures and text messages and other people asking questions aren't going to help."

Chloe recoiled at his harsh reaction, but Emma's tone was firm. "You have no basis for such a claim. In fact, Chloe's application form requesting your death certificate triggered the first memory you recovered."

"But that memory only left me with more questions," David argued. "Talking to Madison myself might actually give me the answers."

Chloe's phone buzzed. She peeked at the screen to see Fred was trying to reach her. She wavered a moment, fearful of the direction the conversation was going but convinced that stepping away would do more harm than good. She hoped whatever Fred needed could wait, and declined the call.

"Amy, do you have any pictures of Madison on your phone?" Emma asked. David started to object but Emma shut him down. "It would be helpful, in my opinion, to confirm that the woman you remember is, in fact, the same Madison that Amy knows."

David took a deep breath, and his agitation abated somewhat. "I thought we already confirmed that."

"Not definitively," Emma said.

Chloe reached for David's hand again, but he pulled away. She turned her attention to the menu, trying to calm her own anxiety while Amy searched her phone for a picture. Chloe had never seen David so worked up. Though he'd had anxiety issues when they were together, his attacks had never been this intense. She worried that something terrible had happened to him, and that bringing back these impossible memories would only make things worse.

"Here's a good one." Amy held her phone across the table for David to see. Chloe looked at the woman on the screen, remembering vaguely from the wedding her attractive smile, tiny nose, green eyes, and petite chin framed by straight, silky, golden hair. The picture had obviously been taken at a party, as Madison was holding a cocktail and surrounded by other people. Chloe didn't remember much about Madison from Amy and Adam's wedding, but a new impression of her as a shallow, self-centered party girl took hold quickly. Her stomach twisted. Even if his memories were true, what could David have possibly seen in Madison?

"Yes, that's Madison." David turned to Emma and asked, "Satisfied?"

"No," Emma said. "Look harder, David. Does the picture of Madison remind you of anything?"

David looked at the screen again. "Not really. It's a nice picture of her." His breath quickened, and he closed his eyes. "Most of the pictures I remember seeing of her were selfies, and she always made this really fake face when she took them.

But every once in a while, someone would catch her in a candid moment, like this one, and those were the pictures I liked best."

He opened his eyes, studied the picture again, and smiled. "When we'd go out with her other friends, she was all about having fun. Everyone around her was always smiling. Privately, she was a little more serious but still really sweet and caring. She helped me through a lot of difficult times."

"Huh." Amy pulled her arm back to put her phone away. "Yeah, that sounds a lot like Madison."

Chloe's heart raced. Hearing David talk about being so close to another woman unsettled her, despite the fact that his memories were impossible. Even if they weren't, she had moved on to a new relationship. Why should she be jealous of him for doing the same thing?

She managed to keep her emotions in check until David turned to her and said, "When I was missing you a lot, Maddie would sit with me and just listen while I told stories about us. We even had the Woodburn Hall painting hanging in the front room of our condo."

An image formed in Chloe's mind of her painting—*their* painting—hanging in front of a couch where David and Madison sat snuggled close together. Heartache slammed into her like a sledgehammer, and she pushed her chair away from the table and stood before she even realized what she was doing. When everyone else at the table looked at her, Chloe made an excuse that she needed to call work and rushed out of the restaurant.

Chloe stared up at the cloudy autumn sky while the cold air settled onto her skin and brought her back to reality. Madison had never seen that painting, because it was hanging on the wall of her bedroom at her parents' house in Stroudsburg, along with several other paintings she'd done during the time she and David were together. Thinking of the paintings reminded her that Fred had called, and Chloe realized she had been holding tightly to her phone ever since. She fumbled with the device until it started dialing.

"Hey babe," Richard answered. "How are things going there?"

Chloe hesitated, surprised that she had called him instead of Fred. "Oh, um, well, it's fine," she said. "I was just, uh, calling to check on the exhibit."

"Fred is taking care of things." Richard sounded unconcerned. "Are you sure you're all right?"

"Sure," Chloe said, trying to convince herself. "I'm just, you know, stressed about the opening and still tired from the flight yesterday." She took a deep breath but coughed when the cold air hit her throat. "Did he get the adjustable walls moved in place around the long sculpture?"

"It looks just like you drew it up." Richard paused a moment before asking, "How's David?"

"He's, um, well," Chloe stammered while she tried to decide how much to tell him. "He's a little confused, I think. He still doesn't really remember what happened to him."

"It sounds like he has a lot to deal with," Richard said flatly. "I hope he understands that you do, too."

Chloe breathed out a short, cynical laugh while she fought back tears. "Yeah, I do, don't I?" Richard didn't even know the half of it.

"Why don't you just come home?"

It was certainly tempting. Chloe had no reason to believe David would doubt her if she said there was an emergency at work, and it wouldn't be completely untrue. He had always felt bad about their plans to move to New York after college falling through. He had told her earlier that she didn't have to stay, and was completely supportive of her ambitions. He would let her go home without argument. She could get the gallery finished, have the opening, and then come back and deal with David afterward.

Except that it didn't feel right. Chloe feared she would be

taking advantage of David's vulnerable state. Besides, she genuinely worried for him and wanted to be near him while he dealt with a situation that grew crazier by the minute.

Chloe sighed. "I can't."

"Why not?" Richard asked, his tone impatient.

"I just can't, okay?" She sniffled and a tear escaped, leaving a freezing trail down her cheek. "It's complicated and it's hard but it's something I just have to do."

"You don't have to do anything you don't want to," Richard said. "Personally, I'd prefer you were here getting ready for the opening, but it's your choice."

"I know." Chloe silently cursed the universe for putting her in a position where she had to choose between a lifelong dream and taking care of someone important to her. "I have a flight first thing tomorrow morning. I'll be fine until then. It would probably be too much hassle to change it at this point anyway."

"Okay," Richard said. "Did you need to talk about anything else?"

Chloe took a deep breath and wiped at her eyes. "No, I'm all right. Thanks."

"Happy to help. Talk to you later." He disconnected the call before Chloe could even say goodbye.

She stared at her phone for a long moment, wondering if she had upset Richard. Did he feel threatened by David? Chloe tried to dismiss the thought as ridiculous. After all, she had no intention of getting back together with David. He was still special to her, but he was more like an old friend than a husband now. She bit her lip and wondered if she had given David the wrong impression by rushing out to Pittsburgh and being so supportive.

Chloe tried to shake the thoughts from her head, and considered calling Fred to take care of whatever had come up. She couldn't bring herself to dial the number, though, worried it would only add to her stress. She took a deep breath and decided to deal with David first. If she could get some closure, she could return to New York with the focus she needed to make her opening happen.

She walked back into the restaurant and took her seat at the table, where the rest of the group was eating appetizers. "Sorry for rushing out like that."

David offered her a plate of potato wedges covered with sour cream, chunks of bacon, and melted cheese. She took one and he smiled at her, but his eyes betrayed the guilt he felt for upsetting her.

Emma dabbed at her mouth with a napkin. "I'm glad you've decided to rejoin us. Now we can proceed with my idea."

"What idea?" Chloe asked.

"Emma came up with a kind of indirect way to see if Madison recognizes me," David explained.

Amy held up her phone. "I'll take a picture of you and send it to Madison, asking if she remembers you from the wedding. It will just happen that David is in the frame."

David took hold of Chloe's hand. "You don't have to do this if you don't want to."

Chloe gave him a little smile to try and assure him she was all right. She still wasn't one hundred percent comfortable with all this talk of David's supposed life without her, but if she could help, she would. He would do the same for her, she was sure of it.

"Let's do it," Chloe said.

Amy took the picture and sent the message. She received a response before she could even set her phone down. "She says, 'Not really. Looks kind of familiar. Cute glasses.'" Amy looked up from the screen. "Should I say something back?"

"Reply as you normally would," Emma said, "but don't mention David."

"Good friend from college," Amy read aloud as she typed. "Artist, lives in NYC now. Big show coming up." She sent the message but didn't set her phone down this time, expecting it to buzz right away. When it didn't, everyone went back to eating.

After several minutes passed without contact from Madison, David shrugged. "Well, it was worth a shot."

"Don't be so quick to give up," Emma said.

As if on cue, Amy's phone buzzed. "'OMG that guy,' all caps," she read. Another message came in, which Amy read silently before announcing, "She's asking who he is."

"Ask if she knows him," Emma ordered.

Amy nodded and typed in the message. Seconds later, her phone buzzed again. "I can't believe this." Amy held the phone so Adam could see, and his eyes grew wide. "She says, 'That's the guy from my dream.'"

eleven

Madison insisted on meeting David despite Amy's concerns. When they finished lunch, Adam returned to his practice and Amy offered to drive Emma, David, and Chloe to Madison's apartment. The drive took over thirty minutes in lunch hour traffic, and Amy weaved through back streets in neighborhoods Chloe didn't recognize. She rode in the back so she could be close to David, ready to comfort him if needed, but he stared out the window the entire trip and felt further away than ever.

"This is it." Amy pulled into a space in front of a little brick apartment building and put the car in park. "We can't stay too long, because I need to pick Beth and Candice up from preschool and Madison has to work tonight."

Chloe nodded, then turned to David, who still stared out the window. She tapped him on the leg. "Hey, are you all right?"

"It's getting easier to remember now." He turned to face Chloe. "It's almost like a regular memory, not some jarring, panicky, overwhelming thing like it was before."

"Okay," Chloe said, wondering what had changed. "If it isn't stressing you out as much, that's a good thing, right?"

David nodded and got out of the car. Chloe followed suit and fell into step with him as they followed Amy up the narrow walk to the building. Emma trailed behind them.

"Are you remembering anything now?" Even as she asked the question, Chloe wasn't sure she wanted to know.

David shrugged. "Oh, just stuff."

"You're being much too specific," Emma joked.

Chloe was about to tell David that he didn't have to hide anything from her, but her phone dinged. Conner's message said the flooring she'd chosen couldn't be installed this week. She huffed and sent a terse reply instructing him to figure it out and assuring him that she trusted his judgment.

"Problem?" Emma asked.

"It's always something," Chloe grumbled as she tucked her phone back into her purse.

David put his hand on the small of her back, causing Chloe to jump a little. He smiled gently at her, and the tension drained from Chloe's mind. That sweet, disarming smile of his had smoothed over many arguments, lifted her spirits when she was sad, and encouraged her when she was creatively frustrated. It was one of the fondest memories she had from their years together, and in that moment, Chloe suddenly realized how much she'd missed it.

"I'm okay," she said, recovering her composure. "Contractors can be frustrating."

The four of them walked up a flight of stairs and down a narrow hallway with dingy paint and stained, out-of-date carpet. "You can hear everything in this place," David said. Chloe gave him a sideways glance, and he clarified. "There was a couple in the apartment next door to Madison's that argued all the time."

"Oh, I remember them," Amy said. "Luckily they moved out a couple years ago."

"Your memories are getting clearer, it seems," Emma said.

"A little, yeah." David crossed his arms and gave Emma an overdramatic glare. "I figured being in a familiar place might help."

"Suggestion can be a powerful influence on memory," Emma warned, refusing to play along. "I see it all the time in court."

When they reached the apartment, Amy knocked and Madison answered almost immediately. She smiled widely and beckoned the group into her apartment. Chloe followed Amy through the small entryway to an eat-in kitchen that reminded her of her apartment in Brooklyn, only larger. She noted the assortment of liquor bottles atop the refrigerator and the crayon drawings stuck to it with magnets.

Madison closed the door and beamed at David. "I can't believe this is happening. I never thought you were real." She approached him to hug and he accepted her embrace easily, even warmly. Chloe's chest tightened.

After she hugged David, Madison greeted Chloe with an awkward hug and a smile that seemed forced. Emma introduced herself and extended her hand for a shake, but like Amy, Madison pushed right past and went for the hug instead. Chloe grinned and shared a look with David. The momentary connection between them helped ease her anxiety about being around Madison, if only a little.

"Let's sit," Madison offered, gesturing toward the living area. She had three well-worn, mismatched couches arranged around a large coffee table that looked like it had been cobbled together from at least two others. The furniture barely fit in the room and seemed out of place for an apartment, reminding Chloe more of a coffee shop or bar.

Madison asked if anyone wanted coffee. Only Amy spoke up, so she offered to make it herself. David walked directly to one of the couches and settled into a corner. Madison followed and sat next to him, practically squealing.

"You always sat like that in my dream," Madison said. "This is so random!"

Emma rolled her eyes and sat on the opposite side of the coffee table from David, and Chloe took a seat next to her.

"We kept this couch." David ran his hand along the fabric. "I remember because it was my least favorite, but when we moved in together we agreed to only keep one of them and I let you pick."

"So, you were having the same dreams as me?" Madison asked.

"Not exactly," David said. "To me, the memories are real,

like it all actually happened."

"But it didn't," Madison argued. "It couldn't have. I've never met you or even seen a picture before today."

Chloe shifted in her seat, unsettled by Madison's quick denial. Was she playing dumb? "I assumed Amy had told you, but David was missing for ten years. We aren't sure what happened to him or why he has these memories."

"I have a ring." David reached into his pocket, then held the wedding band in his outstretched palm. "According to the inscription—"

Madison cut him off. "David and Madison, June 15, right?"

Emma's eyes grew wide. "How did you know that, Ms. Bennett?"

"Because I dreamed about being married to him." Madison said it as if it were obvious. "I had the same ring, duh."

Chloe flinched. "How vivid were these dreams?"

Madison shrugged. "A little more than normal, I guess? The thing that weirded me out the most wasn't that the dreams were vivid, but that I remembered stuff in them. Like, stuff I hadn't dreamt about before." She looked at David. "In the dreams, we met at Amy's wedding and got engaged when I found out I was pregnant, but I didn't actually dream about those things. The dreams didn't start until after Candice was born."

Chloe tried to think of a time she'd remembered something so elaborate in a dream. Failing to come up with anything, she just said, "That's weird."

Madison giggled. "Tell me about it. My therapist says I was just inventing a convoluted narrative as a coping mechanism." She turned back toward David. "I can't wait to see the look on her face when I tell her you're real. You might have to come with me so I don't get committed."

David laughed along with her. "It can be our first real date," he joked.

Madison smacked his leg playfully. "Jeez, Dave, you're even more romantic than I dreamed."

Chloe sat frozen, watching David and Madison act far too comfortable together for two people who had just met. Could they really have known each other in some kind of dream world? If David had shared a connection with someone while he was gone, why had it been Madison and not her?

Emma stayed on point, as usual. "How long did you have these dreams before you went to a therapist?"

"A few weeks," Madison said. "I thought I was just having fantasies, but the dreams kept happening, and they seemed so real. Sometimes I wouldn't remember them after I woke up, but then I'd have another dream and somehow know what had happened."

Amy returned from the kitchen with her coffee and sat on the third couch. "That's when Adam and I suggested she see a specialist, just in case it was postpartum depression."

Madison nodded. "I didn't feel depressed, and I looked up the symptoms and didn't think that was what I had, but it never hurts to be safe, right?"

Madison glanced from David to Emma to Chloe and back again, as if seeking confirmation. David smiled and rubbed her shoulder. "Of course. Better safe than sorry."

The pit in Chloe's stomach grew. She reminded herself that David's connection to this woman couldn't possibly be real. Even if it was, Chloe had moved on and built a new life. She had Richard and Madge and the gallery. There was no reason to be upset.

When that line of thinking didn't work, she distracted herself by toying with her phone, hoping for a missed call or an e-mail or something she could use as an excuse to get out of there. No messages had come in.

"I went to the doctor and he said everything seemed normal physically, and he didn't think I had postpartum depression either," Madison continued. "But he thought I should see a psychiatrist anyway. So I went, and I told her about my dreams, and she asked me if I was having any trouble dealing with day-to-day stuff, and I said no, and she asked me if I had been taking any unusual medication, which I hadn't, and—"

Emma cut her off. "In summary, everything was, in your opinion, normal aside from the dreams, correct?"

Madison's mouth hung open a moment, apparently surprised by Emma's forwardness. She nodded and seemed hesitant to start talking again.

"Don't mind her," David said, squeezing Madison's shoulder. "She's an attorney. It's just how she operates."

"Oh." Madison shifted in her seat and glanced around. "An attorney? Am I in trouble?"

"No, no, of course not," David said. "Emma's a good friend of mine. She just happened to be born with the disposition of an attorney. Our high school guidance counselor suggested she go into professional musical theater, but for some reason she chose law school instead."

Madison's smile returned, then she broke into laughter. Emma glared at David, obviously perturbed by his disarming her. He shrugged and grinned stupidly, and Emma rolled her eyes and gave the tiniest smile possible. Chloe tried to suppress her laughter and glanced toward David, but he had turned back to Madison. Chloe pursed her lips and checked her phone again. Still nothing.

Emma crossed her arms. "I'll have you all know theatrics do play a significant role in the courtroom. Music, not so much, but it's important to remain in control of one's attitude during the course of a hearing. Posture, inflection, nonverbal signals, and other factors must be carefully controlled, in the same way an actor must give a convincing performance."

David and Madison grinned at each other. "She's fun," Madison said. "How long have you known her?"

"Pretty much my whole life," David answered. "We were born on the same day, and our parents met at the hospital. They became friends and Emma and I grew up together, almost like brother and sister."

"That sounds so familiar," Madison said. "You must have talked about Emma in the dreams, but I don't remember actually meeting her." She paused, then locked eyes with Chloe. "He definitely talked about you, though."

Chloe's heart pounded. She had never imagined that Madison's dreams involved her, and now felt like she had been put on the spot. "Really?" That single word caught in her parched throat.

As if sensing her discomfort, Emma chimed in. "What specifically did David say with regards to Chloe?"

Madison took a deep breath. "Dave mentioned you in almost every dream, so I know pretty much everything about you. Grew up in the Poconos, always loved painting, wanted to go to art school but your brother took your savings, how you and Dave met, how you love Chinese food and have your own fancy chopsticks, how you used to wear silk hair ribbons that would fall out all the time, how Dave freaked out when you guys went to New York your senior year..." She trailed off and sniffled, then wiped a tear from her eye. "Pretty sad, huh? I have an elaborate fantasy about being married to this great guy and he's completely obsessed with another woman."

"You never told me you knew the guy's name," Amy said. "And if he was talking about Chloe, we probably could have put the pieces together."

A dark thought shot through Chloe's mind. Could Madison be hiding something? Her alleged dreams somehow aligned with David's sparse memory, and she knew far too much about Chloe. Maybe she belonged to a weird cult like Tommy's.

Madison gestured toward Chloe. "Well, I only met her the one time. How was I supposed to know she was the same Chloe?" She turned back toward Amy. "Plus, it was hard for me to tell the difference sometimes between what I dreamed and what actually happened, especially the stuff about your wedding."

"I suggest we focus on the memories David has recovered thus far," Emma said, bringing the conversation back on point. "That will help us determine how closely your dreams align with David's recollections far better than simply blurting out whatever comes to mind."

"Um, okay," Madison said. "Let me grab my journals."

"Journals?" David asked.

Madison stood. "My therapist told me to write down everything I could remember about the dreams. She never really looked at them, but I guess it was a good thing to do anyway. It helped make them easier to deal with and I didn't have to worry about forgetting them, either." She left the living room and returned moments later with a stack of spiral notebooks.

Emma flipped through her own pad. "Okay, Ms. Bennett, let's start—"

"Call me Madison," she interrupted. "Ms. Bennett is too formal. It makes me feel like I'm in trouble."

Emma smiled at her, and Chloe suspected it wasn't the first time such a request had been made. "Very well, Madison, I'd like to begin with the last thing David remembered prior to his disappearance. In his version of events, this would have coincided with Chloe vanishing. Do you recall him telling you anything related to that?"

Madison nodded and started flipping through notebook pages. "Let me find it to make sure I tell you right. Okay, here. Dave had told me at some point that he had woken up in the middle of the night because he heard something. He looked around but didn't find anything, and even checked outside." She looked directly at Chloe. "Then he went back to bed and when he woke up the next morning, you were gone. It was your wedding anniversary."

"That's how I remember it," David said.

Emma scrawled something on her pad. Chloe leaned over to try and see her notes but couldn't make anything from her scribbles. If Emma suspected Madison of any involvement in what happened to David, she didn't show it.

"That's a lot like what you told me happened to you," Amy said to Chloe. "I didn't think you woke up in the middle of the night, though."

"No," Chloe said. She fought against the memories of that

awful morning. "I didn't hear any noises or anything." Chloe locked eyes with David, who offered a sympathetic smile.

"Okay, moving on," Emma said. "David, do you recall the first thing you remembered about the time you were missing?"

"Let's see," David said. "It was when I was at your apartment, after I'd taken a shower. We were looking through your files and I saw the petition to file for my death certificate, and I remembered filling out the same form for Chloe."

Chloe thought back to the gut-wrenching decision to declare David legally deceased, how she had held onto the forms for months before filling them out, how David's mother objected to the process. It had been one of the most difficult things she'd ever had to do, but claiming their joint assets had allowed her to move to New York.

"Yeah, I remember that one, too," Madison said. She closed the notebook she'd read from previously and opened another, then leafed through several pages. "Dave and I had been married almost two years when that happened." She turned to him. "You said you wanted to set up a college fund for Candice."

David nodded and looked toward Chloe. "I remembered something about Candice when I saw the form."

He turned to Chloe, and looked as if he needed her reassurance that he had made a reasonable decision. Of course, it hadn't actually happened, and Chloe wondered what Madison had to gain by bringing up the money now. Before she could decide what to say, Madison continued reading.

"Emma helped you. Oh, hey!" She nudged David. "You did talk about Emma. The paperwork was set up so it could be easily reversed, but you felt really guilty about it, and we sat down together and looked through your keepsakes."

"Keepsakes?" David asked.

Madison nodded again. "You had this box of stuff that was Chloe's. Whenever you'd get really sad or miss her, you would get out the box and look at the things inside."

Chloe thought about her collection of David's things and

how her heart had ached when she'd first filled the box. The idea of David doing the same for her brought a fresh tear to her eye, which she quickly wiped away.

"What was in it?" David asked.

"If I remember right," Madison said, flipping through a few pages, "it was mostly photographs and little trinkets. There was a necklace you had planned to give her. Your wedding ring was in there, and Chloe's fancy chopsticks."

"Was it this necklace?" Chloe reached into the neck hole of her shirt and produced the heart-shaped pendant.

"Hang on, I tried to draw it," Madison said. She opened the other journal and flipped through until she found the drawing, which she showed to everyone.

"That's definitely a match," Emma said. "Is this triggering any memories, David?"

He shook his head. "Not yet. I can picture the things I'd put in a box like that, but I don't remember a specific time I sat down with Madison and looked through them."

"There was also a painting," Madison said. "We had it hanging in the front room. It was an old building, I think from where you went to college. It had a clock tower."

"Woodburn Hall," David and Chloe said together. They locked eyes as Chloe's mind drifted back to the windy autumn day she'd painted that scene.

"That's where you guys met," Madison said.

"Yeah." David nodded, never breaking eye contact with Chloe.

"It's becoming apparent that your dreams and David's memories do, in fact, line up," Emma said. She asked David to try and focus on day to day life with Madison and Candice to see if he could recall anything new.

David shook his head and broke eye contact with Chloe. "Right, okay. Well, we had moved in together because your landlord raised the rent," he said to Madison. "I don't remember us having a serious or even exclusive relationship until we found out you were pregnant." David's face strained and his breath quickened. "You always loved going out with your friends, but after Candice was born I almost never went with you because I was watching her."

Chloe watched the anguish in David's face as he remembered, and her concern for him quickly gave way to anger toward Madison. How could she use him like that?

"That sounds kind of like me," Amy said. She turned to Madison. "We used to go out together all the time, but since the kids were born I much prefer to be the babysitter."

Madison flipped through a few pages of her notebook. "I did write down some stuff about that, but it wasn't like I was excluding you, Dave. Right here it says you didn't want to go with us on a weekend trip to Erie, even though I asked you to come."

"Was that when you went to that art gallery?" Amy asked.

"Yeah," Madison said. "My friend Sheryl's friend Laura was doing a show, and Sheryl didn't want to make the trip by herself. So what actually happened was Amy watched Candice, but I dreamed, um..." She trailed off, seemingly bothered by something. "I dreamed you watched her, Dave."

"An art show?" David asked. He glanced at Chloe, then back to Madison. "Of course I didn't want to go."

Chloe glared at Madison. Even though she still wasn't convinced anything they were talking about actually happened, the fact that Madison could be so insensitive toward David made Chloe flush with anger.

"Huh." Madison leafed back and forth between pages. "That makes a lot of sense, I guess, but I didn't write down that we talked about it. You just said you didn't want to go."

David fidgeted, looking agitated. "Candice and I could have gone on the trip, but we would have been staying in the hotel a lot, and if I was just going to be staying in with her I figured we'd be more comfortable at home. I don't remember talking about it either, but I have this feeling that every time you'd ask me to come along, I'd just say, 'No, that's okay,' and that was enough explanation."

Chloe gave David a pitying look. "It doesn't sound like you were very happy."

"I was fine," David said. "Candice and I played with her dolls and watched movies that weekend, and it was a lot of fun." To Madison, he said, "And when you got back, you said you'd had a good time that weekend too, and I think we ordered pizza."

"Pizza sounds familiar, and the party for Laura's show was definitely fun," Madison said, then turned to Chloe. "I'm sure it was nothing like the ones you get to go to in New York, though. You probably see celebrities all the time, and have really fancy food and champagne."

David cut in before Chloe could respond. "Chloe is actually having her own debut opening on Friday."

Chloe chuckled nervously. "Assuming the gallery construction gets done."

"Wow, that's exciting! I wish I could go," Madison said. "I love Manhattan. I've only been a couple times."

"We should do a girls' trip sometime," Amy suggested. "I'm sure Adam's parents wouldn't mind watching Beth and Candice for a long weekend." She looked to Chloe. "I bet you know all kinds of fun things to do."

Chloe shrugged. "It's New York City. If you can't find something to do, there's something wrong with you."

Madison and Amy giggled. Chloe noticed David staring at a closed door in the hallway. Candice's drawings clung haphazardly to the door with the aid of abundant clear tape.

"You okay?" Chloe asked David.

He sighed. "Yeah, I just wish I could see her."

Madison pulled out her phone. "I've got *tons* of pictures. Oh, check this out!" She reached for a remote control and switched on the television situated in a corner of the room. Then she tapped her phone screen a few times and a picture of a cherubic, smiling face framed by curly golden hair appeared. "This way, we can all see."

"She looks exactly like I remember," David said.

Chloe glanced at each photo as it appeared, but she paid more attention to David. He smiled and looked fondly at the images of Candice, but somehow seemed uncomfortable. Chloe wished she were sitting beside him so she could comfort him, but instead thought she might be able to ease his tension by saying something. "She's beautiful, and seems really happy."

Madison smiled proudly. "That's my little candy cane."

"You call her candy cane?" Emma asked.

Madison giggled. "Yeah, it's my fun little name for her. She likes that her name sounds like candy and I tell her it's because she's so sweet. Plus, there's a story—"

"She pulled a candy cane out of your mouth when she was two," David interrupted. "Then she tried to hang it back on the Christmas tree."

Madison pursed her lips and turned away.

"What's wrong?" David asked.

Madison rose from her seat and paced near the television. "You weren't there."

David took a deep breath. "I remember being there."

"But you weren't." Madison spun around to face him, a hurt look on her face. "That was just Candice and me, at my apartment, with my Christmas tree."

David shrunk from her. "I know. I mean, I know I wasn't actually there, but I remember it anyway. Didn't you dream about that one?"

Madison sniffled. "Oh yeah, I dreamed it. I dreamed about you when she took her first step, when she said her first word, on her first day of daycare, on her birthday, at Christmas." Tears soaked her face. "I dreaded it. Every time there was a major event in Candice's life, I knew I would have a dream about you. That's why I was so anxious all the time."

Amy rose to bring Madison a tissue. David leaned forward, his elbows on his knees, looking shell-shocked. Chloe had no idea how to react, afraid if she did the wrong thing it would send David into a panic attack or agitate Madison further.

Emma stood. "Perhaps it would be best for us to leave."

Chloe got up as well, and started toward David, but he turned to Madison instead. "I'm sorry."

"You were so good to her." Madison said it like an accusation. "In every dream, you were such a good dad and Candice was so happy, and the next morning I'd wake up afraid I wasn't doing enough for my own daughter. I decided before she was born that I'd rather raise her on my own than with the wrong guy, and every dream made me doubt that choice."

David looked genuinely hurt. "Maddie, I—"

"Don't call me that!" Anger flashed in her eyes.

Amy tried to calm her. "Why don't you go lie down for a bit? I'll help you get settled, and then we'll leave."

Madison looked torn, but relented. "Okay. I'm sorry, this is just a lot to handle."

"It's completely understandable," Emma said. "Thank you for your time."

"Give me just a minute and I'll take you back to your car," Amy said. She and Madison disappeared down the hall, and Chloe heard a door close.

Chloe walked around the coffee table and sat down next to David. Emma received a message and excused herself to the hallway to make a work-related call. They sat in silence a moment before Chloe noticed the picture of Candice still displayed on the television.

"She is cute," Chloe said. David gave her a questioning look and she indicated the screen.

David's breath quickened and his hands shook. "Yeah, just like I remember. Which means there's no way I could be her father."

twelve

Chloe put her hand on David's shoulder to try and calm him. "David, of course you aren't her father."

"But I remember." He wheeled about to face her. "I remember when she was born. I remember taking care of her, feeding her, changing her diapers. I remember watching ridiculous children's shows with her and playing with her toys."

Chloe stammered, unable to come up with anything to say. What David claimed was impossible.

"It was all a lie," David said. "She lied to me."

"Nobody lied to you," Chloe said softly. "Amy told us who Candice's father is. He's a deadbeat dad, and that's definitely not you."

"But this isn't how it happened." His expression was strained, his face bright red, and his breathing quick and uneven.

"Calm down," Chloe said. She leaned back in her seat and encouraged David to do the same. When she noticed Amy watching from the doorway, Chloe motioned for her to give them some privacy.

"I'm not crazy," David said. "I'm not. I remember. I was there. This isn't how it happened." His whole body shook.

"Nobody thinks you're crazy," Chloe said. "I don't think you're crazy." She took hold of his hands and squeezed. "Look at me. I promise, I don't think you're crazy."

"What happened to me?" Tears streamed from David's eyes. "Why do I remember things that didn't really happen?"

"I don't know." Chloe struggled to maintain eye contact, the hurt in David's face breaking her own heart. "We'll figure it out, though." Even as she said it, she wondered how. She briefly considered mentioning Tommy's mystical theories, but decided against it.

"What if we don't?" David asked. "What if we never figure out why I have these memories? I'll just be stuck here, like nothing happened. Like I was in a coma or something, and none of the things I remember about the last decade are real." He shook his head. "But they have to be real! They *feel* real. And I have my ring."

Chloe couldn't fight the urge to wince. It disturbed her that David had a different wedding ring, even though this second marriage couldn't have happened. She wondered what had happened to his ring from their wedding, since the box of mementos Madison had mentioned couldn't possibly exist, either.

She took a deep breath. "I honestly don't know how to explain it, but the most important thing to me is that you're back. You're here again."

David gave a strained smile. "I never thought I'd see you again. That pain, that hurt, has been a part of every single memory I've had so far. I remember all those years that I couldn't find you, that I didn't know what happened to you. I tried so hard to move on."

His words brought back memories of Chloe's own struggle, and her chest turned to lead. "I know what you mean," she said, her voice barely audible.

"But you don't," David said. "Those things actually happened to you. Apparently, you've been fine, and I've been the one missing, and it's freaking me out that what I remember and what actually happened are so different. Except that Madison is the same. And Candice, she's exactly the same. Exactly. That little piece of happiness that I found after all that time, it isn't even real! I have nothing."

Chloe squeezed his hands tighter, sharing his anguish and trying to stay strong for both of them. "You have me."

David shook his head. "You got to move on. You have your boyfriend and your new life. The last ten years of my life are just...nothing."

"Don't say that." Chloe refused to believe he had simply vanished for no reason. "I'm going to help you figure this out."

"I should have just stayed missing." David pulled his hands free and buried his face in them. "Why did I even come back? Why did I have to get pulled away from my life, just to show up and interrupt yours? You've obviously been a lot better off without me."

"Stop it." Chloe's voice quavered. "That isn't true."

"How can you say it isn't true?" David leapt from his seat and paced, ranting. "You have everything you ever wanted. Yes, I'm sure it was hard for a few years, but without me in the way you were able to go live in New York. You get to be the artist you always dreamed of being."

"What, so I'm supposed to feel guilty about moving on?" Chloe's raw emotion bubbled over into anger, and she stood to face him. "Is that it? Or do you want me to feel sorry for you that things were just so difficult? Like they weren't difficult for me. I worked my ass off to get where I am. When you disappeared, I had no idea what to do. I've never felt so alone in my life, and you have the nerve to accuse me of being better off?"

David stopped pacing and turned to face her. "I lost you too. At least, I remember losing you. I feel like I lost you. I remember feeling alone and lost and finding some comfort with Maddie, and then I lost her, too. So, all I get are a bunch of terrible memories and the truth that none of it actually happened. You don't think you're better off?"

"Look, I don't have any more idea than you what is going on with your memory." Chloe took slow steps toward him. "But I still care about you. I still worry about you. I meant it when I said I don't think you're crazy. It sucks what happened. It sucks for both of us. Just because I'm doing okay doesn't mean it was easy for me, either."

"I never said it was easy," David said. "I just meant—"

"Guys!" Amy interrupted them from the hallway, causing both David and Chloe to turn. "How about bringing it down a notch or two? This is seriously not helping Madison."

"Oh, shit." Guilt washed over David's face, replacing the strained anxiety almost instantaneously. "Is she all right?"

Chloe watched his reaction in disbelief. Even after everything he'd just said to her, he still believed he owed something to this woman and her daughter, still felt responsible for them somehow. The sheer absurdity of the situation was too much for her to bear. She turned and strode quickly out of the apartment, nearly crashing into Emma on her way to the stairs.

Chloe got as far as Amy's car before she stopped to breathe. She paced up and down the sidewalk, panting, and tried to come to grips with the situation. She replayed the scene in her mind, fuming over the way David looked at Madison, how he talked to her, how he worried over her. Guilt crept into Chloe's stomach, reminding her she should be sympathetic and happy that he had reappeared. Her phone rang. She declined Fred's call and turned off the ringer. She didn't want to think about what she risked to be here, only to see the man she'd loved and married pining for a woman he'd just met.

"Chloe, wait," David called from behind her.

She wheeled on him. "This is bullshit, David. I know you think they're your family but they aren't. Those things never happened."

"They did happen, they had to," David countered. "I'm not crazy."

"For the last time, I'm not saying you're crazy." Chloe gestured wildly as conflicting emotions sent waves of nervous energy through her. "How the hell am I supposed to feel when you reappear after ten years and start talking about some life you imagined with another woman? Do I not get to be upset when you seem more comfortable with her than you do with me? And worst of all is the fact that, even if these things did happen to you, she was just using you the whole time."

David paused only a moment before retorting with an annoyed, "And?"

"And I think that's wrong! Look I may have moved on with my life but that doesn't mean I stopped caring about you. Even if something happened and you really were with someone else, I wouldn't let them hurt you like that."

David crossed his arms. "You don't know what you're talking about."

"David, please, think about this! Madison doesn't know you. Even in this dream world of hers, she didn't really care about you. It sounds to me like all she ever wanted was a babysitter."

"I was fine with that," he answered.

"So you just let her use you?" Chloe shook her head and blinked back frustrated tears. "Why?"

"Because I used her too. When Madison was around, I didn't feel as sad. She helped me forget about..." He looked away.

"Forget about what, David?" Chloe knew the answer but desperately wanted to hear him to say anything else.

David continued avoiding eye contact. "I'm sorry, I didn't mean it like that."

Chloe balled her fists at her sides and shouted, "Just say it already! You wanted to forget about me!"

"No!" David stepped closer to her, and Chloe backed away. "I couldn't possibly forget you, and I didn't want to, but it was just that the pain was too much. I couldn't handle it. I had to have something to get me out of that, and Madison did it."

"I don't believe this," Chloe said through bared teeth. "You meet some girl at a wedding and she makes you forget all about me?" Chloe shook her head and groaned. "It didn't even really happen! I was at the wedding and you weren't. But even if these are your real memories, I can't believe you would just forget all about me. How long did you even look for me in this fantasy world of yours?"

David closed his eyes, anguish apparent in his features. "I don't remember."

"Of course you don't. Why would you remember a silly thing like that when you could fantasize about getting used by Blondie?" Chloe gestured emphatically toward the apartment building.

David took another step forward, and this time Chloe held her ground. "I didn't want to forget about you, I never could. I loved you. You were everything to me, and I was miserable without you. Don't you get that?"

"Don't accuse me of not being miserable! The only difference is that I kept looking. I kept hoping. I kept you in my mind and in my heart every single day."

"What about Richard?" David asked. "Didn't he make you forget a little?"

Chloe recoiled. "That's different. Richard and I are in a committed relationship, not just using each other. Not only that, but our relationship is based in the real world, not some weird dream or fantasy."

He locked eyes with her in an intense stare. "Do you love him?"

Chloe hesitated. She and Richard never really talked about love. They were affectionate with one another and had been exclusive almost a year and a half, but Chloe honestly didn't know if they were in love. "It's different."

"Different how?" David pressed.

Chloe stammered. "It just is, you know? Just because we care about each other doesn't mean we have to be romantic about it."

"But you do care about him." David never broke his gaze. "This isn't just some fling you're having. So, you couldn't have been hoping every day I would come back, at least not as your husband. You declared me legally dead. You had to have accepted that you wouldn't see me again, right?"

His words dug into her heart, tearing open old scars and

adding a fresh, deep wound. Chloe sobbed, and weakness crept into every muscle in her body. Signing those documents had been one of the hardest things she'd ever done, and now her soul ached anew with both the truth that she had given up on David and the way he'd forced her to admit it. But what else could she have done? She had needed the money to move to New York, and didn't she deserve to chase her dream?

David tried to put his hand on her shoulder, but Chloe pulled away. "I can't do this right now." She turned and started up the street, wiping tears from her eyes. David called after her, but she ignored him. She didn't know the neighborhood and had no idea where she was going, but as she rounded the corner she saw a bus stopping to pick up passengers. She rushed to catch it without checking the destination, and looked back toward the corner as she boarded.

David hadn't followed her.

thirteen

Chloe slumped in her seat on the bus, trying to hide her tears. She took a few deep breaths and got a tissue from her purse. Chloe patted at her cheeks and eyes, ruining her makeup. She dabbed, trying to repair it as best she could, wishing she'd tossed a compact into her purse that morning. But she'd been in a rush, and then they'd gone to see *her*, and she had watched David and Madison act so comfortable, so close to one another in a way Chloe hadn't felt since David vanished.

She stared out the window but paid no attention to the sights as the bus meandered through the outskirts of Pittsburgh. When Chloe realized she hadn't seen anything familiar for a while, she got out her phone to figure out her location. As she brought the device to life, she was surprised to discover it was after 4:30 P.M. Her maps application indicated that she was in McKeesport, a long way southeast of downtown.

"Damn it," Chloe thought out loud. She couldn't remember the name of the hotel where she was staying, so dug in her purse for her room key. As she pulled it free, she accidentally brought with it one of the doodles she'd made earlier that day. Chloe stared into the swirling pen strokes, noting their relaxed, effortless pattern. She spotted places where the ink had sputtered or where a bump in the desk had forced an errant mark, and the exercise soothed her, if only briefly.

She needed more art to scrutinize, something to focus on and clear her head. A destination immediately came to mind, a little gallery somewhere in the cultural district she and David had stumbled upon after seeing a matinee. Chloe couldn't re-member the name or address, but decided she could probably find it if she started at Theater Square.

A few taps and swipes later, Chloe had a route back to downtown Pittsburgh. She had to backtrack a little to catch a connecting bus, then transferred again and settled in for the hour-long ride. She thought about calling Fred back, but froze every time she got out her phone to dial him, afraid to face his judgement, his disappointment. She convinced herself she'd be better able to deal with whatever Fred needed to discuss after she'd visited the little gallery.

By the time she reached her stop, the orange of the sunset had faded to a deep purple, and the dim interior lights cast strange shadows across the faces of the other passengers. She exited the bus and walked quickly up Seventh Avenue, focused on the click of her shoes against the concrete and the blazing marquee of the Benedum Center. She pushed through a decent crowd meandering toward the evening show and turned the corner, hurrying past the tantalizing smells of bars and restau-rants, trying to ignore happy couples strolling hand in hand to the theater. Another block, and the crowd thinned considera-bly. She turned left into a dark alley lit only by the light shining through a narrow glass door at the end, and breathed a sigh of relief that the little gallery hadn't closed in the years since her last visit.

Chloe entered and was enveloped in the too-strong smell of various air fresheners and perfumes—a detail she'd forgotten—but it did not deter her. She stepped into the small space and took in the eclectic decorations, the haphazard lighting, and, of course, the canvases. Paintings of various subjects and styles hung everywhere, crowding each other and arranged in no particular order, the goal just to get them on the walls.

The old woman who ran the little gallery sat in her rocker near the card table she used as a checkout counter. "Take all the time you need. I got nowhere to be."

Chloe thanked her hostess and began browsing the pieces,

which ranged from abstract to photorealism. Traditional land-scapes and portraits competed for space with mixed-media collages, detailed pencil sketches, and surreal watercolors. She studied every stroke, letting herself feel each artist's story, more focused on the act of creation than the creation itself, her emotions flung this way and that by the chaotic collection.

Somehow, she found peace amid the turbulence. While she focused on art, Chloe pushed away the contradicting thoughts and feelings that swirled around David and Richard and her opening. Those were relegated to spectators as the paintings took over, and Chloe let them lead her through her own mind. She gave herself over to each piece, her experienced eye catching the subtleties, brilliantly hidden details and tiny, overlooked mistakes. She absorbed every painting even as they absorbed her, a sort of symbiosis that granted her passage deeper into herself.

"You're an artist," the old woman said, suddenly next to her. It was more a charge than a question.

Chloe nodded. "I paint a little." She surprised herself with her own humility.

"No, you are an *artist*," the woman said. "Anybody can pick up a brush and learn to paint, but you feel it, don't you? You can feel the magic in all these paintings not because of what you see on the canvas, but the sweat that went into making them."

Chloe nodded. "There's a story in every one of these. You have a wonderful collection. I've never been to another place like this, and I live in New York City." She chuckled. "I work for one of the most respected art dealers on the East Coast, and even his gallery doesn't make me feel the way this one does." She suddenly felt very inadequate. As much as Fred praised her work at his premier gallery, Chloe feared she was still coming up short.

The old woman thanked her for the compliment, then asked, "So what's got you out and about alone tonight?"

Chloe shook her head. "Trying to forget."

"Ah, man trouble. I should have known." The old woman scratched at her neck, then nudged Chloe. "You can tell me. What did he do?"

"It's complicated." Chloe sighed. "Please, I really don't want to talk about it. I came here to get away from that mess awhile."

"Okay, okay. I'm sorry." The woman meandered back to her rocker.

Chloe turned her attention back to the paintings, but thoughts of David crept in and stole her focus. She remembered how he would talk sweetly to her, kiss her softly, and hold her in a way that made the rest of the world a blurry, impressionist interpretation of reality. She hadn't realized how much she'd missed that feeling, how much she'd missed him, until she saw how much he cared for Madison. He loved her, and it made Chloe sick to her stomach.

"You're not the jealous type," the old woman chimed in. "I can tell, you know. A lot of good art comes out of jealousy, but that's not your style."

Chloe suddenly felt trapped by the small space and the old woman. She didn't remember her talking so much last time. "I should probably go."

The woman shrugged. "Suit yourself."

Chloe thanked her and stepped back into the chilly autumn air. Despite the uncomfortable conversation, Chloe got what she'd needed from the little gallery. She remembered her purpose, her drive. The east wing and her opening were what mattered now, and she couldn't put her life on hold because David was back. She wondered if she could catch the next flight to New York.

Chloe checked her phone and determined that the hotel wasn't far from the little gallery. They probably had an airport shuttle service, and if not she could take a taxi. She would gather her things, head to the airport, and call Emma on the way to let her know what she was doing. She feared if she talked to David, she might change her mind.

She checked traffic and was crossing the street when Tommy fell in step beside her. "Where are you going?"

"Home," Chloe said. "How long have you been following me?"

Tommy panted as he struggled to keep up with her. "I haven't been following you."

Chloe reached the sidewalk and came to an abrupt stop. Tommy took a step or two past her, then turned back. Chloe crossed her arms over her chest and asked, "Really?"

Tommy huffed. "Okay, fine. I've been following you since you left the hotel this morning."

Chloe rolled her eyes. "I knew it. I knew you wouldn't stay out of this."

"It's important," Tommy said. "I'm trying to—"

"Help me?" Chloe cocked an eyebrow at him. "I don't need your help, Tommy. I haven't needed it my whole life and I don't need it now."

Tommy looked around nervously while people passing by stared at them. "Could we just go someplace and talk? I'll buy you dinner."

"There's nothing to talk about," Chloe said. "My life is in New York now. My career is there. Whatever the hell David thinks he had with that woman..." She clenched her fists and let out a deep breath while her heart trembled on the tightrope between rage and weeping. "It doesn't matter. I've moved on. The sooner he accepts that, the better."

She wheeled around and started down the sidewalk again, and took several steps before she realized how disoriented she was. Chloe ignored it and let the feeling of walking, the sensation of movement, perpetuate her resolve. She wasn't standing still and she wasn't waiting for anyone to tell her where to go.

Tommy caught up to her at the next corner. "You're going the wrong way."

"I don't care," Chloe said without looking at him. The crosswalk sign turned green and she started off at a brisk pace. The wind whipped at her and she hugged herself against the cold, cursing herself for leaving her jacket at Madison's apartment. David would probably just give it to her, she thought darkly. She imagined the two of them sitting next to one another on one of Madison's junky couches, reminiscing about that time Chloe got upset and stormed out into the cold without her jacket.

"You are putting out some serious negative energy right now," Tommy said, his breathing even heavier than it was before. His medallions clinked and pinged off each other as he practically jogged to keep up with Chloe.

"Maybe you could walk a little faster if you weren't wearing all that stupid jewelry," Chloe said, still not looking at him.

"You're really not going to stop and think about this?" Tommy asked.

"Nope."

"You really don't care about what happened to David or why he's suddenly back?"

"Nope."

"Or the potential consequences of walking away from this?"

"I'm more concerned about the consequences of *not* walking away from this," Chloe said. She reached another corner but couldn't cross right away, forcing her to stop. She pulled her phone from her purse to figure out which way she should go while Tommy tried in vain to catch his breath beside her.

"Fine," he said. "You don't care what happened or why or what might happen if you guys don't work this out. But—"

"There's nothing to work out," Chloe cut him off as she struggled to pull up her maps application with trembling, tense fingers. "He and Blondie can live out their little shared fantasy. I've got Richard and my art and the gallery. Everybody wins."

Tommy put his hands on Chloe's shoulders. "Look at me."

Chloe resisted for a long time, still fumbling with her phone. Finally she huffed and looked up, but tried to avoid eye contact. "I don't have time for this."

Tommy's face wore a gentle, calming expression, and he

could have been a younger version of their father, except for the unkempt hair and scraggly beard. He seemed to have recovered from the rush to keep up with Chloe, his breathing steady and his voice even. "You might not care about any of that other stuff, and I know you're pissed at David right now, but I know you can't look me in the eye and tell me you don't care about him."

Chloe shot an intense stare at Tommy. "I..." she started, but something inside her wouldn't let the words form. It was as if saying she didn't care about David were crossing some terrible line, and her heart held her back while her mind frantically waved red flags in her face.

She closed her eyes and fought tears. As much as she hated to admit it, Tommy was right, though she didn't want to give him the satisfaction of knowing that.

"Okay, so I care about him," Chloe said. Before Tommy could speak, she quickly added, "But not because I think we belong together. I just don't want to see him get hurt, you know?"

"I know," Tommy said with a smile. The wind picked up again, blowing their hair around wildly. Tommy took his hands from Chloe's shoulders and used them to hold his hair back out of his face. He closed his eyes, looked upward, and took a deep breath. "Smells like rain."

Chloe pulled her own hair out of her face and sighed as the adrenaline drained out of her. She still didn't want to talk to David, and she was still convinced going home was the right thing to do, but her drive to action had waned somewhat. The cold settled onto her skin and she shivered.

Tommy suggested again that they step inside a nearby restaurant, and this time Chloe didn't argue. They sat at the bar and she ordered a cocktail.

Tommy asked for a glass of water and handed the bartender a wad of folded bills. "I won't be staying. This should cover her."

Chloe wondered where her brother had gotten so much

money. Most of his life he'd actively avoided work and responsibility. Though this group of his seemed to provide some direction and stability, she worried what strings might be attached. "Where are you going?"

"I have a few things to tend to," Tommy said.

Her curiosity got the best of her. "Like what?"

He took a long drink of water before answering. "I'm meeting up with a few local members of the Brotherhood to discuss our involvement in a new business deal. We'll also try to further assess the consequences of David's reappearance."

Chloe imagined Tommy meeting with his colleagues as a strange mix of a drum circle and the mafia. "They don't make you do anything dangerous, do they? Please tell me you aren't hurting people."

"I go where I'm needed and do what has to be done. Sometimes balancing the world energies gets...tricky, but I have the support of the Brotherhood." Tommy offered a reassuring smile. "Don't worry sis, I'm not in over my head this time."

She wasn't convinced, but Chloe held off the urge to parent him. "How many of you are there in this 'brotherhood?'"

"Enough." Tommy chuckled. "Honestly, I don't know for sure. I don't know how many other organizations like ours are out there, either. I do know that there have been other cases of abduction, as well as violence and extortion, but not by us. Where we try to keep the world energies in balance, others seek to do the opposite, usually for political or financial reasons."

Chloe took a deep breath. She was still skeptical, but growing concerned. "And you think one of these other groups might be responsible for what happened to David?"

He nodded and took another drink of water. "It's a possibility I'm looking into. So, about David, I—"

"You're not going to talk to David about this." She stared him down, hoping he'd realize this was not a request. Chloe feared Tommy's theories, regardless of how crazy they sounded, might entice David into some wild goose chase for answers she wasn't convinced could be found.

Tommy shook his head. "I was hoping you would do that for me."

Chloe's cocktail arrived and she took a long drink. Too long, because she coughed as the alcohol burned her throat. Tommy offered his water and it only took a sip or two for her to recover.

"I really should get home," Chloe said. "There's so much to do at the gallery and I don't want to miss this opportunity. I've worked my whole life for this, you know?" She took another, smaller, drink of her cocktail. "I thought I could handle this. I thought I could fly out here, make sure David was okay, and get back in plenty of time for the opening. But now everything's falling apart." She chuckled. "You remember what Dad always says about construction?"

Tommy rubbed his chin and tapped his hand on the bar in thought. "If the job is wrong...something...is right?"

"If something's going wrong, you're doing the job right," Chloe corrected.

Tommy rolled his eyes. "What does that even mean?"

Chloe gave him an incredulous stare. "It means there aren't any shortcuts. Any job worth doing is going to have its challenges, and to do it right you have to work through them." She scoffed. "I must be about the rightest person on earth." She took another drink.

Tommy looked at the bar. Chloe thought he might actually be feeling some sympathy for her, but if so he never vocalized it. Instead he asked, "When's your flight?"

Chloe stirred her cocktail. "Tomorrow morning, unless I can get one tonight."

Tommy took her wrist in his hand. "Don't leave early. Stay here tonight. Talk to David." Chloe started to protest, but Tommy cut her off. "Even if you don't believe me and don't want to tell him about my theories, neither one of you wants to leave things the way they are."

Chloe chewed her lip. It would be awful if something happened to David and the last thing they'd done together was argue. "Did you read in my energy field that we had a fight?" Her tone was only half-mocking.

"I didn't have to," Tommy said. "I heard you guys. I was parked just up the street. I could make out every word."

Chloe buried her face in her hands, embarrassed.

Tommy laughed. "Don't worry about it, sis. It's not like anyone around there knew who you were. Just hang out here until David calls. Talk it out with him. You'll be glad you did."

"What makes you so sure he'll call?" Chloe asked. She imagined Madison comforting him after their argument, and attempted to wash the vision away with the rest of her drink.

Tommy stood to leave, and winked at her. "Let's just call it a hunch."

fourteen

Chloe fiddled with her phone, checking e-mail and browsing her social media feeds, waiting for David to arrive. When Emma had called to find out where she was, Chloe was tempted not to even answer. After she had answered, she was tempted not to tell Emma the truth. After she had told Emma the truth, she was tempted to leave before David got there. Yet here she sat, waiting for him, still unsure what she was doing there or whether she could help him. David seemed so convinced his memories were real, and whenever Chloe thought about him and Madison together her heart raced. Each time it happened, she had a harder time convincing herself that she couldn't be jealous because what David remembered and what Madison dreamed didn't actually happen.

She ordered another drink, hoping the alcohol would help loosen the knot of thoughts and feelings that swung around like a wrecking ball inside her brain. Before her cocktail arrived, David sat next to her.

"Hi," he said.

"Hi," Chloe answered. She had no idea how to proceed beyond that.

"I brought your jacket," David said. He hung it on the back of her bar stool.

"Thanks." She pursed her lips, feeling a little guilty about her prior cynicism.

The bartender arrived with her cocktail and David ordered a beer. "Did you eat?" he asked Chloe.

"I ordered a sandwich but it hasn't come out yet," she replied.

When the bartender returned with David's beer, he ordered a hamburger and some fries. After the bartender left, David turned to Chloe and said, "I'm sorry about earlier."

Chloe sighed, then decided to dive right in. "I don't understand how you could feel so close to her, even though you said she didn't care about you."

David shook his head. "I didn't say that. We were using each other, we were never really in love—at least, nothing like you and I had—but we did care about each other. Sometimes it felt like a relationship and other times it felt like we were just good friends. Candice forced us into more of a relationship, really."

"So, you married her because of Candice?"

"Yeah, we got married soon after we found out Maddie was pregnant."

"But David," Chloe said, "you said yourself that you knew Madison was seeing other people. Why did you think the baby was yours?"

"I think I convinced myself that we were in one of our exclusive periods when she conceived. Besides, none of those other guys were going to give her any stability. None of them would have been a good father to Candice."

Chloe paused, remembering a time she was sick and David, despite being swamped at work, ducked out at every opportunity to come check on her. It was typical, even noble, that he would want to take care of someone who needed him.

After a short silence, Chloe said, "I'm sorry."

David replied, "Me too."

Chloe sniffled and said, "It's okay. But I'm still worried about you. The fact is that Madison doesn't really know you, and you don't really know her. Wherever these memories of yours came from, they don't apply here. It's not like you could just settle in with her and Candice."

David shook his head. "I know. I just really miss them."

Chloe wondered if he missed them more than he had missed her, but didn't say anything. It was her turn to be supportive. "I'll do whatever I can to help you."

"I think we need to figure out what happened to me," David said. "It would be best for both of us to sort this out."

Chloe smiled. "I think so too, but let's take it slow. The most important thing is that you're okay. Maybe you should see a psychiatrist or something."

"Maybe." David swallowed hard before asking, "What about us?"

"What do you mean?"

"Well, what if we never figure it out? You're right about Madison and Candice. I couldn't just start living with them because that's what I remember. And you have your new life with Richard and your gallery. So where does that leave us?"

Chloe thought about the painting Richard had made for her. Should she still consider moving in with him now that David had returned? "I don't know," she admitted quietly.

David sighed and started looking around the restaurant. His hands shook, and Chloe could tell David was on the verge of having an anxiety attack. She comforted him and said, "Let's just take it one day at a time. We'll figure it out together."

"I'm so sorry, Chloe. I know you have work to do, that you need to be home getting ready for your art show. I don't want to screw up your new life."

As upset as she had been with David earlier, Tommy was right: Chloe cared about him too much to abandon him, no matter how much it hurt. She'd have to figure out a way to manage the gallery and prepare for the art show while dealing with this, because that was the right thing to do. It was a lot to take on and she had resented David a little earlier because of it, but not now. Now she felt only sympathy for him.

"You're not screwing anything up, David," she said. "It's complicated, yes, but I'm glad to have you back." True, she didn't know what had happened to him, but she was convinced by now that David didn't leave her of his own free will, and that something strange had happened to separate them. That was enough to help her forgive him, but she was still stressed over the gallery and wondered how she could possibly get everything done in time.

As if on cue, she received a call from Fred. He wanted to finalize the layout for Richard's exhibit, and was upset that she hadn't returned his earlier call about it. Chloe apologized and assured him it would get done first thing the next day.

"You are really pushing it here," Fred said. "You do understand we can't just reschedule this. The work gets done or there is no opening, for either you or Richard."

Chloe ignored his condescending tone. "I understand, and I'll make sure it gets done." She wasn't sure she had convinced him, but it had been enough to get him off the phone.

The food arrived as she put her phone away. David turned to her and asked, "Are you in trouble for being here?"

She took a moment longer than she needed in her purse so she wouldn't have to face him. "No, it's okay." She smiled as she raised her head, hoping to convince David. "Opening weeks are always stressful." Chloe popped a French fry into her mouth.

"Is there anything I can do to help?" David took a bite of his burger and stared at her while he chewed loudly. Even with his mouth full, he couldn't hide the smile that gave away he was doing it on purpose to tease her.

Chloe scoffed and looked away. "Ten years apart, when we get a moment alone together you just had to do that."

David stuck several fries into his mouth, leaving the ends exposed. He leaned in close to her, continuing to make exaggerated chewing sounds while the fries danced around and bounced off his chin. He hummed so it sounded like he asked, "Do what?"

Chloe turned to him with an annoyed smirk, grabbed the ends of the fries, twisted them out of his mouth, and threw them onto his plate. He feigned indignation and reached for the pieces. Chloe stuck out her hand to block him, but he managed to get one and shove it back into his mouth.

She shook her head, and as hard as she tried, Chloe couldn't stop herself from bursting into laughter. "That isn't funny!"

David swallowed and joined in her laughter. "Oh, sure it is. Don't forget, when someone slips on an egg roll..."

"...we are obligated to laugh," Chloe finished. "Oh man, I haven't thought about that in forever."

"Me neither," David said. "We could still do it, you know. Nobody's made a slapstick sitcom about a Chinese restaurant yet." He beamed at Chloe, who smiled back, the two of them sharing a stolen moment and laughing over one of their little inside jokes for the first time in a decade.

"Okay, so now I have to ask," Chloe said. "Did you ever actually learn to use chopsticks properly? Because if I remember right, that whole joke happened because you dropped an egg roll on the floor, and it rolled out from under the table, and you were fretting over someone falling."

David rolled his eyes. "I was trying to show off." He paused, a faraway look in his eyes that Chloe suspected meant he was remembering something. "Actually, I did get much better. I started using yours." His voice lowered, and his laughter petered out. "I could barely look at Chinese food for a while because it reminded me so much of you. Sometime after the trial, I decided to sell the house and move to Pittsburgh, and I found your chopsticks while I was packing. I ordered some takeout and sat down alone with your chopsticks and ate, and somehow managed not to make a complete mess of myself." He chuckled. "I convinced myself that you were there somehow, helping me along."

Chloe leaned over and kissed him gently on the cheek. "That's really sweet of you. You know what's weird, though? When I was packing up the house to move to Stroudsburg, I remember having takeout too, and thinking a lot about you and how bad you were with the chopsticks." A curious thought struck her, one that couldn't possibly make sense but was somehow comforting. "You don't suppose, could we have been doing that at the same time?"

"Huh," David said. "I don't see why not."

"Do you think there were other times, things we were doing together but didn't know it?" Chloe asked. "Assuming, of course, that the things you remember actually happened." Not that she was convinced, but she did like the idea because it made her feel closer to him.

"Probably," David said. "The next time after that I felt really close to you was—"

"Amy and Adam's wedding," they said together.

"I missed you so much that day," Chloe said. "First of all, it took them way too long to get married."

"Oh, I know," David agreed. "All that talk about waiting until Adam was out of medical school was total crap, or they would have gotten married as soon as he graduated. Instead they waited another, what?" He paused and counted on his fingers. "Six years?"

Chloe nodded her agreement with his calculation. "Amy did finally admit to me how scared she was, but that makes total sense. Her dad was married like four or five times and every one of them ended badly."

"Did she tell you how he finally convinced her?" David asked. Chloe shook her head, and he continued, "He told her they'd been living together almost long enough to have a common-law marriage. He said they could either set a wedding date or he'd just file the papers when the time came and they'd be married anyway."

Chloe covered her mouth with both hands, then started chuckling through them. "Is common-law marriage even a thing anymore?"

David shrugged. "I have no idea. It was enough to convince Amy, though."

"That's so mean! But it's so like them. I see why she never told me though. Everyone at the wedding was like, 'Oh finally they got to a stable enough financial situation' and stuff like that. If the truth had gotten out people probably would have made a big deal over it."

"I only found out through Maddie," David said. "She made me swear I'd never let on that I knew." He sighed and took another bite of his burger. This time, he didn't tease her.

Chloe wasn't sure if he felt guilty about bringing up Madison or if remembering the wedding had been somehow painful. She had also been uncomfortable and sad that day, but had done her best to pretend otherwise. As painful as the memory was, talking about it with David dulled the sting a little.

At the risk of reopening the wounds from that afternoon's argument, Chloe asked, "So how did you and Madison go from meeting at the wedding to having a daughter?"

"The long way," David joked.

Chloe looked down at her food, immediately regretting that she'd asked the question. Still, it felt a little easier to talk about since it was just David and not an apartment full of people. "So you've remembered more, then?"

"A little," David said. "Madison and I were just friends for a while. She invited me out to do stuff with her other friends, who were okay but just really weren't my kind of people. They liked to party a lot. I went out with them once or twice and then told her it just wasn't my thing. But she and I had some pretty good conversations, I guess. I really liked being around her." He looked away and took a long drink of his beer.

Chloe fought very hard against mentally completing his statement with, "because she made me forget about you." She took a deep breath, a drink of her cocktail, and a moment to compose herself, then touched his arm gently.

David turned to her, a sad smile on his face. "I'm sorry."

"It's okay," Chloe said. "I get it. I had to move on, too."

David chuckled. "At least with Richard, you guys can talk about art. I still don't know what Madison and I had in common except maybe for drama."

Chloe laughed and they joined hands. "I know you didn't forget about me, just like I could never forget about you. But you found someone who made you forget to miss me every minute of every single day. It was the same for me, when I started painting again, when I moved to the city, when I met Richard. That's what moving on is, you know? It's not forgetting about what you lost, it's about remembering what you still have."

David squeezed Chloe's hand and smiled, and she thought she saw a gleam of happiness in his eyes. He took another bite of his food, then asked, "So what kinds of places do you and Richard go on nights out?"

Chloe wondered if David might be feeling jealous, but his question seemed genuine enough. She decided to let the conversation play out. "We mix things up. He likes to observe people, so we go to a lot of different places. He keeps an eye on social media and if it looks like something interesting will happen, he wants to be there."

"Something interesting? Like what?"

Chloe shrugged. "We've been to a few protests, some political rallies. There was a groundbreaking for a new government building that Richard thought would draw a big crowd but actually ended up being underwhelming."

David took another drink. "So he likes controversy?"

"Not necessarily controversy," Chloe said. "More like human behavior. We go to other things too, like mass weddings and parades. We watched a toddler's funeral one time. That was a rough one."

"What do you get out of these things?" David asked. "Do you just go for moral support, or do you use it in your art, too?"

"Well, you may not remember me telling you this, but all personal experience ends up in art. This, tonight, will end up in my art at some point. It might not be the subject or a very specific piece, but it'll be there." Even as she said it, Chloe wondered whether it would be a positive or negative influence.

David idly dragged a French fry through ketchup. "I used to love watching you, not just when you painted, but even when you talked about art. You always put so much emotion in it, and it would light you up, and I knew all that was coming from the deepest, most honest part of you."

Chloe blushed. "I always liked when you watched me. It was weirdly relaxing. Most of the time it would drive me crazy to have someone looking over my shoulder, but not when you watched me paint."

David flashed a bright smile. "Do you still mostly paint landscapes? What are you working on now?"

"Well, I..." Chloe trailed off and took a bite of food, stalling.

David's smile faded. "What?"

Chloe swallowed, then sighed. "I actually haven't painted anything in weeks."

David looked concerned. "Weeks? You don't paint every day anymore?"

Chloe downed the rest of her cocktail. "Not every day, but even when I'm not painting, I'm usually sketching or doodling. Plus, I'm always studying the pieces we get at the gallery and watching Richard work."

"It must be inspiring to be around so much incredible art all the time," David said. "I'm surprised you don't have hundreds of new paintings."

Chloe recoiled, suddenly feeling defensive. "I'm learning not to dive right in. I'm studying, learning, trying to understand what makes certain pieces stand out, then trying to use the same techniques. Sometimes it takes me awhile to find a good subject for a particular style, because I don't just want to copy work I've seen before."

David turned back to his beer. "Is that how Richard works?"

"Yes," Chloe said. When David said nothing in return, she felt the need to elaborate. "Sometimes he'll plan a series for six months before actually creating anything. He has tons of concept sketches and plans filed away in his studio. Of course, he's a little more diverse than I am because he uses sculpture and mixed-media, but I'm learning those a little at a time, too."

David finished his beer. "Look, I know I'm not an artist, but it always seemed to me like you were happiest when you were painting every day."

Chloe feared that his mood had soured because she was talking about new things she was learning in New York, and she wanted to reassure him that she didn't regret the years they'd spent in Morgantown. She touched David's arm again to get him to look at her. "I was. I was very, very happy."

David smiled. "Me too."

They finished their meals and Chloe settled the bill, careful not to let David know about Tommy's stack of cash. It covered both her and David with plenty to spare, which she told the bartender to keep.

"Should we call a cab?" she asked.

"Nah, let's walk," David said.

fifteen

David exited the restaurant first and held the door for Chloe. She smiled as she passed him. "I like that you still do that."

David let the door close, then fell in step beside her on the sidewalk. "Would you rather I let the door hit you in the face?"

"No, of course not. It's sweet." She stopped and turned to face him, and David mirrored her. With every moment they spent together, he felt less like a stranger, less like an old friend, and more like the husband she remembered.

David smiled. "I can't be the only man who's ever held the door open for you. What about Richard?"

"It isn't just the door," Chloe said. "The whole thing, being out with you, walking together." She looked away, searching for the right words. "After all those years apart, we just fell back into this stuff without thinking, you know? This, tonight, it's almost like you were never gone."

David dropped his head and stared at the space between his feet. Chloe chided herself for even bringing it up. She should have just let the moment be, and wondered why she hadn't. Stress seemed the likely culprit.

Chloe put her hand on David's shoulder, and he raised his head to meet her gaze. "I'm sorry," she said.

David gave her a weak smile. "It's all right. I kind of feel the same way."

They stared at each other for a moment, then turned and continued walking in the direction of the hotel. They talked a little more and while they didn't hold hands, they were never far from contact with each other, brushing arms or fingers occasionally.

A gust of wind picked up, and a few drops of cold rain landed on Chloe's face. She and David quickened their pace, but it was only a moment before those few drops multiplied into a downpour that forced them to take cover in an alcove protecting the entrance to a small photography shop. They stood against the metal shutter that covered the door, as far from the open sidewalk as possible, but each gust of wind brought spray into the alcove, and David and Chloe soon found themselves shivering in thoroughly dampened clothing.

Chloe stared out at the drenched street, wondering how long the rain would last. Her hair clung to her face in places, and David brushed back several strands, tucking them behind her ear, his fingers tracing the ear piece of her glasses. His touch didn't startle her. In fact, Chloe found that each brush of his fingertips melted away a little of her tension.

David chuckled, and Chloe turned to him. "What's so funny?"

"This is so typical," David said. "We were just talking about how it felt like we were never separated, and now here we are hiding from the rain again."

Chloe's laughed out loud and rolled her eyes. Memories of special occasions ruined by bad weather flooded her mind. "When did that all start, our honeymoon?" She thought back to the week after their wedding. They had gone to Florida, and a late-season tropical storm forced them to abandon a lot of their plans.

David joined in her laughter. "There was also that time on your birthday, remember?" His smile beamed, the only spot of brightness in the dark, cold, wet alcove.

"And that time we went to the ballet," Chloe said, leaning toward David and poking him in the chest. He wrapped his arm around her as she approached, and Chloe fell into his embrace naturally, spinning so that her back was to him and his arms wrapped around the front of her.

Chloe took a deep breath, closed her eyes, and let David hug her tightly. "We had some good times," he said.

Chloe reached up and squeezed David's arms. They stood in silence, staring out of the alcove as the rain continued to fall, the wind creating visible sheets highlighted by a nearby streetlight. There were no other people in sight, and it ought to have felt a little eerie. But standing there, leaning against the metal shutter and wrapped up in David's arms, Chloe didn't mind the mist against her skin, or the weight of her drenched clothes, or the biting of the cold October wind.

Chloe didn't think about Madison or Candice or Richard. She didn't think about Emma, the opening, or figuring out what had happened to David. In that moment, her worries were non-existent, the past and future were meaningless, and the whole world ceased to be, save for that alcove and the bit of street just beyond its entrance. Chloe felt something very familiar, something very comfortable, something she hadn't even known to look for.

In that moment, everything just felt right.

She didn't realize it at first, but Chloe slipped back into that feeling easily, one that she and David had shared countless times through college and after they were married. When she did become aware of how good the situation felt, Chloe let herself believe, just for a moment, that nothing had changed. It was like the last ten years were nothing more than a bad dream, the memory of which faded with each heartbeat.

David loosened his embrace on Chloe slightly, and she turned to face him. She met his eyes through the beads of water on her glasses, and they picked up what little light penetrated the alcove such that they sparkled like finely cut diamonds. She wrapped her arms around his back, and relished the warmth of his breath as he lowered his lips to hers.

Chloe closed her eyes and inhaled sharply as David began to kiss her. His lips were cool and damp from the rain, but they were soft, just like she remembered. She pressed her hands into his back as their mouths interlocked, and he squeezed her tightly in return, sending a ripple of pleasure coursing through her body. David extended his tongue and Chloe opened her mouth to accept it, bringing her own to meet his, which he curled upward to stroke the space behind her upper lip.

It was a wonderful, passionate kiss that seemed to slow time itself and left them both gasping for air. The sound of the rain pounding the concrete faded away, as did the bite of the wind and the dampness of the air. Instead, warmth washed over and through her, enveloping her in a blanket of safety so she could let down her guard, relax, and enjoy him.

After a time, their lips parted, and they receded slowly from each other, both of them breathing heavily, neither opening their eyes. Their foreheads met, and they leaned into each other, hot breath showing in the cool air. Chloe lost herself in the feeling of David's body against her own. She fit his embrace perfectly, as if they had been molded specifically for one another. Richard had never held her like this.

Chloe's eyes snapped open at the thought. Guilt drove the pleasure from her, weighing down her thoughts and her chest. She gasped and pulled away. "What are we doing? I can't...we shouldn't..."

David stepped toward her, looking concerned. He tried to pull her back in but Chloe resisted. As much as she cherished regaining this closeness with him, she feared that she'd done something terrible.

They stood staring at each other for what seemed like an eternity. Chloe was at a total loss. What could she possibly say? Being close to David had made her feel better than she had in a long time, a familiar kind of contentment that asked no questions and raised no demands. But at the same time, this was uncharted territory for both of them. Chloe had Richard and the gallery, and neither she nor David knew what had happened to him or where he fit in her life. Why did it feel like she was doing something wrong by yearning to recapture a long-lost passion with the man she had once considered her soul mate?

After an excruciating silence, David tried to speak but

choked on the words. He cleared his throat and said, "I'm sorry." The rain had let up somewhat, and the roar of the downpour had been replaced with splashes of passing cars, the occasional honk, and a distant siren, but all Chloe could hear was the pounding of her own heart and David's apology echoing through her mind.

"Don't," Chloe started, and she also had trouble speaking. She took off her glasses and rubbed them against her sleeve, avoiding eye contact with David, stalling to try and regain her composure. When she finished wiping the rain from the lenses, she brushed away a few loose strands of hair before carefully sliding her glasses back into place. "There's nothing to apologize for. We just, well, we got caught up in some old memories, you know?"

Chloe wasn't entirely convinced of that, and while she couldn't be sure, she didn't think David was either. She didn't want to press the issue, though, as things were already complicated enough for both of them without rekindling that old flame so recklessly. She desperately wanted to ask him what he was really feeling, though she probably couldn't have given a good answer had he asked her the same question.

"Yeah, old memories," he said with a heavy sigh.

"Good memories," Chloe amended. She smiled and David returned the expression, though it seemed forced.

After a moment, he looked away and fixed his gaze beyond her. "How much farther?"

Chloe's smile faded, and she turned to face the street outside the alcove. It was still raining, but not nearly as hard as it had been. The chill of the real world settled back onto her skin, evaporating the warmth she had felt in David's arms. "About two or three blocks, I think."

They stepped out of the alcove and looked both ways down the street, but didn't see any taxis nearby, and the precipitation was now light enough to walk through without feeling terribly uncomfortable.

David shrugged. "We're already wet. Might as well just get

back as soon as we can, right?"

Chloe nodded her agreement but didn't speak. What was there to say? Despite reminding herself that she was in a committed relationship with Richard, Chloe craved the love she felt when David held her, when he kissed her. She hated the idea of cheating, and she loved the life she had built without him, but being close to David seemed so right.

She shook her head and followed David out of the alcove. They quickly walked along the street in the direction of the hotel, Chloe's head and heart warring the whole way.

The deluge began anew just as David and Chloe reached the entrance to the hotel, and they hurried inside. Neither had spoken much on the walk from the alcove, and Chloe knew it wasn't just their brisk pace that kept the conversation minimal. David accompanied Chloe to her room, and she invited him to stay for a few minutes.

"I'm going to go ahead and change, if that's okay with you," she said. She took her pajamas from her suitcase, stepped into the bathroom, and tossed out two large, fluffy towels that David reached for but missed. Chloe giggled. "Sorry!"

"It's all right." David leaned to pick up the towels. "Thanks."

"You don't mind waiting, do you?"

"Not a bit."

Chloe closed the bathroom door and stood staring into the mirror, trying to make herself move. Her heart pounded wildly, and she braced herself against the counter, trying to breathe deeply so she could calm down and try to make sense of the thoughts and emotions battling in her brain. At one point, she feared she might pass out from the stress, but took comfort in the fact that David would come help her if he heard her hit the floor.

David will come help me, she repeated the thought to herself.

Could she rely on that, like she had ten years ago? When they kissed—oh, that kiss!—it had really felt like him, the same man she had loved and married, not some stranger returned from who-knows-where after a ten-year absence. But was he that man? Or was it just a fleeting moment in which they were both swept away?

Whatever was going on, Chloe decided she wasn't going to get anywhere just staring herself down. She had to go out and deal with it, deal with him. After giving her hair a thorough towel-drying, Chloe pushed it away from her face and put on an elastic headband. She changed out of her clothes, grateful that she had packed warm flannel pajamas.

When she came out of the bathroom, Chloe saw that David had started the coffee maker. "I used a bottle of water from the mini bar. I'll pay for it. I mean, Emma will hopefully pay for it." He rolled his eyes. "It's so weird that I have like, nothing. Emma lent me one of her old phones and bought these clothes. The only possession I really have is the ring."

"I sent almost everything of yours to your parents," Chloe said, trying to avoid a conversation about the wedding band. "I don't know exactly what they kept."

"I guess we'll find out when they get back in town." David looked thoughtful a moment. "I remember sending your stuff to your parents, too. I only kept a few mementos and the Woodburn Hall painting."

Chloe stared at the floor. She fought off images of David and Madison together with the painting by reminding herself of where it actually hung, above her bed at her parents' house. Though she had considered taking it to New York, she decided it would make her too sad.

"I always loved that painting," David continued. "Whenever I would look at it, I could feel that wind whipping at me. That was a wonderful day."

Chloe sighed. "It feels like a lifetime ago."

David poured two cups of coffee, and mixed one cream and one sugar into Chloe's, just the way she liked it. He handed her the mug and smiled, and she smiled in return, marveling at how easily he seemed to remember those little details.

"Do you ever wonder what would have happened to us?" he asked.

"Sometimes, yeah." Until David reappeared, it had been some time since Chloe had thought about it. Her once naive ruminations on what their relationship could have been were now murky with doubt.

David looked away, then asked quietly, "Do you think you would have been as happy as you are now, if I hadn't disappeared?"

Chloe took a drink of her coffee, stalling. What did he expect her to say? "That isn't really a fair question. There's no way to tell where we would have ended up, you know?"

"I know." He turned toward Chloe but his gaze was distant, his eyes clouded with confusion and sadness.

"We'll figure this out," Chloe said. "It's going to take time and I know that everything I have going on this week isn't helping. But after the show Friday, things will calm down a bit. We can talk and you can try to sort out what you want to do."

David nodded but didn't say anything. He sipped at his coffee and Chloe did the same.

Finally, he stood and set down his mug. "I should go," he said. Chloe tried to tell him he didn't have to, but he replied, "I need to get out of these wet clothes."

Chloe suspected it was more than that, but decided not to press. "We'll see each other in the morning."

David gave a little smile and headed for the door. Chloe followed, and stopped him before he left.

"Whatever happens, you're still special to me," she said. "I don't know what the right thing is, or how we'll figure it out. We'll give it time and see where we end up. But no matter where that is, I still want you to know that I care about you."

"Me too." David leaned in and Chloe braced for another kiss, but he pecked her cheek instead. "Good night, Chloe."

She locked the deadbolt after he left, unsure whether she

was relieved or disappointed. Chloe turned on the TV and let her mind shut off, losing herself in reruns of home improvement shows until she fell asleep on the couch.

sixteen

The next morning, Chloe called to check in with Conner. She put the phone on speaker and set it on the night stand while she finished packing.

"I think I have the flooring issue under control," Conner said. "It should be installed by the time you get here."

"That's great." Chloe wondered what he'd come up with, but decided against asking for more detail. "What about the walls?"

"The contractor should be here any minute to finish patching," Conner said. "Also, the truck just left for Pennsylvania to pick up your paintings. Richard went with them."

Chloe stopped what she was doing. "He did?"

"Yeah, he convinced Mr. Lumina to let him pick out candidate pieces for your show," Conner said. "Didn't he tell you?"

Chloe hesitated. "Right, sorry. I must have forgotten," she lied, hoping Conner wouldn't pry further. She'd never taken Richard to her parents' house, and it seemed strange that he would go there now without telling her.

"Anything else you need?" Conner asked.

"No, that should do it. Thanks for taking care of everything while I was out of town. See you in a few hours."

Chloe ended the call and zipped up her suitcase. She was about to call Richard when someone knocked on the door. Chloe opened it expecting to see David and Emma, but instead Tommy stood in the hallway.

"What do you want now?" she asked, turning back into the

room. She started double-checking the bathroom, dresser drawers, and under the bed.

Tommy followed her in. "I got a call this morning. One of the more powerful channelers in my Brotherhood just happens to be passing through the area, so you and David can go see him."

"No," Chloe said as she continued checking the room. She had no idea what the hell a channeler was and she didn't want to ask. "I'm leaving to go back to New York."

"What? You can't go back yet," Tommy said. "You have to take care of things with David."

"I don't have time for your nonsense," Chloe said. "David and I will sort things out later."

"It isn't nonsense!" Tommy approached and stood directly in front of Chloe, interrupting her.

"Move!"

"No," Tommy said. "Not until you agree to take this seriously."

Chloe tried to push her way around her brother, but he blocked her path. There was another knock, and she gave him a scowl as she walked toward the door. This time, it was David and Emma. David hugged Chloe as he entered the room, then started when he noticed Tommy.

"I'm glad you're here, David," Tommy said. "Maybe you can convince my sister that we need to work things out between you two before she goes running off."

"I told you last night, I'm not getting in the way of this," David said.

Emma leaned against the door frame, looking bleary-eyed. "What are you talking about?"

Chloe glared at Tommy, then David. "What happened last night?"

"I went back to my room and discovered that Emma had emptied the mini bar," David said. "When I went to get her some aspirin, I ran into Tommy in the lobby. He thinks I was pulled into a parallel universe."

"That's an interesting theory," Emma said, her sarcasm less biting than usual.

Chloe wheeled on Tommy. "I can't believe you went and talked to David. I specifically told you not to."

"Look, whether any of you want to believe me or not, you have to admit something weird is going on here," Tommy said. "You all spent the whole day yesterday trying to find answers to what happened to David, and how did that go, exactly?" He approached David. "I can help you. I know you want answers, and the first step is accepting that you and Chloe belong together."

"Leave Chloe out of this," David said. "She has more important things to do." He pushed past Tommy and picked up Chloe's suitcase from the bed, then asked if she was ready to leave. Chloe nodded and picked up her purse.

"Please, hear me out for just a minute," Tommy said, again lodging himself in Chloe's way. "After we talked yesterday, I had a vision. You two met each other later in life, in New York."

Chloe scoffed. "In an alternate reality?"

"No, more like a different timeline," Tommy said. He turned toward David. "In my vision, you and my sister hadn't gone to college together. Instead, you met in New York after Chloe had finished art school and established a career. She was painting in Central Park and you stopped to talk to her, and things took off from there."

David scowled at Tommy. "Chloe couldn't go to art school in New York because of you, remember?" He shook his head in frustration. "Besides, that's not a vision. You just took what really happened and changed the time and place."

Tommy turned back to Chloe. "No, it was different. Similar, but different. And I think that means you two were always meant to be together. Even if you both take separate ways to get there, you always end up in the same place."

The idea struck Chloe. Was there a chance David could fit into her new life somehow? She closed her eyes and took a deep breath, trying to stay focused on what had to be done. "David and I will sort things out later, but for now I really need to get back to work."

"She's right." David stepped between her and Tommy so she could pass freely. Everyone made their way out of Chloe's hotel room and into the hallway. Chloe and Emma started toward the elevator, and David stayed a step behind, between Chloe and Tommy.

"I'm not just going to let this go," Tommy said loudly. "It's too important. You're going to upset the balance of nature and then you'll all be sorry."

Emma scoffed and rolled her eyes. Chloe apologized for making her deal with Tommy's drama when she obviously wasn't feeling well.

Emma offered a small smile. "This is nothing some strong coffee won't fix. Besides, if I were feeling better I might be compelled to actually engage with your brother and contest his theories. As it stands, however, I'm content enough to simply walk away."

Chloe chuckled. "He doesn't know how lucky he's getting off."

When they reached the elevator, Chloe, Emma and David got into an empty car. David stood at the door and kept Tommy from entering.

"Take the next one," David said.

"You're making a mistake," Tommy warned.

"No, we're not. Just go home, or back to your commune, or wherever the hell you came from," David said. "You haven't changed a bit, have you? Why don't you grow up and do something productive with your life?"

"You're only proving my point, you know." Tommy smiled wryly. "You weren't so defensive until Chloe got upset."

"Goodbye, Tommy." David pushed the button for the lobby level.

Tommy stuck his hand in between the elevator doors to stop them from closing.

"Damn it, Tommy! I'm going to miss my flight," Chloe said.

"Just one last thing." Tommy reached into his pocket and produced a business card. "This is where the channeler and I will be today. My number is on the back. When you change your mind, I'll set up the meeting."

"Channeler?" Emma asked.

"A member of my Brotherhood who is trained to read and predict shifts in the world energies," Tommy explained. He stared at David. "I truly believe he can help you."

David snatched the card from Tommy's hand and pushed the door close button. This time Tommy didn't interfere, and the elevator started down.

"Let me see that number," Chloe said. David flipped it over and held it where Chloe could see while she got out her phone to save the number. She told David he might as well throw the card away, but the elevator doors opened to the hotel lobby before he could respond.

No one spoke during the ride from the hotel to the airport, the absence of conversation filled with a radio news broadcast. Chloe feared she was leaving things in a bad place with David. Even though they had discussed it and were both in agreement that her returning to New York was the right thing to do, they had found no closure. If anything, the situation had only gotten more complicated.

Chloe was still reeling from the night before, how David had kissed her like no time had passed at all. The past two days had brought up feelings she had forgotten all about, and now they pumped through her with each heartbeat, bringing with them new fears. What if David's reappearance was only tempo- rary? What if they had been brought back together only to drift out of each other's lives? What if he decided to pursue some- thing with Madison?

Emma parked the car and the three of them walked silently into the airport. It wasn't crowded, and Chloe had no trouble getting her boarding pass. She turned to say goodbye to David and Emma before heading through security.

Emma hugged her warmly. "It's always good to see you, Chloe. Safe travels, and best wishes for a successful opening."

"Thank you," Chloe said. Just the thought of it started the list of things she had to do building in her head again.

"We should go to her show," David said to Emma. He flashed a sweet smile at Chloe. "I'd really like to be there, if it's okay."

Chloe hesitated. Of course she wanted to share this moment with them, but she wondered if David's presence would distract her. When they went to New York in college, he'd experienced a crippling panic attack that ultimately led them to remain in Morgantown instead of moving to the city, and Chloe feared a repeat of that incident. He had been so supportive, though, and as her eyes met his she knew she couldn't possibly deny him. "Sure, of course," Chloe said.

Emma smiled. "I would love to attend your opening. I haven't visited New York City in ages." She looked thoughtful a moment, then turned to David. "I won't be able to secure you sufficient identification to allow you on a plane by Friday, but it's not a difficult drive."

David chuckled. "I'll hitchhike if I have to."

"You will do no such thing," Emma said.

"You're not the boss of me," David joked.

Emma rolled her eyes. "Why do I even bother?" She grinned and shook her head, then excused herself. "I'll give you two a moment to yourselves."

Chloe said goodbye to Emma again, then stood facing David. He took her hands in his and squeezed gently.

"Thank you for coming to see me," David said. "I don't know why this happened, or why it's happening now, but you being here means the world to me."

Chloe blushed. "We'll figure this out. I'm sorry things are

such a mess right now—"

"Don't," David said. "Don't be sorry. You're amazing, and I'm really proud of you."

Chloe's confidence soared. "Can I call you whenever I need a pep talk?"

David laughed. "Anytime. I wish there was more I could do to help."

Chloe laughed with him. "I know. Thanks."

An awkward silence fell between them. Despite everything that had happened in the past ten years and all the weirdness of the last two days, Chloe honestly had no idea what to say to him.

David glanced at the departures board. "You'd better get going."

They embraced tightly for a long moment, and Chloe smiled as she pulled away. "See you Friday."

"See you Friday," David echoed.

Chloe turned and started toward the security checkpoint. When she reached the back of the line, she looked over her shoulder to see David still standing there. She offered a small wave, and he did the same before turning away.

seventeen

By the time Chloe landed in New York, rain had backed up departing flights to the point that her plane had to wait over an hour for a gate to clear. To make things worse, an accident had bottlenecked car traffic around the airport, resulting in scarce taxis and a very long line. She finally reached her building shortly after noon, and asked the driver to wait while she hurried to her apartment, threw down her carry-on, quickly changed clothes, and grabbed a granola bar on the way back out.

Still flustered and hungry, Chloe entered the gallery through the front door and intended to go straight to the east wing, but Richard greeted her in the lobby. He gave her a quick kiss on the mouth and said, "Welcome back. You're just in time for the big reveal."

Chloe tried to hide both her surprise and frustration with the sudden agenda change. "I didn't expect you back so soon."

Richard ushered her toward the storage room while Chloe fixated on his kiss. Was he always so unaffectionate, or did she just feel guilty about kissing David? Did Richard suspect something? He didn't even ask about her flight, let alone what had happened with David. Chloe took a deep breath and focused on keeping her composure.

Fred stood near a group of boxes leaning against each other. "I was about to show Lumina what I found in Stroudsburg this morning."

Fred smiled. "Richard tells me you have an impressive body

of work at your parents' house. I can't wait to see these."

Chloe thanked him and looked at the stack of packed art. There were a lot more boxes than she expected. "How many paintings did you bring?"

Richard shrugged. "I started by gathering up the Pocono Mountains scenes, the ones Lumina was so excited about. Then I started going through your other work to make sure I hadn't missed any of those, and found quite a few more pieces I thought he might want to see."

Richard opened the first box and Fred asked about Chloe's trip. "Everything's settled with that situation, I hope?"

"Well, not completely settled," Chloe said with a sigh. "But settled enough for now." She glanced toward Richard, who was busy removing packing material from the canvas. When he finished, he turned the painting so Fred and Chloe could see.

"Oh," Chloe said. She'd forgotten about the painting, done the first Christmas she and David spent in their house in Morgantown, a little over two years after they'd gotten married. The scene was dark, with heavy grey clouds and a thick coat of snow on the ground. Chloe remembered embellishing a bit there, as there hadn't been quite as much snow. But the subject, their house, glowed softly against the darkness, punctuated by the decorated tree in the front room window.

Fred stepped in and examined the canvas more closely. "Chloe, this is exceptional. When did you paint this?"

"Almost thirteen years ago." Chloe's emotions raced, and she wondered if the memories the painting invoked were intensified by having just seen David. She treasured the experiences and opportunities she'd fought for since, but did not doubt that she'd been happy at the time.

"You still use the same signature," Fred said. Chloe asked what he meant, thinking he was referring to her name scrawled in the corner of the canvas. Instead, he pointed to a shadow near the bottom of the image, just to the right of center.

"That's just a shadow," Chloe said. "It's not a signature."

Richard rolled his eyes. "He pointed out the same spot in

your other paintings yesterday. I don't think it's significant."

"It is significant," Fred argued, then turned to Chloe. "All of your best work has this same feature. It's subtle, but it's there."

Chloe leaned in and squinted at the painting, looking in the area Fred indicated. "I swear it's just a shadow. I painted this from a series of photos I took, so maybe it just needed some additional texture."

"No, it's something else," Fred said. "Whether you want to admit it or not, it's consistent among your strongest, most meaningful paintings."

Richard set the canvas aside. "My best guess is that you must use that spot as a mixing or test area, and then don't layer enough to hide it. If you had gone to art school, an instructor would have broken you of that habit."

Chloe recoiled and gave Richard a questioning look, but he turned to open the next box. The three of them looked over at least a dozen of Chloe's paintings, several of which she'd forgotten about. Most of the work was from college and the years immediately following, teasing her with thoughts of David and their relationship. As she fought to keep her emotions in check, Richard remained stoic, and Chloe wondered if he knew the impact the images were having.

Fred got a phone call and stepped away, but before doing so he instructed Chloe to have a layout for her work done by the next morning so he could review it. Richard and Chloe continued looking through the paintings.

"Now this one is special," Richard said as he pulled another canvas from its box. "There's definitely a story here."

He turned the canvas around to reveal an autumn scene of a long brick building, set on a curved lawn with two other brick structures flanking it. A clock tower rose from the main entrance in the center, stretching up into a cerulean sky. Chloe was instantly taken back to that day, to the wind whipping at her, the leaves blowing across the lawn, her easel shaking and unsteady until...

Chloe looked away and shut her eyes tight against the tears. "Pack it back up."

"This is easily your very best painting," Richard said. "The lack of sharpness in the details and the way you've blended warm and cool colors suggests you were happy and calm when you painted this, yet the stroke pattern hints at drama or maybe a strong wind."

His detached analysis of the piece, however flattering, grated on Chloe's nerves. Richard wasn't that naive. He had to have known what seeing this painting would do to her. "It's not for sale."

"It could still go in the show—"

Chloe turned back toward him and locked eyes with Richard, fighting the urge to let her eyes drop to the painting. She spoke each word separately as she repeated, "Pack it back up."

"Shouldn't we get Lumina's opinion—?"

Panic shot through Chloe's mind. "Fred cannot see this painting! If he does, he'll want to make it the centerpiece of the show, and I can't deal with that. Please don't argue with me about this. Pack it back up, now."

"No." Richard set the canvas on top of a box and leaned it so it would stand upright, then walked to where Chloe was standing. "As soon as I saw this painting hanging above your bed, I could tell it was about him. And since you haven't exactly been forthcoming about your trip, I needed some way to know if you still have feelings for him. I think I got my answer."

"That's why you brought all those other paintings, just to see how I'd react?" Her jaw quivered as feelings of betrayal began stoking flames of anger.

"Well, it's not the only reason," Richard said. "They are actually good paintings." He sounded surprised.

Chloe fumed a moment, unable to put her warring emotions into words. She finally gave up and strode toward the painting, intending to wrap it and put it back in its box.

Richard grabbed her arm to stop her. "I'll pack it up as soon as you tell me the story behind it."

She turned to him. "Why do you want to hear it? What can that possibly accomplish?"

Richard held her gaze, his expression stoic but with a hint of intensity in his eyes. "Because until you face this emotional trigger, until you understand it and can control it, you're never going to progress as an artist. This is for your own good."

Chloe scoffed. "Really?"

He shrugged. "I take art pretty seriously. You know that. I've been trying to help you push through this block, and now that I know what it is, it seemed like as good a time as any. So, tell me about the painting. Where is this building? It looks like an old college."

Chloe sighed. "It's West Virginia University. Woodburn Hall."

"That's where you went to school?"

Chloe nodded. "I had wanted to study art here in New York, and saved a lot of money, but then this boarding school approached my parents. Apparently, my brother had scored really high on some aptitude test, and they wanted him to enroll. My parents couldn't afford it, but the recruiter convinced them it was such a competitive program that Tommy would ultimately be able to pay them back and more. They used my savings to help send Tommy to school."

She had to pause and take a breath to suppress her anger. Tommy hadn't completed the program and now belonged to a cult, but somehow had connections and plenty of cash. He'd apologized many times over the years and Chloe had mostly forgiven him, but telling the story opened the wounds anew, if only slightly.

"Anyway," she continued, "I was so upset that I stopped applying to art programs. I really had my heart set on New York and if I couldn't have that, I decided nothing else was good enough, you know? My mom had gone to WVU so I applied to the business school there and got a scholarship. Mom felt really bad about the situation but encouraged me not to give up. She made me pack my art supplies when I left for

Morgantown, even though I didn't want to. For the first month or so of the semester, I didn't touch them, but then the leaves started changing and I decided I needed to try painting again. I lugged everything from my dorm room and started setting up, but you're right, it was windy that day. It was so windy that I couldn't keep my easel upright to sketch, let alone prepare my palette. It was a disaster."

Richard turned to the canvas. "It doesn't show."

Chloe ignored the compliment. "I was about to give up. I was going to pack up everything and go back to my dorm room and sulk, but then he showed up out of nowhere." She closed her eyes and smiled.

"He?" Richard crossed his arms. "You mean David?"

Chloe wiped a tear from her eye. "Yes, David. He was walking by and recognized me because we had a class together, so he came over and introduced himself. He asked what he could do and at first, I really didn't want him to do anything, you know? But he insisted. He was always so stubborn. Once David made his mind up to do something, there was never any stopping him." She chuckled. "So, he held my easel and canvas steady while I worked. He asked me a lot of questions about painting. I mean, *a lot* of questions. He never really did understand it, but somehow he got how important it was to me. We talked and laughed, and I painted, and it was like everything in the world was exactly as it should be. It was a perfect moment." Emotion threatened to overwhelm her again. She turned away to wipe the tears from her eyes before they could run down her cheeks.

She recovered and turned back to Richard. "And *that* is why this piece can't go in the show. There's just too much emotion in it, and I can't break down like that at the opening. Plus, with David back I've got him on my mind a lot and seeing that painting doesn't help things."

Richard pulled her into his embrace. "I understand." He paused, then added, "But you really need to get over it."

Chloe pulled away. "Excuse me?"

"This painting represents your old life and that's emotionally confusing for you. You've moved on to bigger and better things, but part of you still wants that." He pointed to the painting. "Part of you still wants him."

The accusation stung, considering how close Chloe had felt to David the night before. She tried to object, stammered, and gave up. "He was my husband."

"Was," Richard emphasized. "He *was* your husband. He's not anymore."

"That doesn't mean I stopped caring about him," Chloe said.

Richard glared at her. "Do you care about him more than you care about me?"

"What? No, it's just..." Chloe pursed her lips as her brain scrambled to translate feelings into words. "It's different, you know? David and I have a history, that's all." Even as she said it, Chloe wondered if she was downplaying how much she missed David.

Richard motioned toward the Woodburn Hall painting again. "And that history is still holding you back. You need to forget about him, and you can start by selling this painting."

"I don't want to forget," Chloe said. "I love this painting and I'll always treasure the day I made it."

"This painting really showcases your ability," Richard argued. "I admire it more than anything else of yours I've seen. Putting it in the show could land you a commission or stir up more interest in your work. You could at least sell prints."

"With everything that's going on right now, I can't possibly show that painting," Chloe said.

"Lumina could put together a list of potential buyers and you could show it privately," Richard suggested.

"No!" Chloe shouted. "Don't you get it? This isn't just a painting to me. It's a part of my life."

"All art is a piece of the artist's life," Richard said.

"Yes, but that doesn't mean we have to give every piece away," Chloe argued.

"I hate to interrupt," Fred called from the entrance to the storage room. Chloe jumped, as she hadn't been expecting him to return. "We have a situation out front."

Chloe started toward the door out of the storage room, but paused after a few steps and turned back to Richard. "Pack that painting up and mark it 'Not for Show,'" she demanded.

Richard rolled his eyes, then nodded and turned back toward the canvas. Chloe followed quickly after Fred, relieved he hadn't seen the painting.

"I don't believe this," Chloe said, staring at the newly-laid floor in the east wing. The laminate pattern looked like cheap wood paneling, and spots along the seams bled into each plank. She knelt down to examine one, and it felt sticky. "Is this glue?"

Richard and Fred both shrugged, and Chloe turned her attention back to the floor. She'd never personally put down a laminate floor, but she was almost completely certain there shouldn't have been glue. When she'd researched her options before ordering, Chloe had looked for a floating floor that could go right over top of the unfinished hardwood without damaging it.

"Who installed this?" Chloe asked. "Where's Conner?"

"I sent him to pick up the show pamphlets from the printers," Fred said. He then poked at his phone and held it in front of him, allowing the ring from the speaker phone to echo through the space. When Conner answered, Fred asked him about the floor.

"The supplier Chloe chose sent back a quote for double what we had agreed upon," Conner said. "When I asked her about it she told me to figure it out, so I found another supplier. It's not exactly the same pattern, but it looks just as nice. Also, one of the drywall guys gave me the number for his cousin, who said he would install the floor for next to nothing."

Chloe flushed with guilt for having not paid more attention

to Conner the day before. "You still should have checked with me before hiring him. Did this cousin even have a contractor's license?" She took Conner's silence as a no. "Please tell me you didn't already pay him."

"That was one of the conditions for getting it done so fast," Conner said. "He wanted paid as soon as it was done."

"Damn it," Chloe said.

"What's the problem?" Conner asked.

"The problem is that the floor is hideous," Fred said. "If I'm not mistaken, it appears to have been installed completely wrong."

"There are glue spots seeping through the laminate," Chloe elaborated. "Why did he glue the floor down?"

"I don't know," Conner said. "How else would you hold it in place? Nails?"

"You should have checked with me," Chloe repeated.

"I tried," Conner said. "It was a little difficult to get a hold of you yesterday. It isn't my fault. This isn't my job."

"It was your job!" Chloe's voice echoed through the space. As she realized how angry she was, she turned away from Fred and the phone, trying to get herself under control.

"We'll discuss this later," Fred said. "Get those pamphlets and get back here as soon as you can. And maybe have this contractor give Chloe a call?"

Chloe recognized that Fred was asking her, and she said, "No, don't bother. This asshole obviously has no idea what he's doing, and he's probably already cashed the check anyway."

Fred ended the call, then approached Chloe and put a hand on her shoulder. "What do you think? Can we fix this?"

She shook her head. "I don't know. I'll need to make some calls, but I think this is all going to have to be ripped up and replaced. Plus, if there's glue under it we might not be able to put down anything new until that's cleaned up."

Chloe bit her lip, knowing she was running out of time. She looked to Richard, who simply stared back at her, expressionless. Though to anyone else it would seem like detached observation, she felt the burning of his unspoken judgment, the silent "I told you so." Chloe realized she hadn't even been through the main exhibit hall yet, remembering the work that needed done just to get Richard's show prepared.

"I'm sorry," she said to Fred. "I shouldn't have left town."

Fred squeezed her shoulder. "What's done is done. Just figure out if this is salvageable and let me know as soon as possible. You know what's at stake here. I'll trust your decision."

Chloe wished she had as much trust in herself. She sighed and dug her phone out of her purse. "I guess I'd better make some calls."

eighteen

Chloe spent the entire afternoon trying to find a new flooring supplier and installer, but no one was available until the following week. She considered purchasing some flooring from a hardware store and installing it herself over the ruined laminate, but was afraid she'd only compound the problem with an additional layer. All the while, she took calls about Richard's show and coordinated arrival and setup times with the caterer and sound engineer. Chloe delegated to Conner where possible, and he seemed glad not to be involved in the construction aspect anymore.

Richard had gone to his studio and Fred had meetings elsewhere, leaving Chloe to handle the situation herself. The responsibility weighed on her, though, forcing her into a pattern of anxiety and indecisiveness. She longed for someone to be her sounding board, someone to talk through the situation with her, someone to tell her whether or not her thoughts made sense.

She was tempted more than once to call David. Not only did she miss him, but she also remembered how well they had worked together. David's analytical, problem-solving mind perfectly complemented Chloe's creative instincts. He had often helped distill her vague, big-picture ideas into actionable goals, and sometimes just hearing his voice had been enough to focus and re-energize her.

Chloe didn't call him, though, fearful of adding to his already high anxiety and her own conflicting feelings. Instead, she pressed on alone, second-guessing every decision and fretting over every call.

Early evening found Chloe no closer to a solution. Richard called to tell her he would pick her up for dinner, and while Chloe was hesitant to leave, she decided a break might do her good. She gathered her things and started toward the lobby when Amy called.

"Hey, Chloe." Amy's voice was less enthusiastic than usual. "You got a sec?"

Chloe worried something might be wrong. "Sure, what's going on?"

"I hate to bother you with this since I know you're so busy, but Madison won't listen to me," Amy said.

"Madison?" Chloe recoiled. "What happened to her?"

"Nothing, nothing, sorry." Amy seemed incredibly flustered. "It's probably not that serious, but she and David have spent pretty much the whole day together."

Chloe froze in place, her face flushed. "What? Why?"

"Beats me. I thought David was going back to Morgantown with Emma today, but apparently he called Madison, and they've been talking about her dreams and his memories. They even went and saw your brother for some reason."

Chloe winced. She regretted not throwing away the card Tommy had given them. "I can't believe Emma just let David go off on his own like that."

"I tried to tell Madison it was a bad idea, but she wouldn't listen. I'm worried she might freak out again. I hate to ask, but could you call David and try to talk some sense into him?"

Chloe didn't want to, but she agreed to help. She ended the call with Amy and then dialed David's number.

When he answered, it sounded like he'd been laughing. "Hey, Chloe. How was your flight this morning?"

It irked her that he was acting so casual. "Fine. What have you been up to?"

David sighed. "Amy called you, didn't she?"

"Why didn't you go back to Morgantown with Emma?"

Chloe didn't want to acknowledge that he was with Madison.

"She had to work. She has a really important hearing tomorrow," David said. "I wanted to see what else I could figure out about what happened."

"But after yesterday, after you and Madison both panicked, why would you think it was a good idea to talk to her again?"

"I had to do *something*," David said. "Emma didn't even have time to go talk to Tommy and this channeler guy, who was interesting, to say the least."

Chloe rolled her eyes. "Why are you even engaging with him? I have no idea what he's up to with this weird cult or whatever, but it can't be good."

"I know it sounds ridiculous, but it's really the only lead I have right now," David said.

"So what, you called up Madison, went to see my crazy brother, and then just decided to make a day of it?" Chloe paced around the lobby, frustrated.

"That's not exactly how it happened," David said. "She sent me a message this morning saying she wanted to talk through the memories a little more. Emma thought it was a bad idea, of course, and I got mad at her because what am I supposed to do, just sit around and do nothing? She had to go back to work and I don't need a babysitter."

"You don't have an ID or any money," Chloe argued. "It's not that you need someone watching you, we're just worried."

"I'm fine," David said. "Emma lent me a little money, and it's not like I'm doing anything stupid. Madison and I are just talking, trying to make sense of whatever's going on with us."

"You went to see Tommy and his cult leader," Chloe said. "That sounds pretty stupid to me."

"It was harmless," David said. "We sat down in front of this young kid, he had to have been like twenty-five or something, all shaven bald with a bunch of weird tattoos. He had me wear the ring and hold Madison's hand, then he said basically the same stuff Tommy had told me before. There's another world and another version of Madison, that I'm not connected to this Madison but I am to the other one, but the two Madisons are connected and that's where the dreams came from..."

He trailed off and Chloe heard Madison's voice in the background. David laughed. "Oh yeah, and he suspects that this was all done on purpose because you and I are soul mates."

Chloe still couldn't understand how David and Madison seemed to be getting along so well, like they had known each other for years. "Well, I'm glad you had fun," she said, trying not to sound irritated. "Please don't tell me you believe any of this."

"No, I mean, I don't know. It was kind of like a psychic reading or tarot cards or something, where you know it's probably not true but there's that little part of you that wants to believe it. And I don't have any better explanation for what happened to me."

"I know." Chloe pinched the bridge of her nose, scarcely able to believe they were having this conversation. "It's just a little weird, you know?"

"Yeah, weird is right," David said.

"No, not the mystical stuff itself, I mean the fact that you'd consider it at all. You never would have before." Chloe's mind drifted back to conversations they'd had back in college about new age movements and superstition. David had always been averse to such things, and to hear him talk seriously about the possibility of being in an alternate reality was a little unnerving.

"I just don't know what else to think," David said, sounding a little defeated. He hesitated, then added, "I mean, what if it's true?"

"It's not," Chloe said firmly. "It can't be."

"Probably not, but what if it is? If there's another world out there, then that would mean the versions of Madison and Candice that I knew would be freaking out right now, wondering what happened to me," David said. "It's bad enough you had to go through that. I don't want to hurt even more people that I care about."

Chloe shut her eyes tight against the vision of David and

Madison together. "So you're buying into Tommy's bullshit? How does spending time with the Madison that doesn't know you help anything? Yesterday you called her a liar."

"I think yesterday it was just a little overwhelming for both of us, but today we've gotten along great," David said. "I kind of get it now, how she and I would have become so close if the stuff I remember actually happened."

Chloe made a fist with her free hand and squeezed, fighting the urge to scream. After their fight the day before, why would David tell her these things? "Well, good for you two," Chloe said through bared teeth.

A knock at the gallery door startled her. Chloe told David to hang on, then walked over and let Richard in. When he asked if she was ready, she held up one finger and tried to hide her face so he couldn't see that she was upset. She walked back toward the center of the lobby.

"Chloe?" David sounded concerned. "Are you all right? How are things going at the gallery?"

"Hectic," Chloe said. She was so upset she couldn't even remember what she had been working on before Amy's call. "I should probably go."

"Okay," David said. "I hope things get better soon. I can't wait to see the show."

Chloe hung up, dropped the phone into her purse, and wiped the tears from her eyes as Richard's footsteps grew closer. She didn't turn to face him, just let him approach and put his hands on her shoulders.

"That wasn't a contractor," he said.

Chloe shook her head. "David."

Richard squeezed her shoulders so hard she had to squirm away. "What did he want?"

Chloe's irritation gave way to curiosity as she magnified Richard's question. Though David was spending time with Madison under the pretense of searching for answers, she wondered if the life he remembered was actually the life he wanted.

Chloe had never rejected the idea of having children, but both she and David had things they'd wanted to accomplish first. David had promised that once he had gained enough experience at his accounting firm and learned to manage his anxiety, they would move to New York so Chloe could pursue her art career. She thought they had been happy, but now wondered if maybe she had held David back from something he'd always wanted, even as she struggled not to blame him for doing the same to her.

The thought brought with it a warm, tingling sensation, and Chloe felt lightheaded. She stumbled slightly and her purse slipped off her shoulder.

Richard caught her. "Chloe? Are you all right?" His voice sounded hollow and distant.

The room and Richard's face spun, and Chloe's entire body felt weak and heavy. Richard eased her to a sitting position on the floor against the closest wall, then rushed off and returned with a bottle of water. Chloe sipped and tried to breathe deeply. It took several minutes for her to recover enough to try standing. When she was able, Richard led her back to the office so she could sit in a comfortable chair.

"I was afraid this would be too much for you," Richard said.

Chloe shook her head. "I'll be fine. It was just a little anxiety." As soon as she said it, she wondered if that was how David felt when he had one of his attacks. It made her feel guilty, which made her feel stressed, and she shook her head against those thoughts, not wanting to repeat the episode. "I could probably use something to eat, too," she added. She hadn't noticed it before, but her stomach was growling.

Richard stared at her, expressionless. "The car is waiting outside, whenever you're ready."

Chloe nodded. "I think I just need another minute. Will you go grab my purse?"

Richard obliged, and Chloe sat in the office and finished the bottle of water. She chided herself for getting so worked up. David could take care of himself, and if he wanted to pursue crazy magic theories and a relationship with a woman who clearly didn't appreciate him, that was his business. Chloe had more important things to worry about.

When Richard returned with her purse, Chloe stood and kissed him. "Let's walk. I could use the exercise."

nineteen

Chloe and Richard left the gallery and walked through the chilly night, along Manhattan streets that glowed with life, and Chloe took stock of everything she had—a great job, a caring boyfriend, her art opening, and living in New York. She loved her life, and the more she thought about it, the more she decided that she wouldn't have any of it if she'd remained in her life with David. It made her feel a little guilty to think it, but David's disappearance might have been the best thing that could have happened to her.

When they arrived at the restaurant, they only had to wait a few moments while the hostess let the executive chef know Richard needed a table. "Clara and I go way back," he explained to Chloe. "We had an on-again, off-again thing several years before I met you. We broke it off for good when she left to go to Europe, but stayed in touch. It helps to know chefs," he said, smiling. "She's great at what she does, too. It isn't just food to her, it's art—the taste, the plating. Clara will even hand-select a wine to match the experience of each course."

Dinner was every bit as impressive as Chloe had been promised, and she and Richard laughed and talked about art and music and Stroudsburg. "I'd never been out there," Richard said. "I never had a reason to go until now." They avoided the topic of her trip and David, while she told Richard about growing up with her hard-working, practical father and her clever, ambitious mother.

"She always wanted us to do better and came up with these

little tricks," Chloe said. "She knew exactly how to manipulate us to do what—well, I guess not what *she* wanted. It was more like she pushed us to be our best selves. Like, when I was a freshman in high school, my dad insisted that I try out for a sport. He didn't care which one, but he said I had to at least try something other than art. I really didn't want to do it because it felt like such a waste of time to me then. And Mom commiserated with me, saying she understood but I should obey my father and all those other things moms say. Then she told me she'd played basketball in high school and I didn't believe her, and she showed me her old yearbook and took me to the park to shoot around a little. We had a lot of fun together, so I decided I'd try out for basketball. I really didn't want to practice though, just maybe go out once in a while with Mom and have fun. But she found ways to make me work at it, to give it my best shot, and I was pretty confident at tryouts."

"Did you make the team?" Richard asked, enthralled.

"No!" Chloe laughed. "I wasn't even close. The other girls had played in middle school and had all these other skills besides running around and shooting. They could dribble and pass and set picks, but when the coach asked me to do those things I didn't even know what she was talking about."

Richard shrugged, grinning. "I don't know either."

Chloe chuckled and took a sip of wine. "So, that should have been it, right? I tried out, I didn't make the team, and I figured I'd go back to painting every waking hour. But the funny thing was I missed that time with Mom, and without any pressure from my parents I started watching basketball and learning, and I asked Mom to teach me some things, and we were having fun and I got in much better shape and I saw that even with all that going on, my art didn't suffer. I always found time for it and I had lots of new inspiration, so it actually got better. And the next fall I tried out again and made the basketball team and made a lot of new friends who—I was surprised to find out—actually thought it was cool I was an artist. That led to the idea to paint this huge mural on the wall of the gym, and a bunch of us worked together on that, and my art kept getting better. That was the one thing I never had trouble working at, but if Mom hadn't gotten me into basketball I would have missed out on a lot. It's weird how that works. Like you can have something you're passionate about and totally dedicated to, but if you only obsess about that one thing it can't become as good, you know?"

"I suppose so," Richard said. "I don't know. I never played any sports or joined clubs in high school, but I went to a lot of games and events and just watched. I watched the players, the coaches, the cheerleaders—especially the cheerleaders." He grinned and Chloe gave him a light smack on the arm. "But I loved watching. I didn't want to be the kid running around sweating, but I wanted to understand him. I'd go home and draw or paint or build something out of junk, trying to focus on one thing at a time until I had the whole experience."

"That makes sense," Chloe said. "I can see that universality in your work, even the one you did for me. Other people won't necessarily get my story out of it, but they'll still get something because somehow you pulled everything in."

Richard chuckled. "Well apparently not everything. I had no idea you were such a jock," he teased.

Chloe rolled her eyes. "You know, I've been borderline obsessed with that painting since you showed it to me."

"I noticed," Richard said, explaining that he'd seen her doodles when he was picking up her dropped purse.

Chloe blushed. "Since I couldn't look at it while I was away, I guess I just kept drawing it over and over. I spent a lot of time on the phone, and you know how I doodle."

Richard looked down, hesitant, almost hurt. "You made some edits."

"Edits? What are you talking about?" Chloe only remembered mindlessly doodling the image, not focusing deliberately on it. "You can't expect it to be exactly the same. I wasn't trying to copy it or anything, just thinking about it and doodling."

Richard shook his head and pulled a scrap of paper from

his pocket. "I kept one, but the others are still in your purse."

Chloe said she didn't mind that he took it. It was just a doodle, and she had a whole shoe box full of them. She explained that she didn't know why she always kept them, but she liked having them to look back on.

"Okay," Richard said, "but really take a look at this. Then look at the actual painting." He pulled his cell phone from his other pocket and displayed an image of the piece. "See how close they are? But there are tiny variations, these strange little loops here and there, and this shadow in the corner."

"That's not a shadow, that's just where I was scribbling," Chloe said, not sure if she believed herself. "And the variations are just where I didn't remember it right or maybe there was a bump in the table or something. You're reading too much into this."

"Am I? I have never known you to buckle under stress the way you did tonight, and I know you have a lot going on, but don't you want this? Aren't you prepared to get your work out there no matter the cost? That's what you always told me before, and that's what I always saw in you. That's why you're so good at what you do for Fred, because of that fire you have for making art. And yet you go out and see this long-lost husband of yours and the fire seems...well, not gone but it certainly isn't burning as bright. I'm worried about you. I'm worried about what he's done to you."

Chloe just stared at him, letting his words sink into her brain. "Where is this coming from? A doodle? No, it's more than that, isn't it?" She didn't want to believe it, but Richard was acting jealous and crazy. He always seemed so above that kind of pettiness and Chloe honestly didn't know how to react.

"This painting," he said, indicating the photo on his phone, "is about you. It's about your life and your journey, and to some extent about the two of us. But the only parts of your doodles that seem to be different are the ones that fall in the 'us' category. How am I supposed to feel about that?"

Chloe started to protest that it was just a mistake, that she couldn't possibly recreate what he had painted exactly, stroke for stroke. But Richard stopped her and said he saw all the drawings in her purse and they're all the same, all changed in the same way.

"This is ridiculous," Chloe said. "Don't you remember what I told you before I left the other day, about this being my future and David being my past? Yes, it's a screwed-up situation and I don't know exactly what sense to make of it, if any. Yes, some old feelings came back and I'm a little overwhelmed, but don't I have a right to be? And now you're accusing me of somehow changing my life story because I couldn't draw your painting exactly from memory? How the hell are we supposed to get through this, to have a real relationship, if you can't trust me or understand when I need a little time to process things?"

She wiped the tears away from her eyes and noticed several other diners staring at her. Chloe didn't realize she had raised her voice so much. Richard looked mortified. Chloe tried to think of something she could do to salvage the situation but came up empty. Instead, she followed her instincts, which told her to stand up and walk quickly from the table, looking straight ahead as far as she could until she reached the door. She turned around to see Richard still sitting there. He hadn't moved an inch, hadn't even made an attempt to stop her or come after her. Most of the restaurant was still staring at her too. Chloe turned and stormed out into the street.

The crowd out in the cool evening paid her no attention, unlike the restaurant patrons. Chloe fumed, thinking about Richard's jealousy and how David never acted like that. Not that David ever painted her anything, either. She wondered if all her doodles were the same, as Richard had claimed, but then she realized that she'd left her purse in the restaurant, and she stopped and stomped her foot. She really didn't want to go back, but she needed her purse. When she turned around, she saw Richard walking toward her, carrying it.

"Damn it, Chloe, what's wrong with you?" he asked, firmly

but with a touch of worry in his tone. "You are so much better than this. And it isn't about me being jealous or anything to do with us. This is about your art. I'm trying to look out for you, to make sure you can continue pursuing your dreams."

Chloe snatched her purse from his grip. "I don't need you to look out for me," she said angrily, but without shouting. "I don't need your help and I don't need your permission. And you know what? If you're so upset about the way I altered a drawing that's supposed to represent my own life, then maybe you just don't know my life as well as I do."

She gave him a moment to answer, and when he didn't she turned around and resumed walking briskly toward the gallery. She turned the corner and felt a hand on her shoulder, and stopped short.

"Let go of me, Richard," she said.

"You aren't walking out on me so easily this time," Richard said. "I let you do that once, and it didn't take very long for me to realize it was a big mistake, one I am not about to repeat."

Chloe pulled out of his grip. "Well, maybe you should start taking me seriously, then."

"I'm taking you more seriously than you are right now," Richard said.

She turned to face him. "No, you're taking my career more seriously. Or at least, you think you are. You're not taking me seriously because you think I'm not taking my career seriously."

Richard squinted. "What?"

Chloe took a deep breath and went over the logic in her head again. Yes, she had said it correctly. "You think I'm not taking this show seriously. I am, and if you took me seriously, and I mean me as a person, me as an artist, not as some intern you're mentoring, you would know that."

"What am I supposed to think?" Richard said, throwing his arms out to the side and nearly smacking a passerby in the face. He apologized, then turned back to Chloe. "You go off to see your ex-husband instead of focusing on the opening, and now he's calling and making you so stressed you can't function."

"It's a stressful situation," Chloe admitted. "I didn't ask for this." A pang of guilt struck her gut. She wondered if she had been given the choice between having her debut and David's return, which she would have chosen. She tried to shake the question away. "What I need is support, not criticism."

"Well maybe I don't know how to do that," Richard said. "Do you know how long it's been since I've been in a real relationship? I thought I was getting the hang of it. I thought I was getting to know the real you, but when I saw your doodles I got scared that maybe I was wrong."

Chloe sighed. "They're just doodles. They weren't meant to be exact recreations."

"I know, I know. It's stupid and irrational." Richard looked her in the eyes and said, "I'm sorry. I'm really sorry."

It was the most genuine thing Chloe could remember him saying to her. While his reaction to the doodles was borderline insane, Chloe had to admit to herself that she had given Richard a very real reason to be jealous. She hadn't told him about kissing David, and she was confident she never would, but she did feel guilty and decided that Richard's feelings were justified.

Chloe kissed Richard gently. "It's all right. You're right that I've been stressed more than usual, and I didn't think you cared that much. I know all about your past relationships and I figured it wouldn't be too long before you tossed me aside too. That's why I felt so conflicted about David. He was always in it for the long haul, you know? He couldn't give me what you can, but he was always stable, dependable. There must be a part of me that still wants what my parents have. I know you aren't that guy, and I've always been okay with that, but seeing David again brought up some old feelings."

Richard shrugged. "Well, if nothing else comes of this, at least you'll have plenty of emotional turmoil to throw into new paintings. You could probably paint another wall at this point. Maybe an entire room."

Chloe imagined what it would be like to paint an entire room, including the ceiling and floor. She wondered if she could paint a 360-degree panoramic landscape, including a sky and the ground. Thinking about the ground, she wondered about texture, whether it would be disorienting to step on a painting of boulders or water, and then something unexpected struck her.

"I have an idea," Chloe said. "We're not going to tear out the floor and lay down a different one."

Richard tilted his head. "But it's hideous. You have to do something."

Chloe grinned and raised her eyebrows. "We're going to paint it."

twenty

"Will paint adhere to the flooring?" Richard asked.

"I don't see why not," Chloe said. "We might need a special primer or something, and we'll have to get started right away. But this will be faster than replacing it, and will save Fred some money."

Chloe made phone calls while she and Richard walked quickly back toward the gallery. She asked Conner to find an open paint store and ask about the primer, and to have a rush delivery of enough to cover the floor as well as two coats of paint. "I need something off-white, maybe twenty percent grey," she said, "along with some ochre, maroon, and forest green. And get a couple gallons of black, too." She also listed off some other supplies they would need, such as tape, brushes, and buckets.

When she finished with Conner, Chloe did a quick search using her phone for mold remediation companies. She found one nearby and dialed the number, but the call went to voicemail. She tried the next on the list with the same result. Determined, she kept trying until she got hold of a one-man operation on Staten Island. She offered him double his stand- ard rate plus mileage, at which point Richard gave her a surprised glare. The man was hesitant, but Chloe talked him into coming out that evening.

"Why do you need a mold contractor? I'm guessing the floor isn't that bad," Richard said.

Chloe chuckled. "I don't need him to clean up mold. I just

need his drying equipment." She explained that during mold cleanup, a plastic barrier can be put in place to create an area of negative pressure and low humidity. "It will dry the paint faster without affecting the other climate-controlled areas of the gallery," she said.

Richard shook his head. "How do you know this stuff?"

"My dad," Chloe said. "He's in construction, and he's done remodels for homes that have fire and mold damage. That, and I watch a lot of home improvement shows on TV."

They reached the gallery and Conner reported that the paint had been ordered and would be delivered within the hour. Chloe told him to get some pencils and a straight edge while she went to the janitor's closet and got brooms and the mop bucket.

"Help me out here," she said to Richard, handing him a broom.

He took it tentatively, but Chloe paid it no mind. She set about sweeping the floor, trying not to stir up too much dust. After she'd gone along the edge of one wall, she looked up to see Richard had barely made any progress.

"Come on, slacker," she joked. "Pick it up a little."

"Are you sure this is going to work?" He looked seriously troubled.

"It's worth a try, isn't it?" she said. Then, seeing how upset he was, Chloe asked, "What's the problem?"

"Aren't you worried that all this practicality is taking away from your artistic side?"

"No," Chloe answered flatly. "And it's not going to take away from yours, either." She didn't know why he didn't want to help other than it being manual labor, and she didn't think he was quite so petty. But she tried to entice him. "It's going to get a lot more fun, and a lot more artistic, once the paint gets here. But first we have to get the surface clean."

She went back to sweeping, working as quickly as she could. Conner returned, left the tools nearby, and joined in. Richard continued to move slowly, but at least he was helping.

After they'd swept, Chloe took the mop and very lightly cleaned the flooring, trying not to get it sopped but at least do enough to pick up the dust.

"I had almost hoped cleaning it would help," Conner said. "It still looks awful, though." He yawned.

"It's okay," Chloe said, feeling energized. "We're going to make it so much better." She asked Conner about the schedule for tomorrow and he said no contractors were due in until afternoon, because they had assumed they'd have to lay new flooring. Chloe said that was perfect and told him that once the supplies were delivered he should go get some rest.

The paint and the mold contractor arrived at almost the same time. Richard and Conner organized the painting supplies while Chloe showed the contractor where they'd be working. He set up the barrier and showed Chloe how to operate the machine, explaining that she could use it to circulate air while they were painting and then switch it to dehumidify when they were done.

"Pretty smart idea," the mold contractor said. "I've never seen anybody use one of these to dry paint. You guys must be under one heck of a deadline."

Chloe thanked him and told him to come pick up his equipment tomorrow afternoon. She took his estimate and the invoice for the paint to the office, then sent Conner home.

"We'll do the primer first," Chloe said, and opened two of the cans. She grabbed two wide brushes from the mountain of supplies. "Start by going around the walls," she instructed. "Make sure to come out at least three or four inches."

Richard frowned. "I thought you said this was going to be fun," he complained.

"Patience," Chloe said. "We need a canvas first."

They set about priming the floor, working from the back in opposite directions around the space. Once the perimeter was painted, Chloe attached some rollers to poles and filled two trays with the primer.

"Lay it on thick, but try to keep it smooth," she said. "We

only want to put down one coat of this if we can."

Richard fumbled with the roller, and Chloe had to work with him closely until he got the technique down. She was actually surprised at how uncomfortable he was with it, and tried to lighten the mood by suggesting he now had a new tool to use in his mixed-media projects. They finished the primer coat relatively quickly, and Chloe turned on the dehumidifier.

She cleaned up the supplies while Richard went for coffee. Chloe pulled two chairs from the office into the lobby, and covered them with drop cloths so they could sit.

"So, what's next?" Richard asked. "This is about as exciting as watching paint dry."

Chloe chuckled, more amused with Richard's rare attempt at humor than with the joke itself. "Once this dries, we'll mark off some borders with the black paint. Then we'll have to wait for that to dry so we can tape it off, but hopefully it won't take long to do in the first place. After that, we'll fill in the marked off areas with color and use a nice off-white as the background."

"Okay," Richard said. "I still don't see how this is fun. Or art."

"Oh, come on. We'll lay down the color pattern so it flows through the space, drawing attention to where the paintings will hang. It will be inviting, keep people moving, and give them something to talk about while they wait to see their favorite pieces again."

"That's traffic control, not art," Richard said.

Chloe backhanded Richard's upper arm gently. "Stop being so negative. Maybe it's not as expressive or emotional as painting a canvas, but we're still making something here."

"Don't you get it?" Richard asked. "Art can't be just a side gig to you. It has to be your everything. It has to completely consume you. Doing this kind of work kills that. Even Fred knows that if your show on Friday is a success, he's going to have to start looking for your replacement."

"But I care about this work," Chloe said. "I care about the

gallery. I don't see why I can't do both."

"You always want to do both. You always think you can do everything," Richard said. "But you can't. It just isn't possible. If you want to be a great artist, and I think you can be, you have to give it everything you've got."

"And clawing my way out of debt, working in a prestigious gallery, and getting an opening doesn't show enough dedication for you? Leaving my husband, who vanished for ten years, alone to deal with whatever weird memories on his own isn't enough?" Mentioning David only compounded Chloe's frustration, as she worried anew about his getting mixed up with Tommy's cult. David also would have been far more helpful when it came to cleaning and priming the floor, she thought bitterly.

"He isn't your husband anymore," Richard said.

"Whatever," Chloe said. "David. You know who I meant. Don't try and disarm me with semantics."

"I've said it before and I meant it, you're an amazing woman, Chloe. I do think it's impressive that you've been able to take on so much and still succeed. But you don't have to do that anymore. This opening is going to give you a chance to finally put all the fighting, all the struggle, behind you. You'll be free to just be an artist, but you have to be willing to accept that."

Chloe looked away from Richard while his words resonated in her mind. Being able to paint and travel and study art without the burden of a day job was what she had always wanted, wasn't it? She couldn't seem to wrap her head around the fact that she'd be giving something up in the process. When Fred had hired her as gallery manager, she had seen it as a better job than retail but still just a means to an end. Somehow it had grown to mean more to her, though.

"Well, I still have this show to do," Chloe said. "It will take at least a couple hours for the primer to dry, so I should probably get to work on the layout."

"Okay," Richard said. "I think I'll go to my studio for a

while. Will you be all right here alone?"

Chloe nodded, then they stood and kissed. Something about it didn't feel right, though. Chloe tried kissing him again, but Richard simply pressed his lips against hers in a meaningless, ritual way, devoid of the tenderness and comfort Chloe desperately needed in that moment.

"I'll be back soon," Richard said as he left. Chloe locked the door behind him, already wondering if it would be easier to just finish the job herself.

Chloe patted the east wing floor with her palm, and the surface felt dry. She smiled to herself and switched the dehumidifier to fan-only mode, then gathered her supplies to lay down an off-white base color over the primer. Her plan was working, and she couldn't wait to get back to work regardless of what Richard said. She decided not to bother messaging him, hoping he'd forget all about the project so she could work alone.

She stirred the paint and poured some into a tray, then dipped the roller in. She pushed the paint across the floor, and the first few strokes looked good. Then, suddenly, a large sheet of the primer peeled off and stuck to the roller.

"Oh no," Chloe said, dropping the pole. "No, no, no!" She knelt down and peeled the primer from the roller and tried to replace it, but the damage was already done. She frantically tried to apply the paint from her roller to the now uncovered floor but it just pushed around, uneven and pooling. More of the primer peeled off onto the roller cover. As she scrambled around, more came off onto her shoes.

Chloe threw the pole and roller onto the floor and it bounced, splattering paint onto her and the nearby wall. She cursed loud enough to echo over the hum of the fan. This was supposed to work. This was how she was going to get her opening, and now it was literally falling apart. Chloe dropped to her knees, sobbing.

How had this happened? Why was it that the universe seemed so intent on keeping her from artistic success? Richard was successful, as were the other artists whose works had graced the Lumina Gallery's walls and floor spaces. Why not her? Did she really not dedicate herself enough to it, like Richard said? Was she really keeping herself from success by insisting on being responsible, holding another job, and being self-sufficient?

And David? She had let herself get close to him, lost herself in his eyes, his smile, and even his kiss. She had risked her lifelong dream to go to him. But now he was spending his time hanging around with another woman and getting suckered into Tommy's impossible parallel universe theory. Chloe fumed, furious at David for what he'd done to her, furious at herself for allowing him to do it. Her rational mind argued that she'd had a choice, that David did tell her to go back to New York, but she still needed someone to blame and he was the easiest target. Her stomach turned as her emotions tottered between anger and guilt. She really had loved and missed David, and a part of her had always held a sliver of hope that he would come back, but why now?

Chloe stood and wiped the paint off her clothes as best she could, then staggered back to the office. She picked up her tablet and started searching the internet for ways to fix the primer, and while some leads looked promising they all involved tearing out what had already been done, and she didn't have time for that. One blogger mentioned using temporary carpeting, so Chloe started researching that option. Eventually exhaustion overcame her, and she fell asleep at the desk.

twenty-one

"Chloe? Hey, Chloe!"

Chloe struggled to open her eyes, and she reached up to rub the sleep from them. When she got her bearings, she found herself in the Lumina Gallery office, with Fred looking down at her, scowling.

"What the hell is going on here?" he asked.

Chloe straightened herself in the chair and yawned. "Sorry, I must have fallen asleep. I was trying to fix the floor, but—"

"It's a complete disaster," Fred cut in. "Yes, I saw it. Not only that, there's a machine running out there and paint supplies all over the lobby. Do I need to remind you we have an opening tomorrow night?"

Chloe's breath caught. She'd never seen Fred so angry before. "No, of course not."

"And these invoices!" Fred picked up the papers from his desk and shook them in front of Chloe's face. "While you do have discretionary funds, when you spend this much money I expect results, not an even bigger mess."

"I'm sorry," Chloe said, fighting to keep her composure. The last thing she wanted to do was break down and cry in front of Fred, but the anxiety and lack of sleep had her emotions on edge. "I thought the paint would work. Maybe I set the dehumidifier too high."

Fred slapped the papers back onto the desk and shouted at her. "I don't care what happened! Get this place cleaned up, now!" He turned and stepped away from Chloe, then took a deep breath. "Rushing the east wing was obviously a mistake," he said, his voice more even but still carrying an edge.

Chloe stood. "We could still make it happen. I found some temporary carpeting—"

Fred wheeled on her. "No! I'm not throwing any more resources at this. After the opening, we'll resume construction according to the original plan."

Chloe looked away and tightened her jaw, fighting tears. "I'm sorry," she whispered.

Fred sighed. "Stop apologizing and do your job. Clean up the mess, then take the rest of the morning off. Go home and get some rest, then be back here after lunch to finish preparing for Richard's show."

Chloe took a breath, then turned back toward Fred. His expression had softened a little, but he still looked angry. She nodded and forced an "okay" from her parched throat, then started toward the office door.

Fred called to her before she got out of the room, and she froze in place. "I'm disappointed, but I'm a man of my word. When the expansion is complete, I will debut your paintings albeit with considerably less fanfare. And I expect you to prepare a small, private showing of your work in the auxiliary room, to be held just before Richard's opening."

It was better than nothing, she knew, but Chloe couldn't fight the weight of failure that seemed to hang from her shoulders. "Thank you," she said.

Fred said nothing in return. Chloe heard him turn and drop himself into his desk chair, and she left the office. The lobby was messier than she remembered, with brushes and paint cans strewn about haphazardly. The hum of the dehumidifier grated her already fragile nerves, so she switched it off. Then she stacked all the painting supplies inside the east wing, called a cab, and stepped outside into the foggy morning.

Chloe yawned as the driver pulled away from the curb. She let her forehead rest against the window and watched absentmindedly as the city passed by, trying not to think of what she'd lost. What an opportunity Fred had given her, and she'd squandered it. She knew she'd have her debut eventually, but to miss out on this chance to have a large and diverse crowd viewing her work was crushing. A tear ran down the side of her nose and settled in a salty pool on her lips.

Her phone rang, startling her. Chloe wasn't sure, but she thought she'd fallen asleep for a few minutes. She pulled the phone from her purse and looked at the screen. David. Just seeing his name made her shoulders tense. She wanted to decline the call, but couldn't bring herself to do so. What if something had happened to him?

"Hello?" Chloe tried not to, but she sniffled.

"Chloe? What's wrong?" David asked.

"I just..." She swallowed a sob. "I don't want to talk about it right now."

"Is it the construction? Did something happen?"

"I said I don't want to talk about it," Chloe snapped.

David took a deep breath. "Chloe, it's going to be all right. I'm on my way there."

"You're what?" Chloe's breath quickened as she imagined having to cope with his obsession and anxiety on top of preparing for the opening.

"I'm at the bus station," David said. "I didn't want to wait. I spent the night with Madison and—"

"You what?" Chloe's immediate assumption that they'd been intimate and corresponding knee-jerk reaction surprised her. The woman had three couches for crying out loud. "I mean, why would you do that?"

"Hey, it's not what you think," David said, his voice defensive. "Like I said yesterday, we were trying to find some answers."

"It's always been about finding answers with you," Chloe said. "Everything had to have some kind of explanation. Why this? Why that? You know what, David? It doesn't matter."

"I think it would be nice to know something," David argued. "I mean, it's been ten years. But—"

"Right, it was ten years ago," Chloe said. "I want to know what happened to you too, but I have more important things to worry about right now."

David sighed. "I know."

"Really?" Chloe scoffed.

"Really," David said. "Look, I'm sorry about the other day. I want to make things right. Madison helped me realize that I was so focused on what happened when I disappeared that I didn't pay attention to what's happening now."

"Well, congratulations," Chloe said sarcastically. "What a breakthrough. Maybe you and Blondie are right for each other after all."

"I told you, it's not like that," David said, sounding hurt. "I thought trying to give you some closure was the only way I could help you, but it just made things worse. I get that now, and I want to fix it."

There was a moment of silence on the line, until Chloe's irritation waned enough to allow a pang of guilt in. "I'm sorry," she said.

"Me too," David said. "You gave up a lot to be here for me, and I didn't appreciate it. Now I want to be there for you."

Chloe winced, tears starting anew in her eyes, which were strained from fatigue and dry contacts. "David, no—"

"I'm coming, Chloe. I'll be there this evening, around six."

"I don't want you to do that," Chloe said.

"Don't worry, I'll be fine," David said. "We can talk more when I get there, and I'll help you with whatever you need to get ready for your big debut."

"It's not happening," Chloe whimpered.

"What?"

"I said it's not happening." Chloe wiped away her tears. "Just forget it, okay? I blew it. Nothing has gone right all week, and it obviously wasn't meant to be."

"Wait, slow down," David said. "What happened? Maybe I can help."

"No," Chloe said. "I'm in enough trouble as it is already. I need to focus on getting Richard's show ready or I'm going to lose my job."

David exhaled sharply. "This is my fault, isn't it?"

Chloe took a deep breath and spoke slowly to stop herself from snapping at him. "I need a little time, David. I need to get through this opening. If you want to help, just give me some space."

"I'm sorry," David said.

"Stop," Chloe said. "It's fine. I'll be fine. We'll talk in a few days, when things calm down."

"Fine," David said quietly.

Chloe sighed. "It isn't all your fault. And I'm glad you're back, it's just..." She swallowed the lump in her throat. "It's just really shitty timing, you know?"

David chuckled. "Not exactly a first for us."

Chloe rolled her eyes and laughed. "No, I guess it isn't."

"Remember that time we got all dressed up to go to that fancy steakhouse, and when we got there it was closed?"

Chloe smiled. "Yeah, I remember. It shut down like three days before that." As the conversation fell away, her mind also drifted to another case of bad timing, when they'd been caught in the rain Tuesday night.

"We'll talk soon," David said. "I miss you."

"I miss you too," Chloe said. As she hung up the phone, a small part of her regretted telling him to stay away. As much as she longed for his comfort, though, she feared his coming to New York would only make things worse.

During their last semester in college, David had applied to all the major accounting firms in the city and lined up several interviews. They decided to stay in Manhattan instead of making day trips from Stroudsburg, but David couldn't handle it. Chloe helped him navigate to his first interview, then went sightseeing. He was supposed to meet her when he was done, but got lost and panicked. When Chloe finally caught up to him, he shook with anxiety and could barely function.

David canceled the rest of his interviews and they left for Chloe's parents' house that evening. They decided to settle in Morgantown, much to Chloe's disappointment, but David always promised he would give it another try someday. Then he vanished.

A tear slid down Chloe's cheek as she watched the buildings and people pass, wondering how things might have been different if she'd chosen the city instead of him.

Chloe entered her apartment to find Madge sitting at the kitchen table, drinking juice and studying an art history book. "You don't look so good, Mrs. S. Are you okay?"

She shook her head and told Madge what happened at the gallery. "I blew it. I shouldn't have gone to see David."

"No, you needed to do that," Madge said. "Seeing him again made you happy."

"I guess, but now this big thing that I've always wanted is ruined, you know? It's really frustrating to work so hard on something only to have it fall apart."

"Sounds like my last project in mixed-media," Madge said. "And the group project isn't going well either."

"Did you guys decide on a subject yet?" Chloe asked.

"Nope," Madge said. "We all agree we want to do something that's unique and different from everybody else, but we can't figure out what that is."

"I wish I could help more," Chloe said. "Not only am I way behind at the gallery, I'm also in a slump myself."

"It's okay," Madge said. "We're all supposed to come up with some more ideas and meet tonight."

Chloe trudged toward the bathroom. Madge stopped her. "Is Mr. S still coming?"

"I told him not to," Chloe said. "But don't be surprised if

he shows up anyway."

"You don't sound too happy about that," Madge said.

"It's not that I don't want to see him, I just don't need the distraction, you know?"

"I guess that makes sense," Madge said.

Chloe took her contacts out and then went to her bedroom. She plopped down on the bed without even undressing, then pulled out her phone and set an alarm for noon. She tossed and turned, unable to stop thinking about her failure. What if she'd done things differently? Would it have mattered? Was there more she could do?

It was a long time before Chloe fell into a fitful sleep.

When she returned to the gallery, Chloe could barely focus on the finishing details of Richard's exhibit. Fortunately, Conner was more help than he had been with the east wing construction, allowing Chloe to move at a slower pace than she normally would. By late afternoon, she'd finished all the paperwork and sent Conner home.

Richard arrived as she carried the last of the paintings she had chosen for her private show to the auxiliary room. Despite wanting him to stay away the night before, Chloe was still a little irritated that he hadn't even bothered to check in with her. She tried to remain professional, though. She needed a final sign-off on her layout of his exhibit, and hoped his company might help keep her mind off David and the east wing.

He scanned through the canvases while Chloe set up easels. "Did Lumina choose these pieces?"

"No, I did," Chloe answered.

"So, I take it he still hasn't seen all the paintings I brought from your parents' house," Richard said.

Chloe suspected he wanted to discuss the Woodburn Hall painting again, so she tried to avoid the subject. "The pieces Fred liked initially were the landscapes from the Poconos, so that's what I pulled."

Richard picked up the first canvas and helped Chloe position it on an easel. They worked in silence for a few minutes, until the first four paintings were in position. Chloe planned to arrange a semicircle of ten paintings in the auxiliary room, using the layout she'd drafted for the east wing as a guide. She stepped back to make sure the ones they'd placed so far still worked in that order.

After a moment's analysis, she noticed Richard watching her. "What do you think of this order?"

He shrugged. "I see no problems with it."

Chloe scanned the paintings again. The second canvas featured bare, snow covered trees, while the third depicted a sparkling lake and branches laden with green leaves. Loneliness and isolation prevailed in the winter scene, whereas the summer painting exhibited energy, life, and hidden potential. In the original layout, there had been two other pieces between them, but in the smaller space of the auxiliary room she had cut those. Now she wondered if the transition between the paintings was too jarring.

She asked Richard about her specific concern, and again received a noncommittal answer. "Each of these stands on its own. There's nothing linking them aside from the style and the fact they were done in the same geographic region. We hadn't met when you painted these, so you didn't know about tying a series together with visual cues yet. Unless, of course, you count that shadow Lumina pointed out."

"There's an emotional link between them," Chloe said. "You don't feel that as you go from one to the other?"

Richard paused a moment. "I think we should set up everything, then we can reassess the layout. Otherwise we'll just be doing this over and over again."

Chloe sighed. He was right, and she wondered if her irritation had more to do with his failure to connect with her work or her own exhaustion. They worked together to set up the rest of the paintings, speaking very little. When they finished, Chloe stood in the center of the arrangement, the pride in her work marred by the nagging regret of failing to finish the east wing.

Richard stood next to her. "This looks good, but your best work isn't in here."

Chloe rolled her eyes. "I am not showing the Woodburn Hall painting."

He turned to her. "I think you should. It's an anchor holding you to your past, but it's also an exceptional piece. I took the liberty of sending a photograph of it to some potential buyers, and—"

"You did what?" Chloe's eyes went wide and she spun to face him, her muscles tense.

Richard ignored her, though. "There is a lot of interest. If you showed it here, you could make a considerable amount."

Chloe crossed her arms. "I told you, it's not for sale. How could you shop it around like that? Not only did you go behind my back, you went behind Fred's."

"Lumina hasn't even seen the painting," Richard said.

Chloe stuck her finger close to Richard's face. "Which would only make him more upset if it got back to him that you were taking offers. Not that it matters anyway, because *it's not for sale.*"

Richard didn't flinch. "It was only a suggestion."

Chloe's chest tightened, his words stoking the fire of her anger. Before she could lash out at Richard, though, she heard what sounded like someone pounding on the gallery's front door. Her thoughts shifted to wondering if she had forgotten to cancel a contractor visit, allowing her irritation to abate somewhat.

She turned to leave the auxiliary room, but paused to put in the final word with Richard. "Do not bring up that painting again. Do not offer it to anyone. I'm not showing it. I'm not selling it. Is that clear?"

"Your loss," he said.

Chloe took a deep breath, collected herself, then strode out into the lobby. She was so preoccupied that she didn't even register who had knocked until she was two steps from the door.

David stood on the sidewalk outside the gallery, smiling and waving sheepishly at her.

twenty-two

Chloe opened the door and motioned David in. "I knew you wouldn't listen to me."

David smirked. "Then why did you bother telling me not to come?"

"Old habits, I guess." She put her hands on her hips and shook her head at him, but David's only reaction was to smile at her. After a moment, she gave up on being upset with him and extended her arms, inviting a hug.

David shifted the duffel bag that hung over his shoulder, then leaned in to embrace her. "How are things going?"

She returned his embrace, then pulled away. "Could be better, but at least I've got things mostly under control now." He didn't seem nervous at all. "You're handling the city okay?"

David shrugged. "I guess so, but all I've done so far is ride a cab from the bus station."

Though she was glad to see him relaxed, Chloe still felt a touch of bitterness that he hadn't been able to control his anxiety like that during their ill-fated trip to New York in college. She squeezed David's shoulder and they shared a smile. "I'm glad you're doing all right. Just set your bag down anywhere and I'll show you around."

She checked the lock on the front door while David put the duffel bag on the floor and stretched. They turned toward the reception area when Richard emerged from the auxiliary room.

"Who's this?" Richard asked, his tone betraying his suspicion.

Chloe introduced them, and David and Richard eyed each other warily as they shook hands.

"Chloe was just going to show me around the gallery," David said. "Is this a bad time?"

"I think we're about finished here," Richard said. "I just need to review my layout."

Chloe yawned. "We'll make it a quick tour." She led David and Richard to the center of the main lobby. "This is where the reception will be tomorrow night. There will be a podium and a string quartet—"

"Strings?" Richard asked. "I thought we agreed on a DJ."

"When there was the possibility of a joint show, Fred decided to bring in a quartet. Don't worry, though, this isn't the usual classical and wedding music group. The quartet that's coming tomorrow covers modern rock and pop songs, so you'll still get the higher energy you prefer for your show."

Richard rolled his eyes. "You could have at least told me."

Chloe gave him an indignant glare. "Well, it was a crazy week, after all. I could barely keep up with Fred's music and catering selections in the wake of Conner's handling of all the construction." She noticed David glancing around nervously and asked if he was all right.

"Yeah, just taking it all in," he said. "So, the stuff on the walls...?"

Chloe smiled. "Pieces from Fred's personal collection. We rotate through a few different sets of paintings. Normally there would be sculptures out here too, but we moved them out of the way for the reception. Also, when the gallery opens back up to the public next week, we'll move some additional tables and racks into this space for selling prints, art books, stuff like that. We even have miniature versions of Richard's centerpiece sculpture on order."

"Chloe manages all this," Richard said, putting a hand on her shoulder. "All the planning, setup, sales. You even do a little scouting, don't you?"

Chloe winced at Richard's obviously forced smile and condescending boasts. "A little. Fred's so well connected that he usually knows what he wants well before I've even heard of it."

David looked around and settled his gaze on the east wing entrance, which was blocked by a temporary construction divider. "Is that where your part was supposed to be?"

Chloe sighed. "It will get done eventually."

David turned to her. "And there's nothing we can do to finish it?"

She gave him a sad smile. "No, it's too late for that. But I appreciate you offering to help."

"It is a shame, though," Richard said. "I was looking forward to seeing her work in the gallery. At least you'll get your private showing though, so it won't be a total loss."

"Private showing?" David asked.

Chloe explained about setting up a small exhibit in the auxiliary room for a hand-picked group of collectors. David insisted on seeing it, so she led the way.

"These are great," he said as he browsed the paintings. "Is there a reason you put them in this order, though?" David indicated the winter and summer scenes she'd asked Richard about before.

Chloe gave Richard a knowing glance, but he didn't react. "I'm still playing with the layout."

David nodded. "Well, they're all amazing. I'm sure it'll be a sellout." He winked, emphasizing that he remembered the proper meaning of the word.

Chloe grinned and led them back through the lobby toward the main gallery and Richard's exhibit. She got a phone call and needed something from the office, so Richard went ahead into the show while David excused himself to the restroom, blaming the long bus ride.

Chloe dealt with the call, a final confirmation from the sound engineer, then hurried to rejoin David and Richard before they got too irate with one another. She was relieved to see David waiting for her just outside the restroom, but tried not to show it.

"You didn't have to wait," she said.

David shrugged and smiled at her. "Just thought I'd hang around in case you needed anything." He paused, then added, "Richard seems nice."

Chloe chuckled at his obvious discomfort, but decided not to press the issue. As the two of them walked toward the main gallery, Richard was walking out.

"What did you think of the layout?" Chloe asked Richard.

"I think it's perfect," he replied, leaning to kiss her. "As usual, you've set me up for an excellent flow of conversation."

Chloe doubted his answer. Something about the space bothered her, and she had hoped Richard would catch it. "You didn't see anything that was off, anything that needed tweaking?"

"What do you mean?" Richard asked.

"What she means," David chimed in, "is that you're lying."

Richard crossed his arms and glared at David. "And what the hell would you know about it?"

David took a step back. "I admit I'm not an artist, all right? I never have been. But I know Chloe, and what she's trying to say is that the way these paintings are arranged doesn't feel right." He looked to Chloe, who stood listening intently, then back to Richard. "Like I said, I don't really understand art, but I don't think the art is the issue. Chloe wants the exhibit to be the best it possibly can, and to do that she needs to play with it more, tweak it until she finds the magic."

"You're right." Chloe took a deep breath, then stood beside David. "Richard, I think we need to reconsider how we present the show."

"It's too late for that," Richard argued. "I've been through the space already. I have a flow of conversation going in my mind. If you change it now it will completely throw me off."

"Oh, come on," David said. "If you're anything like Chloe, you know everything about every one of these paintings and sculptures from where you got the idea to which paint you used to how long it took you to make it. It's not like you have to do research. It's *your* work."

"The art isn't finished until it's properly presented," Richard said. "You think I just make a painting and that's all there is to it? When someone buys a piece tomorrow, they'll remember what was said about it. My presentation is part of it."

"Okay, fine," David said. "But it's not like changing the arrangement of the pieces changes how you present each one."

"It changes things," Richard said. "Subtle things. Things you don't understand."

Chloe stepped between them, afraid their argument would only grow more heated. "That's enough. What's important is that we get this show working, and the sooner the better."

"You chose this layout," Richard said to Chloe.

"Yes, but normally I have more time to experiment with everything," Chloe said. "This hasn't exactly been a normal week." She glanced at David apologetically.

"I'm fine with it," Richard said. "I see no reason this would cause any problems." He stared directly at David and added, "Unless you see something specific that needs to change, I vote we leave it as is. I trust your original instinct, Chloe."

"Then you don't know her at all," David said.

"Better than you ever did," Richard shot back. "Did you just come here to make her doubt herself?"

"Of course not. Chloe's instincts are great, but they aren't everything." David turned to her. "How many times have you started something, then got part way in and changed things? It's not a criticism, it's just that you tend to narrow your focus as you go. You don't start out with all the details, just a big idea that you improve along the way."

Chloe took a deep breath. David had a point, even if his abrasiveness with Richard was less than helpful. "You're right, but so is Richard. We can't change things too close to the opening."

Richard crossed his arms and waited for Chloe's decision with a neutral expression. David eyed Richard uneasily, then turned to Chloe.

"Walk me through it," he said. "Take me through the space step by step and let's talk it out." Richard started to protest, but David cut him off. "We'll do it once. If we can't figure it out after one try, we'll just leave it."

Chloe was thoughtful a moment. "That sounds fair. Let's do it."

Richard's blank expression didn't change. "Fine."

The three of them walked toward Richard's exhibit. At the entrance, Chloe turned to Richard and asked him to wait in the lobby.

"It's my work," he said. "I deserve an opinion."

Chloe shook her head. "You're too close to it. David's not. And while he may not be an artist, he has an eye for detail and I trust him."

"An eye for detail?" Richard scowled at David. "What did you do for a living again?"

"I'm an accountant," David said.

Richard scoffed and turned to Chloe. "Finding out-of-place pennies has nothing to do with art."

"Look, I know how important this is," David said. He glared at Richard and added, "For both of you. I'm only trying to help."

"Fine," Richard said. He turned and walked out into the middle of the lobby.

Chloe led David into Richard's exhibit. It began with two sculptures, one of a man and one of a woman, that were slashed and smeared at different places on their bodies. The sculptures, placed in the middle of the entrance to the exhibit, blocked much of the view from the lobby and forced the audience to walk around them. Beyond that, the space opened up, with a large abstract sculpture in the middle of the room and paintings along the outside walls. A few dividers broke up the perimeter, but for the most part a visitor could travel in a circle around the room and see everything.

David walked straight ahead to the large sculpture, which was made from the twisted and charred remains of wrecked cars. "This is weird."

Chloe chuckled. "I think it's supposed to be. People come to Richard's shows expecting shocking socioeconomic and political commentary. This really doesn't say anything at all. I think he made it to throw them off."

They circled around the amalgamation of wreckage and David joked with Chloe about demolition derbies and traffic in Morgantown. She let her stress float away on their laughter and eased into a comfortable, relaxed stroll through the exhibit.

Behind the central sculpture, a dividing wall separated the main flow of foot traffic around the perimeter from people encircling the massive centerpiece. Two paintings of different styles hung on the back side of the dividing wall.

Chloe indicated the one on the left. "This one is acrylic on canvas. See how it matches these others? They're from the same series."

David turned around to face the main wall, and Chloe followed his gaze past several paintings in the same style and palette as the one on the left side of the partition. The other series featured central carvings surrounded by tinted plaster details.

"I would have liked it better if the partition wall were V-shaped," Chloe said. "That would have created more separation between the two series. We don't have any like that, though, and putting two partitions this size next to each other would have closed things off too much."

David looked at the short wall again, nodding. Chloe waited while he walked to the corner and started back, glancing at the paintings in the acrylic series. He didn't speak, but Chloe could tell from his expression he was studying, analyzing, and looking for a pattern. She smiled as she watched him, remembering how well his rationality and her instincts complemented one another.

He stopped, turned, and pointed to the two pieces on the partition wall. "What if you switched these?"

"I thought about that, but then it breaks the series," Chloe said. "The flow of the paintings is right, I think."

"Maybe the flow of the paintings is right, but not the flow of people." He moved back toward the corner and repeated walking to center. "If I'm walking down this wall, then when I turn toward the middle of the room I see that side first." He pointed to the side of the partition opposite him.

Chloe went to the outer wall and mimicked David's motion. "I see what you're saying, but then you have to do a full circle to get back to the other series."

"It's only weird because we went to the center first," David said. "Do you think most people will do that? If you come into the space and start along one of the outside walls, then when you get here you see the partition, go out around the statue, and then come back to the partition."

"Oh, so make a bigger loop." Chloe paused and considered the idea, then walked past the partition to stand between the statue and a side wall. A vision of patrons moving through the space formed in her mind, and she pointed out where to place rope barriers to keep the main circuit around the perimeter. "We could also put a short one at the entrance to keep people from going right to the central sculpture. That would hint at where to go while still keeping the space open."

She walked around the space a bit more, then asked David to help her move the two pieces on the back of the partition wall. The painting on the left was large but not too heavy, but the one with the protruding parts was far more awkward. They managed, however, and switched the two pieces relatively quickly.

Chloe returned to the entrance of the room and David followed. They walked around the perimeter to the back, past the partition, around the sculpture, and back to the rear wall. "This works for me," Chloe said. "It's great, actually. Let me go get Richard."

David smiled at her, and she returned the expression. Despite her exhaustion and anxiety, her mood had lightened considerably. She glanced around the exhibit as she walked toward the entrance, and pride swelled in her. Though the east wing remained closed, she had still managed to put together an impressive layout for the featured artist.

She called to Richard from just inside the lobby, and he followed her back in. Along with David, they followed the new proposed path while Richard rehearsed his notes.

"I'm worried about that partition wall," Richard said when they completed the circuit. "If people are crossing past each other, it could be a problem."

"I think there's enough room to accommodate groups at each piece and walking space," Chloe said. "Besides, most people won't spend a lot of time back there. They tend toward the open areas more, especially at the beginning when it's crowded and most people are trying to socialize rather than study all the work."

"I do like the loop better," Richard admitted. He turned toward David. "And this was your idea?"

David's smile was mostly gracious, though Chloe detected just a hint of hubris. He motioned back and forth between himself and Chloe. "It was a joint effort."

It had been a joint effort, and Chloe took comfort in the fact that she and David still made a good team. She was glad he had come, and relieved that he didn't seem to be suffering from the debilitating panic that gripped him the last time he'd been in New York.

Richard's phone dinged and he announced that his car was on the way. "What are your plans this evening?"

"I have a few last things to put in order here," Chloe said. "After that, I think I'd like to get some sleep." Aside from a few fitful hours earlier that morning, Chloe hadn't slept in her own bed since Sunday night.

Richard nodded. "And what about you, David? Looking to explore the city this evening, see what you missed out on all those years ago?"

Chloe elbowed him. "Stop it."

Richard shrugged. "I only asked an honest question."

She didn't care for his jealous behavior, and offered to walk him out to wait on his car. "I'll be right back," Chloe told David. "Do you mind waiting?"

David smiled and shook his head.

twenty-three

Once they were outside, Richard turned to Chloe. His face wore little expression, as usual, but he spoke with impatience. "Why is he even here? How long are you going to let him distract you?"

Chloe rolled her eyes. "He came to help. You're going to have to accept the fact that David will always be important to me. He's been through a lot and I want to make sure he's all right."

Richard's face suddenly twisted with anger. "Don't you dare feel sorry for him!" Chloe shrank away and he regained his composure. "I'm just saying, the guy left you and now you're just letting him walk back into your life? He's getting in the way and that's not right."

Chloe scowled. "David did not leave me."

"That's crap and you know it," Richard retorted. "What, was he kidnapped by the mob or something? Abducted by aliens? Please!" He threw his arms into the air for emphasis.

Chloe set her jaw and dug her fingernails into her palms. "Stop it."

"Look, I'm not trying to be the bad guy here," Richard said. "I'm just looking out for you."

"There's no need for you to be acting so jealous. We're just trying to figure some stuff out, that's all. He and I are..." She paused and shook her head, searching for the words. "We're different people now."

"That's a good thing," Richard said. "You're far better off

now than you ever were with him."

"What's that supposed to mean?"

"I mean, David held you back. You were married to him for what, five years? And in that time, did you ever sell any paintings? Did you have a gallery to manage? Contacts? Prospects? Anything resembling an art career? You didn't, and it was because of him."

"No, that's not true," Chloe said, again angry at Richard for attacking David. "He tried. He made me a studio in our house and helped me find little shows around Morgantown. He wanted to make it to New York eventually. Even if he couldn't give me all this, David supported my art."

"No, he appeased you," Richard accused. "All he did was give you shiny baubles to distract you from the truth, which was that he never believed in you."

"You don't know what you're talking about!"

"Why are you defending him?"

"Because you're out of line, Richard! David was my husband, and he loved me, and I know that his support wasn't a lie. What do you think I am, some kind of idiot? Do you really think that if David was just leading me on that I wouldn't be able to see it?"

"Well, he's obviously good at playing on your emotions," Richard said. "Look at how much attention he's gotten from you this week. All this drama got in the way of having your big show tomorrow night, and he won't even give you the courtesy of explaining where the hell he's been all these years. You know what? That's fine. Go ahead and let him get close to you again. Just throw away what we have and run back to him, and see how long before he 'disappears' again."

Chloe stammered. Hurt and rage boiled inside her, and she wanted to smack him across the face. "How could you? Are you really so jealous and angry at David that you don't care how hurtful you're being to me?"

Richard crossed his arms. "I am angry, but I'm not jealous."

"Oh, whatever." Chloe let out a frustrated huff. "Fine,

you're angry. But you don't have to attack me like that."

Richard sighed. "I'm worried about you. That's what's going on here. He's so clueless. He doesn't understand anything about art or the gallery. It's distracting to have him around."

"Maybe a little, but he did help this evening, you know?" Besides helping with the layout of Richard's paintings, David had also calmed Chloe down and restored a little of her confidence, but Richard didn't need to know all that.

"And now you need to rest, but do you think he'll actually let you?" Richard scoffed. "You should just send him to a hotel and spend the night with me."

"What about your pre-opening solitude?" Chloe wondered if he was actually willing to let go of his rituals to help her.

Richard shrugged. "I have a guest room."

Chloe rolled her eyes. "I'll be fine. Besides, David and I should probably talk about how to move forward."

Richard took Chloe's hands in his own. "You know how to move forward. Paint. Create. Use this setback as a springboard to new challenges."

Chloe saw a rare sincerity in the glint of Richard's eyes. He genuinely worried for her, though whether he cared more about her heart or her career was anybody's guess. She kissed him lightly on the mouth.

"You're right, painting is my way forward," Chloe said. "It always has been."

"I still say you should give yourself a little time away from David tonight," Richard said. "You can use my studio. Go play around, make something, free yourself from all the tension that's been consuming you this week."

It did sound tempting, but Chloe shook her head. "David doesn't know the city. I'd rather not send him off alone."

"Leave him with Madge," Richard said, grinning.

Chloe laughed. "She would love that, actually."

Richard's car arrived, and he kissed Chloe again before letting go of her hands. "Let me know if you want to use the studio."

Chloe agreed and said good night, then watched as the car pulled away. She took a moment to think before going back inside. Richard had a point about David being a distraction, but a part of her still wanted to be around him. She considered a compromise approach, to take David back to her place and leave him with Madge for a bit while she painted, and then they could talk afterward. It seemed feasible, even though she caught herself once again trying to do everything. At least there was less pressure this time.

Chloe walked back into the gallery, but stopped short as the odor of something burning teased her nostrils. "David?"

"I'm in he—oh shit!" His voice came from the east wing. "Bring a fire extinguisher! Hurry!"

She ran to the far side of the lobby, where an extinguisher hung from the wall. Chloe broke the glass, pulled the cylinder free, and rushed into the east wing, hoping she would make it before the alarm started blaring. She didn't.

As the repetitive, high-pitched screech echoed through the entire gallery, David's attempts to smother the flame with a drop cloth met with little success. Chloe pulled the pin from the extinguisher and doused the fire with foam, filling the air with particles that quickly found their way into her throat. She and David coughed and tried to fan the cloud away with their hands.

"What the hell were you doing in here?" Chloe asked.

"I just wanted to see what it looked like," David answered between coughs. "It's not so bad." The foam cloud dissipated enough to reveal a large scorched area on the floor. "Well, it wasn't."

Chloe stared at the damage. It looked like the primer had peeled off the floor when David entered, and a piece of it caught on one of the portable work lights. "You could have burned the whole building down."

"I'm sorry," David said. "I just thought maybe if it wasn't so bad I could help you finish it."

Chloe dropped the fire extinguisher and crossed her arms

over her chest. "I told you to forget it. I told you I needed some space, and you came to New York anyway. Why won't you listen to me?"

David took a step toward her. "I came here because I wanted to help you. I wanted to see your new life and try to make it up to you for dropping everything and coming to Pittsburgh." He spread his arms. "I wanted to see your paintings in here."

Chloe shook her head. "You can't just show up after ten years and think you know what's best for me."

"I know you always wanted this," David argued. "I know how hard you were busting your ass to make this happen, and I can't figure out why all of a sudden you're ready to give up."

"You don't know anything about what I've been through!" Chloe's whole body shook with anger. "I don't care what you think you remember, you can't understand what it was like for me when I figured out just how much I relied on you and how scared I was, not knowing how I was going to survive. But I did. I fought through that, and it took years for me to finally go after what I wanted, and I was so close. I was so close, and then..."

Chloe's face twisted as she fought back tears. She blamed this all on him, but couldn't bring herself to say it out loud. Her cell phone rang, and she turned away from David to answer.

"What's going on over there?" Fred asked. "I got a notification that a fire alarm went off."

"I've got it under control," Chloe said. "It was just a small incident in the east wing. No major damage."

"The east wing?" Fred's voice took an angry edge. "I thought we agreed you would close it off."

Chloe's chest tightened. She wanted to take care of the situation and get out of there, and that would go quicker if she took responsibility and didn't tell Fred the whole story. "I was in the process of doing that, but one of the work lamps overheated. The fire's out, but we'll need a new extinguisher in the lobby."

"It's not like you to be so careless," Fred chided.

"I know," Chloe said. "I'm sorry."

"Thank you for taking care of it." Fred's exasperation gave way to a frustrated sigh. "I won't tolerate these kinds of mistakes. I hate to say it, but another incident like this might be the last."

Chloe set her jaw, refusing to break down despite the overwhelming shame that gripped her. "Of course. I understand."

When Fred hung up, Chloe led David back to the lobby. A fire truck arrived, and she ordered David to wait while she pointed one fire fighter to the east wing then led another to the alarm panel. He told Chloe to leave the building and she complied, taking David with her.

They waited outside in silence for a few minutes. Finally, David spoke up. "I'm sorry about everything."

Chloe hugged herself against the cold. "You're lucky the whole floor didn't catch fire."

"I know," David said. "I guess you were better off without me, after all."

Chloe wheeled on him, simultaneously incensed with David for starting the fire and horrified imagining how much worse it might have been. "Don't you dare talk like that! You could have been trapped in there and died, you idiot!"

David dropped his gaze to the sidewalk. "I'm sorry. I really did come to help."

Chloe refused to engage with him on the subject any further. She turned away and forcefully wiped the tears from her eyes and cheeks.

The fire fighters emerged from the building after a few minutes and told Chloe she could go back inside. They removed the burned work light and recommended the peeling primer be cleaned up as soon as possible. Chloe thanked them and went inside. David followed, but he waited in the lobby while Chloe proceeded to the office, where she called to order a new fire extinguisher.

With that done, Chloe removed the remaining work lights and extension cords from the east wing before closing it up. David offered to help carry them to the storage room, but she turned him away. After checking the office and main exhibit space, she ushered him out, turned off the lights, and locked the door.

Chloe hailed a cab and sat in the back seat, leaving the door open. David stared at her, seeming unsure of what to do. "Where are you going?" he asked.

"Home." She hesitated, closed her eyes, and ground her teeth in frustration. As tempting as it was, Chloe couldn't bring herself to leave him behind. She sighed and said, "Come on," then slid over on the seat.

David got in and closed the door, and Chloe gave the driver her address. She spoke to David without looking at him. "You can stay at my place tonight. I'm going out, though."

"I can get a hotel," David said.

"No, don't do that. You probably owe Emma enough money as it is."

David pursed his lips, looking as if he were debating whether or not to say what was on his mind. Finally, he blurted out, "I still think we can fix it."

Chloe threw him an angry look. "Drop it."

He turned away and stared out the window. "Fine."

Chloe and David didn't speak the rest of the way to her apartment building, and he followed silently into the elevator and down the hall. Her anger had cooled somewhat, but she was determined to get through the evening without a lengthy discussion about where they stood and whether or not it was David's fault the east wing didn't get done. She wanted to drop David off, change, and get out of the apartment as quickly as possible.

As soon as she unlocked and opened her apartment door,

Madge appeared in the doorway between the kitchen and living room. A big, toothy grin appeared on her face as soon as she saw David. She bounced up and down, seemingly unable to keep her excitement in check.

"You must be Mr. S!" she squealed.

"David," he said, offering a small wave. Madge rushed toward him, her bright red hair flying behind her. She collided with David and threw her arms around him in a tight embrace. David's eyes grew wide, and he gasped for air.

Chloe couldn't help but giggle. "This is my roommate, Madge."

"This is so exciting!" Madge said, finally releasing David. "Mrs. S told me all about you, but I never thought I'd get to meet you in person."

David took a deep breath, recovering from Madge's squeeze. "Nice to meet you, too."

For a brief instant, Chloe reconsidered going to Richard's studio. Madge had such a positive energy about her that Chloe wondered if talking through things with her roommate around might be easier, even fun. When she looked at David, though, her conflicting irritation and yearning for him stirred again, and she excused herself to change.

Chloe tossed her work clothes into a pile on the bed and pulled on some warm leggings and a sweater dress. Then she grabbed some old, paint-covered sweats and put them in a tote bag. After hesitating a moment, she grabbed her pajamas just in case she decided to stay in the little apartment at the studio. She cursed at the thought of having to take a toiletry bag, but then she noticed her carry-on from the trip to Pittsburgh, still packed. She pulled the plastic bag with her essentials free and added it to the tote.

After one last check, Chloe decided she had everything she needed and pulled her door open. A startled Madge stood just outside, her fist raised as if she were about to knock. "Hey, Mrs. S, I was just about to ask if you wanted to order Chinese for dinner. You told me all those stories about you and Mr. S and how you taught him to use chopsticks, and——"

"Do you mind if David hangs out here for a bit?" Chloe blurted out, unwilling to be pulled into nostalgia.

Madge started. "Of course not." She looked Chloe over and noticed the tote bag. "Are you going somewhere?"

"I need to get out of here for a little while," Chloe said.

Madge pouted. "You're really just going to leave Mr. S?"

"Only for a little while," Chloe said. "I need to paint. I'd like to get my mind off of things, and Richard said I could use his studio."

"You can use our studio," Madge said. "The super left a message earlier saying we could get back in now. I haven't been down to see it yet, though. Hey! We should take Mr. S down there."

Chloe looked away. "I was really hoping for some time to myself."

Madge put her hands on her hips and locked Chloe in a firm stare. "No."

"Excuse me?"

"No, Mrs. S, I won't let you go off by yourself tonight."

Chloe failed to recall a time when Madge had been so assertive with her, and almost laughed. "You can't stop me."

"Mr. S came all this way," Madge said. "He wants to see you. He wants to see what you do."

"He came to the gallery. I showed him around, I introduced him to Richard, I brought him here to meet you," Chloe said. "Then he insisted on 'helping' when I asked him not to, and started a fire in the east wing."

Madge gasped. "OMG! Is everything okay?"

Chloe waved off Madge's concern. "Yeah, it wasn't a big fire. But still, I can't deal with him any more tonight. I need a break."

Madge went back to pouting. "He just wants to be around you. Don't you want to be around him?"

"Yes, of course," Chloe said. "You know how much I missed him. But that doesn't mean we need to spend every second together."

"It's not like he's been demanding all your attention. When you guys were together, did he ever stop you from painting?

Chloe sighed. "No."

"So why would he now? Let's just go downstairs and you can paint. Mr. S can help me organize my supplies or something if you really think he's that much of a distraction."

Again, Chloe hesitated for a moment. Maybe Madge's suggestion would work, and Chloe could both get some painting done and visit with David. Maybe they could even go out, since he seemed to be handling the city well. But just the thought of talking about old times made her cringe, and a tingling sensation crept into her arms. They needed to move, they needed to create, and she couldn't risk any distraction.

"Sorry, I just can't," Chloe said. She pushed past Madge and rushed out of the apartment without saying goodbye.

twenty-four

Richard greeted Chloe when she arrived at his studio. "I'm glad you decided to come over."

Chloe set her bag down and hugged him tightly. Richard wrapped his arms around her and asked if she was all right. "Did David do something to you?"

Chloe told Richard about the fire. "I don't understand why he doesn't get it, why he keeps insisting that he knows what I need better than I do."

"He probably can't stand that he has nothing and you've moved on to something better than him," Richard said.

That didn't really sound like David, but how well did she know him anymore, anyway? "I don't know. I know he didn't do it on purpose, but what was he even doing in there?" He had accused her of giving up. They had fought. She'd had a chance to think on the ride back to Manhattan, and David's words were sinking in.

"Do you think there's more we could do?" Chloe asked. "Is there any chance at all we could save the east wing?"

"I thought Lumina was pretty adamant about you focusing on my show," Richard said. "I don't want you to lose your job."

"But it seems wrong, doesn't it? To be this close to finishing and just stop?"

"Are you as close as you think you are?" Richard asked. "There was obviously more to do this week than you anticipated. Besides, if you take your time then you can bring in a general contractor to take care of the coordination so you can get back to what you need to focus on: your art."

Chloe sighed. "Maybe you're right." She still couldn't shake the nagging feeling that she should be working on it, though.

"Stay here tonight. Paint something." Richard gestured to his supply cabinets. "Help yourself to anything you need. I'm sure this space is a lot better stocked than that basement room you were using. I'll stop by in the morning."

"You're not staying?"

Richard shook his head. "It's the night before a show. I need complete focus, and that means I have to be alone. You know that."

Chloe did know that, but had also hoped he would make an exception, just this once, for her. "I thought maybe we could relax together."

Richard kissed her forehead. "I'll take you out for a nice lunch tomorrow. In the meantime, you should paint. Forget about David and work through your stress on the canvas."

Chloe agreed and Richard left. She dragged her bag back to the apartment and sat on the sofa for a few minutes, still struggling with her emotions and conflicting thoughts about what to do. Growing restless, she went back into the studio and found an easel and canvas, set them up, and stood staring into the blank surface, waiting for an image to come to her. Too many thoughts were in the way, about David, about Richard, about the gallery. She busied herself looking through Richard's cabinets for paints and found a bin full of acrylics that matched her preferred palette. She surmised these must have been the paints he used to create *Chloe's Journey*. She grabbed some brushes and set up a table near the easel to place everything on. She squeezed paint onto her palette board, took a deep breath, and faced the canvas.

Again, nothing came to her. Chloe stood frozen, desperate for a flash of inspiration or, at the very least, an idea of where to begin. Over a month had gone by since she had created anything she was proud of. Slumps happen, Richard had told her.

Chloe had even seen him go through one a few months ago. The difference was that Richard's slump had only lasted a couple weeks, and once he came out of it he had thrown himself headlong into his work, painting and sculpting for ten, twelve, and sometimes sixteen hours a day.

Chloe looked around the large, well-organized space that probably rivaled the studios at Madge's art school. It was set up almost too perfectly, giving the room a cold, surreal atmosphere that reminded her of a stage or movie set. Chloe shuddered at the thought of being watched, but suspected that Richard liked the idea of putting on a show. With him, everything seemed to be about appearances.

On the contrary, Chloe preferred a cozy studio space. Though sometimes inconvenient, the basement room she shared with Madge had character and felt safe. When she'd lived with her parents, Chloe had only been allowed a corner of their detached garage in which to paint, but she'd made it work. She remembered fondly the time and energy she and David had put into converting a spare room of their house into her art studio.

Despite her intention to escape him, David lingered in Chloe's thoughts. She imagined his easy smile and the twinkle in his eyes. David would never have allowed Chloe to go so long without painting. In fact, he encouraged her to paint every single day, and had been shocked two nights ago when she told him she didn't anymore.

Chloe smiled, remembering what he would say to her: "Just paint. Anything you paint will be better than anything I could paint, and there are definitely more people on my skill level than yours. So just paint anything, because it will automatically fall in the 'good' category. Plus, you're guaranteed to have at least one person tell you it's amazing."

His words flew through space and time to settle in her heart, loosening the knots of doubt that held Chloe captive. She exhaled, gripped her brush, and threw strokes around the edges of the canvas, instinctively starting with a deep forest green. She blended in a rich brown, then took her knife and added some detail lines in gold. The shapes weren't clear in either her mind or on the canvas, but she kept going, pushing her anxiety into the empty space around her, letting the sound of her breath and the weight of her palette board and the smell of art supplies blur and congeal together with her memories of David, putting her in almost a trance, a meditative state that reached into her soul and transformed every thought and emotion she couldn't voice into a brush stroke, into a quick jab of texture or an aggressive slash of color. She blended her paints with reckless abandon, ignoring every formula and ratio she had memorized. She attacked the canvas until she was spent, then took a step back. Before the whole picture could settle into her brain, though, she touched up a shadow near the bottom, just right of center.

It was a sloppy, raw amalgamation of images and themes, natural and urban elements clashing among vague, abstract shapes that connected to each other with jagged, aggressive lines. Chloe wasn't sure what to make of it, but it felt good. She had poured herself completely into the act of creation for the first time in a long while, and a tingling high coursed through her arms and down her spine.

Chloe stared into the painting, her confidence building with each heartbeat. She had stood her ground against doubt and created something. She had worked through adversity to reach her goal. Finishing the east wing should be no different.

But how? Fred had made it clear he didn't want to spend any more money. Chloe decided she could use her own funds and lay out the bigger expenses on credit in anticipation of her commission. She had neither the time nor desire to deal with any more contractors, but it was too much work for her alone. If she could just get a couple people to help, she felt sure the east wing could be ready for the opening.

Surging with energy, Chloe practically ran to the apartment to fetch her phone. She hoped Madge and David could forgive her for the way she'd acted earlier, and that they would be willing to come to her aid.

"Hey, Mrs. S, everything okay?" Madge asked above what sounded like the din of a crowded room.

"Yeah, sorry about before. Where are you? Are you busy?"

Madge hesitated. "I'm, uh, working with my group on our project."

"Oh." Chloe remembered Madge had been having trouble with the project, and didn't want to interrupt. "How long do you think you'll be doing that?"

Again, Madge hesitated before answering. "I don't know for sure, but it could be an all-nighter. Do you need something? Maybe I could get away for a little bit."

"No, I don't want to stop your progress. What's David doing? Is he with you?"

"Yeah, Mr. S tagged along. He's actually been kind of a big help."

Chloe flinched with surprise. David had never been too hands-on with art projects, though she supposed he could be helping in other ways. "Do you think you could spare him for a while?"

"What do you need, Mrs. S? We'll help out as much as we possibly can."

"I'm going to the gallery," Chloe said, her heart pounding. "I'm not going to give up on this opening. If you or David can help me, I think we can finish the east wing before the gala."

The background noise on Madge's end of the line died down suddenly. "Uh, you know what? We can totally meet you. How long until you get there?"

"I'm leaving Richard's studio now. Shouldn't be more than fifteen or twenty minutes."

"Okay, see you then!" Madge sounded absolutely giddy.

Chloe laughed, her confidence bolstered by Madge's enthusiasm. "All right, don't rush. Get to a stopping point on your project and message me when you're on your way."

"Can do, Mrs. S. See you soon!" Madge giggled and abruptly hung up, leaving Chloe a little taken aback. She shook it off, gathered her things, and left Richard's studio. There were no cabs in sight, so she started walking, letting her adrenaline build and pump through her. No matter what it took, she wasn't going to let her big chance slip away.

After a couple blocks, Chloe flagged down a taxi. Once inside, she pulled the tablet computer from her purse and began planning her night's work.

The lights were on when Chloe's cab pulled up to Lumina Gallery. She chided herself, thinking she'd forgotten to turn them off when she'd left in a huff after the fire. To her surprise, Conner came out to meet her.

"What are you doing here?" she asked. "Is something wrong? I thought everything was set for tomorrow night."

"Almost everything," Conner said, grinning. "I got called in for a special project."

"Special project?" Chloe worried out loud. Had Fred really lost that much faith in her? Confused, she followed Conner into the lobby.

Madge stepped out of the east wing as they approached. "Hey, Mrs. S!"

Chloe recoiled. "I thought you were working on your group project."

Madge giggled. "I am! Come see!" She grabbed Chloe's arm and led her into the east wing.

Chloe gasped. Over a dozen people, most of them looking to be Madge's age, worked on various projects around the room. One group spread and shaped plaster on the wall, followed closely by another group with air brushes. An older man arranged tiles on the floor below the space where a painting would hang, and several others fed colorful cloth through sewing machines. The colors all tied into Chloe's usual palette.

"What is happening?" Chloe asked.

"It was Mr. S's idea," Madge said. "I took him with me to

meet with my group at school, and we were trying to figure out what to do for our project. He said we should do a whole room and I didn't understand what he meant at first, but then he explained it, so we went to the professor and he said it was a great idea, and we even got some other groups to help since we only had one night."

Chloe turned to her. "This was David's idea?"

"You were so upset. After you left, all he could talk about was trying to help you," Madge said. "Once he had this idea, he got so excited. He called your friend Miss Emma and she agreed to send some money for supplies, and the school offered to pay for some too as long as you put up a little sign saying they helped."

Chloe stepped further into the room, still in disbelief. She spotted David in a corner, working with two students to hang one of the tapestries. Tears formed as she strode toward him, and he turned as she approached.

"You're here," he said, smiling. "This was supposed to be a surprise, but—"

Chloe grabbed him by the shirt and pulled him into a firm kiss. David was caught off guard, but quickly relaxed and wrapped his arms around her. When nearby students began to cheer and tease, Chloe and David both laughed and locked eyes, and she knew in that moment that everything was okay between them.

"Thank you," Chloe said. "Thank you so much."

"I couldn't have done it without Madge and her classmates," David said.

Chloe turned away from him to face the room, all of whom were staring at her. "This is incredible, and you have no idea just how much this means to me. Thank you all so much!"

Madge tugged at Chloe's arm. "Come on! I want to introduce you to everyone."

She looked back at David, who laughed and then returned to work on the tapestry. Madge led Chloe around, introducing her to classmates and explaining the project. "I showed everybody the pictures of your paintings I had for the layout, and when we got here Conner let us see the actual canvases so Jackie"—she pointed to a short, thin Latina with a shaved head—"could make the plaster look just like your brush strokes."

"It's thin so it dries fast," Jackie explained. "I wanted to do something more elaborate but we don't have time."

"It looks great so far," Chloe said.

The textured walls served as a frame for each painting, and conveniently covered some of the sloppy work the drywall contractor had done. Between the textured spaces, the walls were being painted to match the air brushing, and Chloe was happy to see some of the paint she'd bought for the floor being put to good use. The primer had been cleaned up and Madge explained that temporary carpeting would be delivered in the morning.

Next, Madge introduced Chloe to Bo, the older man setting tiles on the floor. He turned to them and pushed his long, white hair out of the way to reveal a matching beard, glasses, and a gentle smile. "I'd do the whole floor if I could, but it wouldn't be ready to walk on by tomorrow night," he said. "Instead we're making a little mosaic below each of your paintings, almost like welcome mats for them."

The last member of Madge's group was Meni, a soft-spoken young man with a round body and a thick Indian accent. He directed the students with the sewing machines and pointed out the placement of each tapestry. "One in each corner," he said to Chloe. "Also, we'll put one at the middle of three walls, all except the one with the door. The entrance gets a big, grand curtain." He gestured to indicate that it would open like a circus tent and showed Chloe the cording that would be used to tie it back.

"Mr. S said it wouldn't be hard to take down the boards you had over the entrance," Madge said.

"He's right," Chloe said. She glanced over her shoulder to see David finish hanging the tapestry, then high-five his helpers. She smiled. "I still can't believe you guys did this for me."

"You deserve it, Mrs. S." Madge pulled Chloe into one of her tight hugs, but this time Chloe squeezed back equally as hard.

They laughed and pulled apart. Chloe again looked back toward David. He was positioning another tapestry, smiling widely and talking with the students. She felt terrible for the way she'd talked to both him and Madge before she left the apartment. "Listen, Madge, about earlier—"

Madge waved her off. "Don't worry about it. You were upset, it happens." She pursed her lips a moment, then asked, "So where's Richard?"

"Home," Chloe said. "He wouldn't even stay with me at the studio."

Madge's shoulders sagged, and she looked at Chloe sympathetically. "That sucks."

"Yeah, well..." Chloe shook her head, unwilling to make an excuse for him. "I did paint, though."

"You did?" Madge perked up. "The slump's over?"

Chloe smiled. "I think so, yeah. It was kind of amazing, like something just opened up inside and poured out onto the canvas. I haven't been that inspired in forever, you know?"

Madge squealed. "I bet it has something to do with Mr. S being back."

"I don't know," Chloe said. "I was pretty mad earlier. Maybe I just needed a release from the stress. That could have pushed me though whatever was blocking me."

Madge rolled her eyes. "Denial isn't just a river in Egypt, Mrs. S."

"I'm not in denial," Chloe said. She thought back to before David vanished. "I mean, sure, when we were together David always relaxed me. He made me feel confident and yes, that helps me paint. But I obviously did okay without him, you know? Look at the pieces Fred picked for my opening. David wasn't around when I did a lot of those."

"I'm not saying you can only paint when Mr. S is around,"

Madge said. "I'm saying that Richard put your painting in a funk. You were overthinking it and getting yourself stuck, and Mr. S got you out of that."

"Not to change the subject, but why do you call Richard by his first name?" Chloe genuinely wanted to know.

Madge didn't hesitate. "Because I don't like him."

Chloe flinched. "You never told me that."

"Yes, I did," Madge said. "I told you that a bunch of times. I'd say, 'I don't really like Richard,' and you'd say, 'Oh you just don't know the real him,' or something like that. But I always thought you could do way better. You know who else thinks that? Mr. S."

Chloe tried to remember when Madge had said she didn't like Richard, and a few vague things came to mind. She wasn't exactly happy with Richard at the moment, but was he really that bad? The fact that David didn't like him came as no surprise. "What did he say?"

Madge's face lit up. "Oh man, Mr. S is so super jealous. He called Richard's art fake and trashy."

"No way!" Chloe couldn't help but grin. It was an unusually bold—if petty—statement on David's part.

"Oh yeah, he said that. In those words. He also said that if you were going to be with an artist it should at least be someone who gets you. He said he'd feel better if I was dating you instead of Richard." Madge started giggling uncontrollably.

Chloe tried to keep a straight face as she said, "I like you a lot, Madge, but not in that way." Then she, too, broke out into laughter.

Madge put the back of her hand to her forehead. "Oh, Mrs. S! Whatever shall I do now that you've spurned my heart?"

"You're still so young and beautiful," Chloe said in her best soap opera voice. "The right one is out there, I just know it. If only it could have been me!" They laughed together until they heard someone clear her throat behind them, prompting them to turn around.

Jackie stood, arms crossed, a scowl on her face. "I hate to

interrupt, but this is a *group* project, remember? I could use a little help over here."

"Sorry, I'm coming," Madge said. Jackie nodded and walked back toward where she was working, but before Madge followed she said to Chloe, "I like Mr. S a lot, and I know he cares about you. Just talk to him and I know you guys can work it out."

Chloe smiled and watched Madge walk away, then looked to David again. He was still fussing with the tapestry, focused and engaged and obviously trying to get it just right. Her heart leapt at the idea that maybe the two of them could still have the life they dreamed about all those years ago.

Conner approached and interrupted her line of thinking, saying food was being delivered and he could use some help carrying it in. Chloe obliged, eager to join the project.

twenty-five

They worked through the night, fueled by pizza and energy drinks, cookies and coffee. Chloe fought the urge to take control and let Madge and David continue coordinating the project, though she did offer small suggestions here and there. She assisted some of the students with their techniques and even learned a little herself.

By midmorning, the temporary carpeting had been installed and the last of the students had meandered out. Chloe and David stood side-by-side at the entrance to the completed east wing, arms around each other's backs, admiring their work. Her landscapes hung majestically amid the plaster, paint, fabric, and tile that made the room itself a work of art.

Chloe thought it interesting that the paintings in the exhibit were born from her need to move on from David's disappearance, yet the exhibit itself reached its full potential as a direct result of his return. Neither experience had been easy, but both had been transformative, pushing her life forward, leading her down new paths.

She kissed his cheek, and they smiled at one another for a long moment. The twinkle in David's eyes made the bags below them seem to disappear.

"I'm sorry this week was so hard for you," he said. "I didn't mean to be such a distraction, and I don't want you to think I'm trying to force my way into your life."

"I want you in my life," Chloe said. "I've missed having you in my life."

"Me too," David said. "But no matter what happens, I wanted to make sure you had this. You waited so long and worked so hard, and the thought of you missing out on it was unbearable. And just so you know, I never thought you couldn't do it on your own. I wanted to help because you deserve this and I want you to be happy."

"I am." Chloe leaned into him, rested her head on his chest, and felt her heartbeat settle into the rhythm of his. "This is by far the happiest I've been in a very, very long time."

David gave her a squeeze, then took a step away and sighed.

"What's wrong?" Chloe asked.

"It's just..." He took a deep breath, but kept his back to her as he continued, "I want to share this with you. I want us to be close, like we used to be, but..."

"But what?" She put a hand on his shoulder. "You don't need to worry about Richard. Things aren't going to work out between us."

He still wouldn't look at her. "I'm sorry."

"No, don't be. I'm not sure we were ever really right for each other, you know?" She sighed. "I guess you don't really know someone until you've gone through a crisis with them."

David's voice was raspy. "You'll find the right one someday."

Chloe couldn't believe what she heard. She had finally opened her heart up to the possibility of being with David again, yet it seemed he was rejecting her. What was happening? She asked him as much.

David reluctantly confessed. "Tommy said there's a chance, and I doubt it's really possible, but he said I might disappear again. He thinks my connection to Madison and Candice could pull me back into the other world."

Chloe stared at him in disbelief. "What? David, no, that's crazy."

"I know, but Tommy's afraid it could happen soon. He said something about the energy being unstable since it's our—"

David shook his head. "I mean, it's the anniversary of when I vanished. He wants me to meet him this afternoon to do some kind of experiment."

"This afternoon? Aren't you coming to the opening?" Chloe asked.

David looked away.

"Please, you have to be there," Chloe begged him. "You and Madge worked so hard to make it possible. How could you even think about missing it?"

"Knowing you're happy is enough," David said. He turned back toward her, smiling his sweet smile, his eyes misty. "But I know this is important to you, so if you want me there, I'll be there."

Chloe hugged him. "Please."

He nodded. "Okay. I'll send Tommy a message and tell him it will have to wait."

Chloe pulled away. "Do you really believe all that nonsense about another world?"

"I don't know what to believe. I have no idea how I ended up wherever I was all those years. It's probably bullshit, but what if it isn't? I can't take that chance. I can't let us get close only to vanish and leave you alone again. And besides, if there's a chance any of that was real...I have a daughter. I can't just abandon her. As much as I want to share your life, it's *your* life. It's what you've worked so hard for, and I don't want to be in your way."

"How can you say that?" Chloe asked. "Look at what you were willing to do to help me. You aren't in the way."

"But you never would have made those paintings if I hadn't disappeared," David said. "We might never have moved to New York. You have so much to look forward to here, and I can't even tell if my memories are real or not."

Chloe had wondered about those things herself. Where would she be and what would she be doing if David hadn't disappeared? It wasn't fair. Why did she have to choose one or the other? There had to be a way to know for sure that she was making the right choice.

"Tell me if this feels real." Chloe pulled him in close and kissed him hard on the mouth. He wrapped her in his arms and returned her affection, leaving trails of warmth where his fingers pressed into her back. Their mouths locked in a familiar dance, and Chloe welcomed the surge of excitement that came with each caress of his lips.

Would she trade her paintings and grand debut for ten years of these kisses? After everything they'd been through, could they pick up loving each other now that things were so different? Would Chloe be a one-hit wonder and fall back into painting only as a hobby? And what if, in spite of all that, she chose David only to lose him again? Her head spun as she savored him, hoping that the passion they had for one another in that moment would lead her to clarity.

"Am I interrupting something?"

Chloe and David turned to see Richard staring at them, his arms crossed but his features neutral. Chloe slipped from David's embrace and turned toward Richard, unsure of what to say. Though she'd come to accept things were over between them, she hadn't wanted to end it like this.

Richard walked past her and stood in the entrance to the east wing. "I see you've been busy," he said, eyeing the room. "I stopped by the studio earlier and saw your painting. It's impressive."

"It felt like a breakthrough." Chloe swallowed in a failed attempt to ease her suddenly dry throat. In all the excitement last night, she'd forgotten about her invigorating painting session.

"It's a marked improvement," he said. "I could tell you've been working on those techniques we discussed. Personally, I think you could continue improving and Lumina would invite you to show in the main gallery, but I see you had other ideas."

Chloe and David shared a wary glance. "We should talk," she said to Richard.

He ignored her. "This isn't the direction I thought you were going with the renovation."

"I had some unexpected help," Chloe said.

"I suppose it's fine, if you're all right with a bunch of strangers altering your artistic vision," Richard said.

"It was David and Madge, not a bunch of strangers."

"I didn't see you trying to help," David said. "Why are you being so negative about this?"

"It's embarrassing," Richard said. He turned to Chloe. "You are an unknown. You rode into this opening on my coat-tails and now you dare to upstage me at my own gala?"

"Lumina offered Chloe this opening because of her paintings," David said. "She's not your intern or your understudy."

Chloe was calmer. "No one is upstaging you. It's still your opening, and the east wing is simply a bonus for those in attendance."

Richard rolled his eyes. "Oh, come on. Look at this place. The tapestries, the plaster work, the mosaics. The whole room is a show piece, and what do you think people will be talking about after tonight, my art or your gallery?"

"Madge and her classmates get credit for that," Chloe said.

"But you and Lumina allowed this. You allowed these kids to come in and create a space that draws attention away from my exhibit."

"None of this was about you," David said. "It was about making sure Chloe got to have her opening."

"It is *her* opening now, isn't it?" Richard smirked. "Fine then. Have your opening, but you'll have it without me."

"What are you talking about?" Chloe asked. "The gallery's set up, the arrangements are made. All you have to do at this point is show up and sell."

"I don't think I can possibly do that with any dignity considering this last-minute addition to the venue," Richard said. "I'll spread the word on social media that I won't be in attendance, that my show will be closed during the gala. And then we'll see how successful your debut is. We'll see how much of it was really about you and not about me."

"You're bluffing." David stepped forward and got in Richard's face. "If you pull out of the show, you don't sell any art either. Plus, you'll piss off Lumina and he'll never invite you to do a show here again."

Richard cackled. "Oh no, looks like you got me," he mocked. Then, to Chloe, "Is he seriously that clueless? And you'd rather be with him than me?"

"Stop it," Chloe said. She turned to David and told him to back off. "I can handle this."

"He can't seriously mean it," David said.

Chloe nodded. "I'm afraid so." She turned back to Richard and glowered at him while she explained. "There's enough time that he could line up another gallery. Due to his fame, they'd bend over backward to get his pieces in there. The exhibit wouldn't be nearly as professional, the gala wouldn't be anything close to what I've planned, but it wouldn't matter. The crowd follows the artist, not the gallery."

Richard gave a satisfied grin. "So now that the remedial class is over, let's say we open negotiations. What are you willing to give me to keep my work at Lumina Gallery?"

Chloe tried to remain stone-faced. She had already secured Richard a lower commission rate than most artists, purely on the basis of their relationship. "I could try to squeeze another percent or two off the gallery commission. Fred wouldn't be happy but I could probably talk him into it."

Richard scoffed. "Please. You think a percent or two of commission concerns me?" He pointed to the east wing. "This is the issue. This exhibit is detrimental to my opening."

"She's not giving up her opening, not after she worked so hard," David cut in. His eyes narrowed, a scowl creased his face, and his breath came in audible huffs.

Chloe again motioned for David to calm down and stepped between him and Richard. She sighed. "What about a percentage of my sales?"

"Tempting," Richard said. "Actually, I'd settle for the full sale price of one particular painting."

"One painting? That doesn't sound so bad," David said. He

stepped forward to stand beside Chloe, looking to her for confirmation.

Chloe's heart sank, for she knew exactly which painting Richard was talking about. "No," she said, her voice quavering.

"I've made up my mind," Richard said. "You'll have to choose between selling that painting or having a debut that's... underwhelming."

"Which painting?" David asked.

Chloe turned toward him, tears standing in her eyes. "Woodburn Hall."

David threw a smiting glare at Richard. "You are such an asshole."

"Oh, now I'm the asshole? I'm not the one who left his wife, then showed up a decade later to ruin her career. I suppose I can't stop Chloe from backsliding, but I can at least remind her that you've been in the way the entire time. Now she has to make a decision." Richard stared Chloe down. "So, what's it going to be?"

"Please, Richard," Chloe said. "Don't do this to me."

"Sorry, but this is your last chance. It's him or your art. Which is more important?"

Chloe stammered. If she lost Richard's show, not only would her own debut be ruined, but Fred might fire her. But how could she possibly part with a painting that had captured one of the most meaningful moments in her life?

David put his hand on her shoulder. "Sell it."

Tears streamed down her cheeks as she turned to David. He was smiling his sweet smile for her, the anger gone from his face and not a hint of sadness in his eyes. She rubbed her eyes and started to protest, but David stopped her.

"It's just a painting," he said. "It's my favorite of everything you painted while we were together and I love it more than all the pieces hanging in the east wing combined, but this is a once in a lifetime opportunity. I know how much that piece means to you and what it represents, but it isn't worth missing your big chance. Sell it."

His words reaffirmed what Chloe knew in her heart to be the only correct choice. "Okay, as long as you're sure."

David nodded. "We'll always have the memories of that day. That's what matters."

"How touching," Richard mocked. "So that's your decision, then?"

Chloe took a deep breath and nodded. "I'll have Fred arrange a private showing this evening. The gallery will take a minimal commission, and the rest of the sale price is yours."

Richard grinned wickedly, then motioned toward the gallery office. Chloe understood he wanted a contract drawn up immediately and led the way across the lobby, but David stopped short when his phone dinged.

"Emma just landed. I'm supposed to meet her so we can go shopping for a suit." He looked up at Chloe. "Is a suit okay for the gala, or should I just rent a tux?"

"A suit is fine," Chloe said with a sad smile. "Just don't wear a tie."

David looked confused. "I thought this was a really fancy event?"

"It's an *exclusive* event," Richard said. "That means invitation only, not black tie. The only people there in tuxedos will be the waiters." He snickered.

"Most of the women will be in dresses, but the men will be all over the place," Chloe explained. "It's what they call 'cocktail casual.'"

"Of course, the more famous you are, the more people will forgive poor fashion choices," Richard said. "Being a nobody, a suit is probably your best bet."

Chloe scowled at Richard, then turned and kissed David on the cheek. "See you tonight."

"See you tonight," David echoed. He smiled and walked toward the exit, typing on his phone as he went.

Chloe sighed and continued toward the office, Richard in tow. While David was right about selling the Woodburn Hall painting, it would have been much easier to do if she'd known for certain he would remain in her life. If something happened to David or they drifted apart somehow, she would have to go on without both him and the painting that had come to embody everything they'd meant to one another.

twenty-six

Chloe took an hors d'oeuvre from the tray before sending the waiter on his way into the boisterous crowd that filled the gallery lobby with mingling and eating, laughing and drinking. She tried to convince herself it was just like any other of the dozen or so openings she'd hosted since becoming the gallery manager, but she simply couldn't shake her nerves away. She watched people stroll by the entrance to the east wing and eye the closed tapestry with curiosity and excitement. Chloe almost wanted to peek herself, still in disbelief that her art was in there, about to be shown in such a prestigious venue.

Near the curtain, *Chloe's Journey* stood affixed to an easel, displayed without a title card to maintain the surprise. Richard had demanded at the last minute that it be placed there, almost like he was taking credit for Chloe's entire exhibit. She tried not to look at it, since even a glance reminded her of his smugness and tightened her chest with anger.

She decided she should go about business as usual to try and calm herself. Fred had brought in extra help to handle sales that evening so she wouldn't have to worry as much about it, but Chloe felt that the natural thing to do now was to work the room. She greeted socialites and collectors she'd met already and allowed the regulars to introduce her to their guests. She talked about art and politics and the striking, highly topical work Richard always did. She discussed the few pieces visible from this side of the velvet rope and promised that what lay further in was even more exciting. Whenever someone asked about the east wing, she only said that Fred had prepared a surprise and she wasn't about to lose her job by spoiling it.

As she made her rounds, Chloe searched the crowd for David and Emma, but didn't see them. She considered calling one of them to make sure everything was all right, but was pulled into a conversation before she could decide.

Eventually, Conner fetched her from a rather lively discussion about couture furniture coverings and directed her to meet Fred in his office. Chloe excused herself politely and walked toward the back section of the gallery, carrying a half-empty flute of champagne. She knocked and let herself into the office where Fred and Richard waited.

"There she is," Fred said, grinning widely. "You look stunning. Ready for your big night?"

Chloe took a deep breath and nodded. "I'm as ready as I'll ever be."

Richard stepped forward and kissed her lightly on the cheek despite her attempt to dodge it. Chloe glared at him, and he reacted by smiling and extending his elbow to escort her. Chloe declined the gesture and turned to Fred, who didn't seem to notice or mind the tension between her and Richard.

"All right then, let's get this opening started." Fred strode past them and led the way to the small stage where the string quartet was set up. He motioned to the musicians to stop playing, and then signaled the lighting technician. The overhead lights in the lobby dimmed, and the track lights pointed at the stage intensified. The crowd noise faded to a hushed murmur.

Fred took a wireless microphone from the sound technician and stepped to center stage. Chloe and Richard flanked him on either side, two steps behind. Again, Chloe knew the position well, but the excitement of the moment was almost too much for her. Almost. She breathed deep and held her composure.

"Ladies and gentlemen, welcome to this evening's opening." Fred paused for applause, then continued. "Tonight, we have another outstanding collection from world renowned artist Richard Harlin, whose turbulent and thought-provoking works are currently on display in at least fifteen countries." He gestured to Richard, who took a step forward and waved to the crowd, drawing another round of applause. "Richard has sold out shows at the Lumina Gallery before, so if you see something you have your eye on, don't hesitate. We are honored to have your latest work here once more."

Fred turned and shook Richard's hand, and the crowd applauded again. Richard stepped back and Fred continued his welcoming remarks. "Many of you also know my gracious and lovely gallery manager, Chloe Sullivan. Not only has she done a remarkable job of showcasing Richard's work for tonight's event, but she has also worked tirelessly and in the midst of incredible personal difficulty to complete our gallery expansion over a month ahead of schedule."

Fred motioned toward the east wing while the audience clapped. Chloe searched the crowd, Fred's remark prompting her to look again for David and Emma, but the lights shining in her eyes made it impossible to see beyond the closest faces.

"Not only are we opening our east wing tonight," Fred continued, quieting the applause, "but we are also proud to debut an incredible artistic talent who was, I'm embarrassed to say, right under our noses and managed to stay undiscovered for quite some time."

Fred turned and smiled wide at Chloe. She held her breath.

"Ladies and gentlemen, the Lumina Gallery proudly presents Richard Harlin, and for the first time anywhere, our very own Chloe Sullivan!"

As Fred said her name, the curtain covering the east wing was pulled open, revealing the space beyond. Chloe trembled as the applause and cheers rose from the crowd and she saw her paintings adorning the walls, arranged and lit perfectly. She gasped and blinked away a tear. It was her dream come true, a spectacular, breathtaking moment she had worked for since she'd been old enough to hold a paintbrush.

Suddenly, Fred was in front of her, urging her to breathe. He beamed and patted her shoulder. "I still don't know how you pulled this off. Now, get out there and enjoy it."

Chloe nodded and smiled. The lights readjusted and the attendees flocked into both the main gallery and the east wing. Chloe followed Fred and Richard into the throng, but she'd only just gotten off the stage when she heard Madge.

"Mrs. S! You did it!" Madge pulled Chloe into a tight hug. She feigned being crushed and they laughed together.

"I couldn't have done it without you and David," Chloe said. "Have you seen him?"

"Right behind you." Madge giggled, then turned and practically skipped toward the east wing.

Still dazed from the excitement, Chloe stared after her roommate a moment before turning around. David and Emma both smiled at her.

Emma leaned in first. "Congratulations, Chloe! This is a remarkable achievement."

"Thank you," Chloe replied, grateful that Emma didn't squeeze nearly as tightly as Madge.

Emma turned and eyed Richard, then stepped aside without acknowledging him. David and Chloe stood facing one another, grinning. She felt an overwhelming urge to be close to him, but held herself in check. She still wasn't sure what to think about David being back or whether his disappearance had led to this moment, but for now he was in front of her, smiling, and that meant the world to her. She spread her arms, inviting his embrace.

He pulled her in close, and that familiarity crept into Chloe's heart once more. He gave her one warm, loving squeeze and kissed her near her ear. "I always believed you could do this," he whispered. "I am so proud of you."

David leaned away and released her, and Chloe could tell he was crying even though he tried to hide his tears. She had to wipe one of her own away. David took a handkerchief from his pocket and offered it to her, and Chloe dabbed at her cheek.

A couple of regular collectors approached to congratulate Chloe. David and Emma went ahead of her toward the east wing, while Richard and Fred headed toward the main gallery. At first, the amount of praise and attention Chloe received embarrassed her, as she knew these people to be collectors of exquisite taste, but she eventually relaxed enough to talk freely about her work.

Madge introduced Chloe to a few of her art school instructors, and they had a good laugh about choosing good influences as roommates. The crowd thinned after a time, and Chloe sought out a tray of food as soon as she was able. Her throat was sore from talking, and she sipped at a glass of champagne in an attempt to ease it.

Emma approached and congratulated her again. "This must be exhausting work during a typical opening. I don't even wish to speculate how you must feel tonight, having been responsible for nearly its entirety."

"I'm sure I'll crash later," Chloe admitted. "But right now, I feel great."

"As you should," Emma said. "I believe your work is selling quite well. Every piece is impressive, though there was one painting in particular that caught my attention. It felt familiar somehow."

"Which one?" Chloe asked. Emma began describing it, but they decided to walk over to where it hung instead. On the way, they each fetched a fresh flute of champagne from a passing waiter.

The painting was one Chloe had done not long after moving back to Stroudsburg. "I didn't sleep well for a while," she explained, "so I started leaving the house before sunrise and driving around town. One morning I ended up here, and I sat watching the fog creep around this old train depot. It reminded me a little of a trip David and I had taken down to the New River Gorge. The fog was thick and the tops of the mountains were like islands on a lake of clouds. I wanted to paint it but didn't have my supplies, and he wouldn't let me take a picture to paint it later."

Emma looked surprised. "That seems unlike him."

Chloe nodded and took a drink of champagne. "He said he didn't want to take it with us. He said he wanted that moment to be private. It was strange because I'd never heard him talk like that before. And then..."

Chloe took a deep breath and bit her lip. Emma turned to her inquisitively.

"And then," Chloe said, "he proposed."

Emma grinned. "Are you saying that lovely steak dinner, at which David's parents and I were in attendance, and his classic down-on-one-knee gesture were simply a ruse?"

Chloe laughed. "That was the public version. Truthfully, we were engaged long before that, though David hadn't bought a ring yet or anything." She turned to look at the painting again. "No, we were together early in the morning on a hilltop, watching the fog, when he told me he wanted to marry me."

"I hardly think that constitutes a proposal," Emma teased.

"It was," Chloe said. "I know it was. It was strange, like it was a moment made for us even though we weren't ready for it. But we took it anyway. And when I saw this"—she indicated the painting—"it reminded me of that morning, of him. But instead of making me sad, like almost everything else did back then, I felt weirdly compelled to capture it."

"That may explain why it feels so familiar," Emma said. "It does remind me of David. Speaking of whom, where is he?" She glanced around, looking for him.

Chloe also scanned the crowd. "I haven't seen him since the show opened. I thought he was with you."

Emma shook her head. "He's been distant today. I pressed, but he refused to disclose what was bothering him. After the gala began he seemed content to browse the exhibits alone, so I gave him some space."

"He and I sort of ended things earlier." Chloe pursed her lips. She hadn't really had a chance to process it, and surprised herself with the finality of her statement.

Emma scrunched her face. "Ended things?"

"I mean, not really *ended* like forever, just, um..." Chloe wagged her hand, searching for the words. "We decided to limit our expectations, you know? To take the pressure off while I get my art career moving and he looks for portals to other worlds with my brother."

Emma gave a concerned stare. "How is Thomas involved in this?"

"He's harmless." Chloe made a brush-off gesture. "Tommy just got in David's head a little. I think David still believes he has some obligation to Madison and her daughter."

"And you're fine with this?" Emma arched an eyebrow.

Chloe shrugged. "I don't know, maybe? You know how David is. He won't be satisfied until he either gets an answer or pursues every possibility. As long as he's okay, I'm okay." The words came out easily despite her racing heartbeat. Maybe she had accepted it, after all.

Emma looked about to argue, but Fred interrupted. "Things are going very well tonight," he said. "I know this wasn't an easy week for you, but you've pulled things together quite impressively."

Chloe blushed and thanked him, then introduced Emma.

Fred turned to Emma and shook her hand. "It's a pleasure to meet you in person. You deserve due credit for your investment in this project, as well."

She smiled wide. "I was more than happy to assist. Chloe has been a good friend and I fully understand the importance of this expansion. Her passion has been an inspiration as long as I've known her."

Chloe's blush deepened and Fred winked at her. "I know exactly what you mean. Well, since I have you both here, why don't we proceed with the private showing you requested?"

Chloe's mood fell from elation to dread in an instant. "I suppose it would be best to get it over with." She glanced around the room. "I think David should be there, too."

"Perhaps we'll spot him on the way," Emma said.

Fred led them through the throng from the east wing to the auxiliary room. They stopped several times to receive compliments on both exhibits, and Chloe even took a few offers for her paintings. The success of the opening provided considerable levity, but she still didn't see David, and her anxiety about parting with the Woodburn Hall painting grew with each step.

Emma entered the auxiliary room first, followed by Chloe. Fred closed the door behind them, and they stood in front of a single, lonely easel placed directly below an adjustable track light. The lump in Chloe's throat grew as she stared into the scene, and goosebumps formed on her arms. She closed her eyes and allowed her mind to drift back to that perfect moment when David arrived to help her, how his winsome smile alleviated her frustration and allowed her to create an amazing piece of art that was as much a part of her as the hands that made it.

A tear rolled down her cheek. She wiped it away and turned to Fred. "I don't think I can do this."

"I'm sorry, Chloe, but the painting has already been sold," Fred said.

twenty-seven

Chloe's entire body trembled, and her voice broke as she desperately asked, "What? How?" She looked around the nearly empty room and whispered, "There isn't even anyone here."

"That's an inaccurate assessment, I'm afraid," Emma said.

Chloe turned to her, confused, panicking. "What do you mean?"

Emma remained stoic only a moment more before breaking into a smile. Fred stepped around Chloe and shook Emma's hand. "Congratulations on your acquisition."

Chloe's gaze bounced between them and finally landed on Emma. "You?"

Emma nodded, her face aglow. "I'm purchasing this painting as a gift for some very dear friends of mine."

Chloe's sobs broke into a laugh, and she threw her arms around Emma. "Thank you! Thank you so much!"

Emma squeezed Chloe in return. "You are most certainly welcome."

"When I saw the contract you'd drawn up on my desk this morning, I had a feeling something was amiss," Fred said. "Because Emma had invested in finishing the east wing and I knew she was a friend of yours, I contacted her to ask about the painting."

Emma and Chloe separated from their embrace. "I informed Fred of my opinion that you would never willingly sell that particular piece, and we came to an arrangement."

"The gallery will compensate Emma for her investment in

the east wing with funds in the amount of her contribution plus one Chloe Sullivan original painting," Fred said.

Chloe still couldn't believe it. She hugged Fred and thanked him and Emma profusely.

"David told me what transpired this morning," Emma said. "I find it absolutely despicable that Richard would force you to execute a contract on such a meaningful piece."

Fred pressed for an explanation, and Chloe rolled her eyes. "He threatened to pull out of the opening tonight unless I agreed to sell that painting."

"Why this particular painting?" Fred asked.

"I suspect Richard became aware of that piece's significance in Chloe's history with David," Emma said.

Fred scowled and balled his fists. "That son of a bitch! I gave him the best commission rate in the country for this show, and he would cross me for a petty lovers' quarrel?"

Emma put a hand on Fred's shoulder. "Fortunately, circumstances developed in our favor."

Fred took a deep breath and relaxed. "Very true. Still, when I spread word of this attempted stunt he'll be hard pressed to negotiate favorable terms in this city for quite some time." He turned to Chloe. "You, on the other hand, will always be welcome here. I realize this opening could be your first step toward a full-time art career, but I hope you'll stay on as gallery manager awhile longer. Even if you don't, please contact me first any time you're ready to do another show."

"Thank you," Chloe said, blushing. "And yes, I plan to continue managing the gallery." She laughed and added, "Who else is going to do it? Conner?"

Fred joined in her laughter. "Maybe one day, if he pays attention and learns from your example." He turned toward the painting. "So, I'm dying to know now, what's the story behind this piece? The technique is excellent, by the way. There's so much more to it than the building. I can tell it was windy when you painted this, and yet there's a tranquility here."

Chloe's breathing quickened, and her heart pounded against

her ribs like a desperate prisoner against iron bars. "It was the day we met," she said. "David was with me while I painted it." She told him about the wind, David stopping to help her, and how they talked and shared a perfect moment together.

"I have always adored that story," Emma said.

Fred didn't react at first. He squinted and analyzed the painting instead. "You said David was holding your easel?"

Chloe sniffled. "Yeah, why?"

"Where was he standing?"

Chloe hesitated, then allowed herself to be taken back to that day in Woodburn Circle, even as she resisted her feelings for David. She remembered his easy smile, his gentle admiration and encouragement, his genuine desire to help and to get to know her. She walked around to the backside of the easel, situating herself such that when viewed from the front she would be behind the right side of the canvas. "He was about here. Where are you going with this?"

Fred's face lit up with a wide grin. He turned to Emma and asked, "Do you see it?"

Emma shook her head. "I'm afraid not. See what?"

Fred raised his eyebrows and turned to Chloe. "David is in this painting. He's in all your paintings."

Chloe squinted at him. "What are you talking about?"

Fred motioned with his head, beckoning her to come around to the front of the easel again. "Do you remember when we were discussing the signature in your work?"

Chloe flinched. "The shadow thing? I told you, it's not a signature."

Fred chuckled. "Right, right, it's just a coincidence there was a shadow the same shape and size in the same place in all those paintings." As Chloe arrived beside him, he pointed to an area near the bottom of the image, right of center. "And I suppose it's also a coincidence that the very same shadow in this painting corresponds exactly with where David was standing."

Chloe leaned in closer to the canvas. The shadow was indeed there, and like her other paintings she'd not noticed its presence before Fred pointed it out to her. She mentally mapped the area around Woodburn Circle, placing the buildings, trees, and light posts, accounting for the time of day and the weather, trying to figure out anything else that could have made that shadow.

"Admit it, Chloe," Fred said. "That's David's shadow."

"I'm convinced," Emma said.

Chloe sighed. "Okay, fine. You're right, there's nothing else that could have made that shadow. But David was there, and if he cast a shadow I would have painted it."

"And when he wasn't physically there, you felt him, and you added his shadow," Fred said. "You're a talented artist, but your finest work comes out when you open your heart and give yourself over completely to the moment, and David is obviously what helps you do that. He brought out the very best of you."

Chloe thought back to her time in the Poconos, the long hikes and painting sessions that reinvigorated her passion for art, when she thought she was getting over David's absence. She had been able to completely let go then, to open her heart to the moment and feel her way through each scene, placing colors and strokes by instinct, losing herself in a rush of emotion that drove her to levels of expression she'd never touched before. As she recalled those moments, she tried to focus on the spot Fred had identified in her paintings.

An overwhelming presence coursed through her, flooding her body with warmth. "He was there," Chloe sobbed. "He was always there." She quaked with the realization that she had succeeded in spite of David's disappearance, not because of it.

"I now understand why all the work in your exhibit feels so familiar." Emma dabbed at her own eyes.

"We have to find David," Chloe said. "I have to tell him about this. I have to tell him I still love him."

Emma laughed. "Someone told me earlier you two had decided to 'end things,'" she teased.

Chloe rolled her eyes. "Someone obviously didn't know

what she was talking about." She led the way out of the auxiliary room and into the gala crowd. Emma headed for Richard's exhibit while Chloe searched the east wing, and when they met back in the lobby neither had found David.

Madge approached, munching on an hors d'oeuvre. "Is something the matter, Mrs. S?"

"Have you seen David anywhere?" Chloe asked.

Madge looked thoughtful. "Not for a while. He looked like he was stepping out to make a call last time I saw him."

"Oh no," Chloe said. "He probably went to meet up with Tommy."

Emma pulled out her phone. "I should be able to determine his location using the tracking app I installed on the phone I lent him." A few taps and swipes later, she frowned. "He's in lower Manhattan, just outside the financial district." She stared at Chloe. "Why would he leave without saying anything?"

Chloe groaned in frustration. "He and Tommy wanted to figure out if he could somehow be pulled back to the place he remembers."

Madge gasped. "And you just let him go?"

"You should have mentioned this before," Emma said.

"What?" Chloe asked defensively. "Why are you taking this so seriously? It's not like any of my brother's cult mumbo jumbo is real."

"You said yourself that David is desperate for an explanation," Emma said. "In my experience, desperate people make poor decisions, and we have no notion of just how far Thomas will go to justify his beliefs."

Chloe scoffed. "Tommy doesn't have the initiative to do anything dangerous."

Madge's brow furrowed. "Are you really willing to take that chance?"

The question fanned a spark of worry in Chloe's chest. She took in the scene around her, a portrait of the life and career she'd worked so hard to achieve. This time, she held no reservations about rushing to David's side, her urgent need to tell him how she felt driving all doubt from her mind. "You're right, I should go."

"I'll accompany you," Emma said.

Chloe thanked Emma, then turned back to Madge. "Do you mind working the floor until we get back?"

The young redhead saluted and winked. "It's under control, Mrs. S."

Emma waited by the door while Chloe told Fred what was going on. He implored her to be safe and return as quickly as possible. She had nearly reached the exit when Richard called to her.

"He left you again, like I told you he would." Richard smirked as he stepped closer to Chloe. "And now you're going to abandon your career yet again, to go chasing after a pitiful excuse of a man who doesn't care a thing about your dream."

"You know what?" Chloe took an aggressive step toward him, only to have Emma's arm bar her from going any further.

"I advise against striking him, though I would gladly testify on your behalf should you choose to do so," Emma said.

Chloe grinned at her. "Don't worry, the only thing I'm going to hurt is his ego."

Richard crossed his arms. "This should be good."

"Ah yes, the wildly successful artist thinks he has it all figured out," Chloe taunted. "You spend so much time and energy observing and analyzing people, but you never really understand them. Do you want to know why?"

Richard rolled his eyes and gestured for her to go on.

"Because you're always looking at them and never through them," Chloe said. "All these stories of social strife and political unrest are told from a single viewpoint: yours. It's the same reason you can't maintain a serious relationship, because you only measure the other person against your own expectations. I really thought you wanted to see me grow as a painter, but now I know your idea of an artist is someone exactly like you."

"I think I have a pretty good idea of what an artist is,"

Richard argued. "If you don't believe me, ask any one of these fine people who came to see my opening. They certainly didn't attend this event hoping some unknown landscape painter would show up instead."

Chloe heard someone make an "ooooh" sound, and she noticed a crowd had gathered around their argument. Richard reveled in the attention and invited Chloe's retort.

"The only art you understand and appreciate is your own," Chloe said. "You'll never be any more than what you already are."

"What I already am is pretty damned good, if I do say so myself. All you've ever done is talk about how you always dreamed of being an artist," Richard mocked. "You keep dreaming, but I'd rather live it."

"My dreams are bigger than you," Chloe said. "Your one-note song will get old eventually, and then what will you do? What happens when people don't want to be shocked any-more? Do you think your art has ever made anyone weep? Laugh? Ever tried to give your audience a sense of peace? Of purpose? Of joy? No, because your art is all about what you can see. Mine is about what you can feel, and I can create that be-cause unlike you, I understand that there's more to this life than making things that sell."

The crowd grew as Richard's and Chloe's voices got louder, and the gala guests murmured among themselves and looked to Richard for a riposte. His narrowed eyes betrayed his otherwise neutral countenance.

He walked toward the entrance to the east wing, where *Chloe's Journey* was displayed. "What about this piece? This isn't shocking or social commentary. In fact, you told me yourself that you loved it."

Chloe joined Richard in front of the canvas. "And when you saw my doodles of it, you went insane because they didn't match exactly what you had painted. You accused me of alter-ing your vision, when it was supposed to be about my life."

"Why don't you enlighten us, then?" Richard looked

around. "Where's Lumina?"

Fred stepped forward from the crowd and crossed his arms, looking stern. "I hope you two are enjoying this little spectacle."

As Fred's gaze met hers, Chloe mouthed the word, "Sorry." Fred then fixed his scowl on Richard.

"I'll just need a moment more, and then we can all get back to the party," Richard said. He asked Fred if anyone had purchased *Chloe's Journey*.

"Not to my knowledge," Fred responded. He called for Conner, who confirmed that no offers had been made on the painting.

"Thank you." Richard turned back to Chloe. "Since no one else has claimed it, the painting is yours. Let's not forget that when I first showed it to you, you didn't want me to sell it at all."

"I assumed it was a gift," Chloe said, making sure to speak loudly enough for the crowd to hear. "How silly of me."

"Well, it is now. It's yours. You can make whatever alterations you want. So why don't you show us all how you would improve upon my work?" Richard stared at her, waiting, his face fixed in that expressionless way that Chloe now saw as a mask.

He'd put her on the spot, and Chloe needed to say or do something. She looked to the crowd, then back to the painting, and as she followed the swirling strokes of color stolen from her own palette, the work felt less like an homage and more like derision. Richard didn't actually understand her or what she'd been through; he had simply copied elements from her own paintings and taken ownership of her struggle.

She hated it.

Chloe balled her fists as anger quickened her breath and tightened her muscles. She glowered at Richard, and he offered a smug smile in return. Lashing out at him would be futile, and punching him would only lead to more trouble, but her rage demanded release. Chloe's eyes drifted back to the painting, and she found her outlet. She bent down, removed her right shoe, and slashed through the canvas with the heel. The crowd gasped.

"What are you doing?" Richard's mouth hung open.

Chloe grinned wickedly. "I'm just adding my emotional response to your work, like you asked."

She continued hacking at the painting, her teeth gnashing, her rage boiling over. When she finished there was little left but the wooden frame. She put her shoe back on and glared toward Richard, who eventually broke her gaze and looked downward. Satisfied, Chloe turned and left the gallery with Emma.

twenty-eight

Chloe leapt out of the car as soon as it stopped, leaving Emma to pay the driver. She rushed toward the derelict storefront where they had tracked David's phone, convinced by the light leaking through the boarded-up windows that he and Tommy must be inside. The blacked-out glass door stuck at first, then came open with a loud squeak. Without waiting for Emma to catch up, Chloe charged in and called for David.

"Chloe?" His voice came from farther inside, beyond where Chloe could see. There was little light, as most of the overhead fixtures had been stripped of bulbs, and high piles of boxes and various junk blocked her view in all directions.

She picked her way through the mess as quickly as she could without tripping. "Where are you? Are you okay?"

"Chloe, get out of here!" David yelled, his voice closer.

"I'm not leaving without you," Chloe called back. She stepped around a few high shelves that had been pushed together, then fear brought her to an abrupt halt.

David stood with his hands raised in the air. He slowly turned his head and looked apologetically at her.

"Don't move!" Tommy stepped into Chloe's line of sight, his small pistol leveled at David's chest. He kept his eyes on David and asked, "What are you doing here, sis?"

Chloe could hardly believe what she was seeing. "Tommy? What the hell are you doing?"

"Cleaning up your mess," Tommy said. "I didn't want it to come to this, but if you and David are both still alive and not in love it creates some real problems, and I can't let that happen. I swore an oath—"

"But I am in love with him," Chloe cried. David turned and met her gaze, and tears formed in her eyes. "I never stopped. I know that now."

"Chloe, I—" David started.

"But he's not in love with you," Tommy said, his eyes wild. "He still wants to go back to the other world." Tommy poked David in the chest with the pistol. "Don't you?"

"Stop it!" Chloe had to stop this somehow. She stepped toward them, but froze when Tommy pointed the gun at her.

"Don't come any closer," he ordered. "I can't have you interfere with this." He aimed the pistol back toward David.

"This is insane!" Chloe shouted. "It's all bullshit, you know. There's not some kind of mystical power, there's not another world, and there's no reason to kill anyone."

"David believes in the other world," Tommy said. Then, to David, "I'm sorry I couldn't send you there. This is the only option left."

David's expression mixed fear and regret. "I should have listened to you. I just wanted to know for sure that I wouldn't hurt you again."

Chloe's heart pounded. After everything she'd been through to rebuild her life, deal with David's reappearance, and finally understand how much he meant to her, she wasn't about to lose him now. She strode toward David, eyeing Tommy the whole time, not stopping even as he pointed his pistol at her. She stood between Tommy and David, her arms spread.

"What are you doing?" David asked.

"I'm not going to let him kill you," she said. Then, to Tommy, "You'll have to kill me first."

"Chloe, don't do this," David said.

Tommy grabbed one of Chloe's arms with his free hand and tugged her out of the way. She resisted, but he was stronger than she expected. Chloe lost her balance and fell to the floor. Tommy hesitated, and a worried look crossed his face.

David took the opportunity to try and wrestle the gun from Tommy's hand, forcing his arm upward. A shot fired into the ceiling.

Tommy gained the upper hand and knocked David away from him. He leveled the pistol at David's chest again. "Nature must be kept in balance. I'm sorry."

"No!" Chloe screamed.

Suddenly, Emma stepped behind Tommy, emerging from out of nowhere, wielding a piece of two-by-four. She swung the board and connected with the back of Tommy's head, knocking him to the ground, unconscious. David kicked the gun away and it slid across the floor, lost under a pile of junk.

Chloe scrambled to her feet and threw herself on David, squeezed him as tightly as she could, and kissed him hard on the mouth. He returned her affection, and the two of them held each other close for a long moment.

"Are you okay?" David finally asked.

Chloe nodded. "You?"

"Yeah."

Chloe looked over David's shoulder to where Emma had knelt down to check on Tommy. She pulled out of David's embrace. "Is he...?" As awful a thing as her brother had done, Chloe still hoped he was all right.

Emma smiled. "He'll have a nasty bump and an excruciating headache when he wakes, but he should be fine."

David turned and pulled Emma into a tight hug. "Thank you." He let her go and turned back to Chloe. "Both of you. I honestly had no idea Tommy would do anything like that."

"Me neither," Chloe said. She was still catching her breath from the excitement, but as the adrenaline abated her original purpose for finding David came back into focus.

She took his hand in both of hers. "I need to tell you something. When we were looking at the Woodburn Hall painting tonight, I saw something I'd never noticed before. I realized that no matter how many years it's been or what we've had to go through on our own, we belong together. I'm just not me without you."

David smiled and tears glistened in his eyes. "But look at what you accomplished without me. I always wanted you to be happy, but I held you back."

Chloe shook her head. "You never did. I only got to where I am because of you, because of what you opened up in me. If it hadn't been for you, I couldn't have created the pieces that got me the show. You helped to push me, to make me dig deep down into my heart and have the confidence to be totally honest in every stroke."

"No, you're talented on your own. You don't need me to create amazing paintings," David said.

"It's not about talent," Chloe said. "It's about having someone believe in you. It's about having someone push you. It's about having someone in your life that makes you want to be the best person you possibly can. And you're my someone. You always have been. Ever since that day in front of Woodburn Hall, you've been able to bring out something in me I didn't know was there. When you disappeared and I had to move on, all the love and support you gave me was still there. You were still there. You are in every single painting hanging in my show tonight."

"You're my someone, too," David said. "There's never been anyone else."

Chloe wiped away her tears and kissed him again. As she stepped back and remembered where they were, a sinking thought settled in. "What about Madison?" she asked quietly.

David sighed. "I care about her. I mean, I could never love anyone the way I love you, but..." He closed his eyes tightly and pursed his lips. "It's Candice I'm worried about. Even though I know I'm not her biological father, I still think of her as my daughter. It makes me sick to think I abandoned her."

Emma approached and put a hand on David's shoulder. "The Madison and Candice you think you know are not real. You didn't abandon anyone."

David spun away and took several steps. "They're real to

me. I know it sounds stupid, but if there's no other world then what the hell happened to me? Where was I?"

Emma shook her head. "I don't know."

David wheeled around to face them again. "So, what you're saying is that ten years of my life are just gone. I vanished from the face of the earth for a decade with no explanation and no reason, yet I have all these memories of another life. How the hell are we supposed to move on together if I keep remembering things that never happened?"

"I'm certain there must be some explanation," Emma said. "However, without proof I cannot accept these memories of yours as anything but fabrications."

"I remember the day I met Madison," David said. "I remember the day we moved in together and the first time she told me she loved me. I remember when Maddie took the pregnancy test and we found out she was going to have a baby, and I remember seeing Candice's heartbeat on the ultrasound. We brought her home from the hospital together. I remember her first word, her first step, the first time I read her a bedtime story, the first time she got really sick." He paused and shook his head. "All those moments feel so real, so how could they not have happened?"

Chloe fought tears. It broke her heart that David seemed so happy in a life without her, but she had to be strong for him if they were ever going to move past it. "I can't explain it either, but I'll do whatever I can to help you figure it out."

Emma crossed her arms. "Let's establish some ground truth based upon something we can all agree actually happened. Tell me about being married to Chloe."

David shrugged. "You know all about that." He looked to Chloe. "We were happy, weren't we?"

Chloe smiled. "Very."

"Be more specific," Emma said. "Tell me some distinct memories from the time period in which you were Chloe's husband."

"Well, let's see..." David rubbed at his chin a moment. "We

got this bread maker as a wedding present, and we didn't use it for almost a year. When we did finally try it, the stupid thing shorted out halfway through making the bread, so we put it back in the box and tried to return it." He chuckled. "It would have worked, too, if the store clerk hadn't smelled the fried circuit board through the box."

Chloe laughed along. "I told you we needed to let it air out another day."

"Good," Emma said. "What else?"

The bread maker story reminded Chloe of another kitchen-related incident. "Remember that time we tried making pasta from scratch?"

"What a disaster." David rolled his eyes, then told Emma the story. "We tried to do the thing with the pile of flour and mixing the eggs in right on the counter. Well, the first attempt ended up on the floor, and our water was boiling so we hurried up and mixed some more in a bowl and cut it into these ridiculously wide strips. We threw those in the water and then started cleaning up the mess we'd made, and before we knew it the water was boiling over!" He laughed out loud.

"Then you tried to move the pot off the flame," Chloe added, also laughing. "It's a wonder you didn't burn your hands off."

"I panicked, okay? It seemed like a better idea than trying to scoop the water out with a plastic cup."

Chloe feigned indignation. "It was the first thing I could get my hands on, you know?"

"I have a new understanding of why I wasn't invited to more dinner parties at your house," Emma joked. As their laughter petered out, she asked David to tell her something about Chloe's art.

David thought a moment. "You remember how we remodeled the den in our house to be her studio? A lot of times she'd close the door while she was in there, but not always. I remember how sometimes I'd walk by and see her in there, so focused, so happy, and I'd just stand and watch, and I never thought she noticed me doing that, until this one time I caught her winking at me. She told me later she'd always winked at me. Every time. And she thought it was hilarious that it took me so long to notice."

Chloe's lip quivered. "I had forgotten all about that."

David took her hand and squeezed. "It's okay. It was just a little, silly thing."

She wiped away a tear. "I know, but it really was funny. I loved those little moments we had together."

David smiled lovingly. "Me too."

They stood spellbound by one another until Emma interrupted. "So, do you notice any differences between the memories you have of this alleged other world and the memories of your marriage to Chloe?"

She didn't follow Emma's line of questioning, but it did comfort Chloe to know David remembered their relationship so fondly. She believed he would choose her over Madison in a heartbeat, but that didn't solve the Candice problem.

"Chloe and I were together a lot longer," David said. "Plus, once Candice was born everything pretty much revolved around her."

Emma smiled. "That's not an answer, David."

He put his hands on his hips and gave Emma an impatient look. "You already know, don't you?"

"Of course I do," Emma said. "However, I believe it's rather important that you reach this conclusion yourself."

David sighed and looked to Chloe, who shook her head. "Sorry," she said. "I've got nothing."

He turned back to Emma. "Can I at least have a hint?"

"When you started listing memories of Madison and Candice, you named a lot of milestones," Emma said. "Then you told me a story about you and Chloe and a bread maker. Is there an equivalent story with Madison?"

"We didn't have a bread maker," David said wryly. He paused before adding, "At least, I don't think so."

He looked troubled, and Chloe squeezed his hand. She

tried her best to comfort David while steeling herself against whatever story he would tell about a mishap or everyday adventure involving Madison and Candice. It didn't help matters when she noticed he was wearing the wedding band.

"I can't come up with anything," David admitted after a long moment.

Chloe exhaled and tried not to let her relief show.

Emma paced slowly, her courtroom demeanor fully engaged. "The stories about the bread maker and the pasta both involved unfortunate circumstances, yet you think of them with fondness. Why do you suppose that is?"

David and Chloe turned to each other and answered instantly, simultaneously. "Because you were there."

A sob escaped on Chloe's breath, and she buried her face in David's chest, pulling herself as tight as she could against him. His hands caressed her back while she listened to his heart beating fast and strong.

"And?" Emma asked. Chloe turned her head to see Emma gesturing him to elaborate.

"And because we were in love," David said. "And when you're in love, it's the little things that stay with you. Even when everything goes wrong, there are always those little moments you can laugh about later, and they make the best stories."

Chloe loosened her embrace just enough for her lips to reach David's. They smiled at one another, and then his eyes went wide and he staggered backward a step.

"Madison and I never had any of those, at least not that I remember." David raised one hand to his forehead and squeezed. "I can't remember anything like that with Candice, either. Not a single one. You'd think there would be a funny diaper change story or something but..."

He trailed off, and Emma finished the thought for him. "Whoever provided you with these false memories only gave you the outline of the story. You were given milestones, including a fake wedding ring, and left to fill in the blanks with assumptions."

David's breathing quickened and he staggered again. Chloe rushed to his side and attempted to hold him up. Emma found a box sturdy enough for him to sit on, and Chloe lowered him onto it.

"It's okay," Chloe said. "We're here. Just breathe." She couldn't even begin to imagine what must be happening in his mind, his belief in the other world having been picked apart and challenged by Emma's clever argument.

David recovered enough to lift his gaze to them. "So, it was all some kind of trick?"

"That is my hypothesis, yes," Emma said.

"It's getting blurry now, all of it," David said. "It's almost like it was all a dream, somehow. And I think I get it." He looked directly into Chloe's eyes. "What I really wanted the whole time was you. All the little moments we had, all the good and bad times we went through together, all the code words and inside jokes we shared, those somehow got mixed up and rearranged into these fake memories. But in my heart, I think I always knew that it was you, that it was us."

Chloe's heart overflowed with joy. He hadn't stopped loving her, either. She pulled him into another firm kiss that left them both gasping for air.

twenty-nine

Chloe and David turned when they heard Tommy moan. He sat up and reached for the back of his head, wincing as his hand made contact. "What happened?"

Emma stood over him. "You attempted to kill David, so I was forced to subdue you."

Tommy squinted. "What? No, I didn't."

"You had a gun," Chloe said, exasperated.

Tommy tried to lean forward and look for the weapon, but groaned and closed his eyes. "It was loaded with blanks."

"Blanks?" Chloe exchanged a look with David and remembered how scared she'd been when she thought he might be killed. "Why the hell would you do something like that? Did your cult put you up to this?"

Tommy attempted to stand but couldn't get to his feet on his own. Emma and David helped him up and guided him to sit on a box while Chloe stood there fuming. She wanted to smack her brother, but seeing him hurt stayed her anger.

"It was a last-ditch effort to push the two of you together. While we feared a grave imbalance in the world energies if you didn't choose one another, the Brotherhood doesn't murder people." Tommy looked apologetically toward David, then back to Chloe. "I'm sorry, but it was the only way."

"Only way to what, give me a heart attack?" Chloe turned away, replaying the encounter in her mind, her adrenaline surging anew. She wheeled on Tommy. "You threw me down!"

David put an arm around her shoulders, pulled her close,

and kissed her forehead. She leaned into him, still angry but calmer.

"I'm sorry I had to take things this far, but it worked." Tommy smirked and pointed at David and Chloe. "You guys are back together, the way it should be. Balance has been restored."

Chloe groaned. "Will you stop with all this talk about energy balance and alternate realities? This isn't funny!"

"I know the other world isn't real," David said. "Emma helped me accept that, and the memories are starting to fade away."

Tommy shot a glare at Emma. "How else do you explain everything that's happened?"

"David's memory was falsified," Emma said. "I theorize that he was abducted and forcibly subjected to some kind of suggestive stimulus, though the motivation to do such a thing still escapes me."

"You said yourself that there are other brotherhoods out there," Chloe said. "One of them could have kidnapped him."

"That was my original suspicion, but I ruled it out for a couple reasons," Tommy said. "First, David's memories were scattered and incomplete. If you're going to all the trouble of abducting someone to alter their memories, you probably want those memories to stick."

"That doesn't completely eliminate the possibility, as there are numerous other factors," Emma said. "The memory alteration process may have been flawed, for example."

Tommy turned to her. "That brings me to my second reason. Madison's dreams were vivid enough to remember, but didn't convince her to pursue a romantic relationship with David. The dreams made her just comfortable enough to allow them to talk through the situation as friends, but nothing more. If I were a shady group trying to keep David and Chloe apart, I'd want Madison to be a viable temptation."

Chloe tensed at the thought of David settling into a life with Madison and Candice. She wondered if those jealous feelings would ever go away.

David gave her a reassuring squeeze. "I know it was a little weird, but talking things through with Madison on Wednesday actually helped a lot. She could relate to what I remembered, which let me relax and accept that I had somehow changed over the last ten years. My anxiety doesn't bother me as much anymore, and I even felt comfortable enough to take the bus to New York so I could help you."

"That's exactly my point," Tommy cut in. "Rather than drive a wedge between you and Chloe, Madison's dreams actually did the opposite. She helped you accept the passage of time and empathize with Chloe's struggles in your absence. Plus, when you and Madison met with the channeler, I didn't sense any malevolent energy. Therefore, I concluded that another organization didn't send you away to create an imbalance."

Emma rolled her eyes. "Thank goodness you cleared that up. I'm certain your alternate explanation will be just as fascinating."

Tommy ignored her and addressed Chloe. "Remember the vision I had the other day, about you and David meeting later in life? Your getting together in college was probably not just the result of an imbalance in the world energies, but also caused a further shift. I believe fate took corrective action to make sure you two were not just together, but together at the right place and time. The resulting anomaly manifested as David's other world."

Chloe flinched. "So, to be together now, we had to be apart for ten years?" She glanced at David, who looked equally confused. "That doesn't make any sense."

"Plus, I know the other world wasn't real," David added.

Tommy addressed Chloe first. "You're soul mates; it's your destiny to be together. However, to properly affect the binding forces and reestablish balance, fate decided that you had to be separated for a while so you could reconnect here and now." Turning to David, he continued, "Our current theory is that the other world isn't a physical place so much as an arrangement of energy, like a lucid dream or a very immersive simulation. Though you were physically removed from this world, nothing you experienced there was real. Now that balance has been restored, the energy is dissipating, and your memories are fading."

"This is all superlatively far-fetched," Emma said.

Tommy squinted at her. "And your theory about an evil entity that abducted David, partially brainwashed him, and ineffectively altered Madison's dreams isn't?"

"I never held that to be a definitive conclusion," Emma said. "It is, however, vastly more plausible than your supernatural fantasies. You might as well have claimed that extraterrestrials absconded with David to another galaxy."

David chuckled, and Chloe grinned at him. As crazy as Tommy's ideas sounded, she did appreciate the sentimentality behind them. It had only taken her and David a week to feel as close as they had before he vanished, despite the fact that he'd reappeared wearing a ring with another woman's name on it.

The thought gave her pause, and prompted her to ask Tommy, "If nothing in the other world was real, where did David's other wedding ring come from?"

Tommy faced David and broke into a mischievous grin. "Have you looked at it lately?"

David held his left hand in front of him. "What, the ring? It's right he—" He froze a moment, and his eyes went wide. "No way," he whispered.

Chloe leaned in to look, but just caught a glimpse before David pulled it from his finger. He held it closer to his face, turning it to study the inscription inside the plain gold band that looked a lot like...

Chloe gasped. "Is that...?"

David turned to her, shock lingering in his eyes even as the corners of his mouth crept into a wide smile. "Yeah. It is."

He handed her the ring, and Chloe examined it closely. Without a doubt, she now held the very token she had given David at their wedding, engraved with the words, "I'll Stand By

You 10-27-2002."

"Well?" Emma asked, sounding impatient. "What's so exciting?"

"It's our wedding ring," David said. "From when Chloe and I were married."

Emma approached and Chloe handed her the ring. She inspected it briefly, then looked at David with disbelief. "Where did you find this?"

He took the ring back and shook his head. "I was wearing the other one, the fancy ring with Madison's name inside," David said. "Tommy had me put it on while he tried to sense the other world."

Chloe, David, and Emma all turned to Tommy, who crossed his arms and wore a smug smile. "You had it the whole time. The influence of the other world changed the ring's appearance. Now that the energy has dissipated, you can see its true form."

David shared a bewildered look with Chloe, and she knew they were wondering the same thing: could Tommy have been right all along?

"This is preposterous," Emma argued. "Your statements about metaphysical energies and alternate realities are firmly rooted in mysticism and completely without merit." Though her tone was firm and her jaw set, doubt haunted Emma's eyes.

Tommy swept his arms outward dramatically. "There's more to heaven and earth than...something...and philosophy?" He looked to Chloe for help with his faltering Shakespeare.

She sighed. "Close enough. We'll blame the concussion."

Emma took a step toward Tommy and demanded to know, "Who put you up to this?"

Tommy shook his head, and his smile wilted under Emma's accusing glare. "No one put me up to—"

"This is obviously some sort of trick, and I refuse to believe you acted alone," Emma said, her voice quavering. "I refuse to believe any of this nonsense."

David grasped Emma's shoulder. "Hey," he said with a

soothing voice. "It's okay. Calm down."

Emma spun to face him, her expression intense. "Thomas had multiple opportunities to handle and switch that ring, did he not?"

David offered her a patient smile. "Yes, but you'll never get him to admit he did."

Emma glanced over her shoulder at Tommy, who had tensed for another volley. She took a deep breath and turned back to David. "I suppose you're right," she said, sounding defeated. "At this rate, we may never ascertain the true cause of your disappearance."

"Maybe we'll figure it out someday." David shrugged and smiled at Chloe. "Or maybe we won't. It doesn't really matter." He extended his arm and kissed Chloe as she stepped into his embrace. "The most important thing is that we have each other, no matter what happens from here on out."

A warm wave of happiness washed over Chloe's entire body. She beamed at David, soaking in his easy smile through tear-laden eyes. She leaned in to kiss him again, but her phone rang. She and David froze, looked at each other, and burst into laughter.

Emma chuckled along. "Any call that interrupts such a poignant moment must be exceptionally important. I recommend you take it."

Chloe wiped her eyes and tried to suppress her giggling. She pulled out her phone and gave David a quick kiss on the lips before answering.

"Chloe? Is everything all right?" Fred sounded concerned, but not upset.

"Yeah, we found David and everything's fine," she said, smiling at David. "We were going to head back soon."

"Take your time," Fred said. "Things have calmed down significantly since you trashed Richard's painting."

Chloe winced as a pang of guilt struck her. "About that, I'm really sorry. I was just so upset, you know? I hope I didn't embarrass you."

Fred chuckled. "Don't worry about it. We'll be the highlight of the weekend gossip columns. If you don't mind, I'd like to leave the shredded canvas on display for a while."

Chloe hesitated. She wasn't sure she wanted to see the ruined painting again, but she didn't feel in a position to argue. "Sure, I'll even put one of my shoes on display with it."

Fred laughed. "We'll have to rename the piece *Chloe's Fury.*"

"I'm sure Richard will call it derivative," she joked.

"Well, he had it coming," Fred said. "Anyway, I was going to wait until you got back to tell you this, but what the heck? Conner just told me that your show sold out."

It took a moment for Chloe to fully comprehend the words. "I sold everything?"

"Every single piece," Fred confirmed. "Not only that, but most of your paintings received multiple offers. It's one of the most successful debuts I've ever seen."

Chloe's breath caught and her face lit up with joyful disbelief. David's excitement seemed to match her own, and he gave her a squeeze and a kiss on the cheek.

"You did it! You really did it!" David laughed and tears formed in his eyes.

"Once the gala officially ends, we are going out to celebrate. My treat," Fred said. "And Richard is most certainly not invited."

Chloe laughed. "Sounds good to me." She ended the call and kissed David.

Emma pulled Chloe into a warm hug. "Congratulations! What an incredible achievement."

Tommy stood, but still seemed unsteady. Chloe rushed to his side and put an arm around him. He smiled weakly at her. "Way to go, sis."

"We need to get you to the hospital," Chloe said.

"I'll escort him to the nearest ER," Emma offered. "You and David should return to the gallery, and I'll meet up with you once Thomas has been admitted."

Tommy grinned at her. "I look forward to continuing our

conversation. I'll get through your skepticism yet."

David shared a look with Chloe, then raised an eyebrow at Emma. "How hard did you hit him?"

Chloe chuckled and turned back to Tommy. "Good luck with that. Call me after you see the doctor, especially if it's anything serious." Tommy nodded, and Chloe gave him a little nudge in the side. "I mean it. If you don't, I'll tell Mom and Dad you pointed a gun at me."

David and Emma cleared a path through the abandoned store, removing as much junk as they could so Chloe could help Tommy follow them. They stepped out into the clear, cool night, and David hailed a cab for Emma and Tommy. Once they were on their way to the hospital, David flagged down another taxi for Chloe and himself.

As the cab pulled away from the curb, Chloe looked back at the old boarded-up building, the last place she would have expected to find her true love again. Even though they'd spent much of the week together, she decided that night, when they completely reopened their hearts to one another, was when David truly returned.

"I'm sorry again about leaving the opening," David said. "I should have said something, but I didn't want to ruin your moment. I wanted you to be happy with this incredible life you have."

Chloe took David's hands in hers. "How could I possibly be happy with everything I have if I didn't have you to share it with?"

David squeezed her hands. "I would love to share this life with you." He chuckled and added, "I'm sorry you don't get much out of the bargain. I have pretty much nothing. All you get is me."

Chloe kissed him lightly on the cheek. "It's enough," she said. "It always has been."

THE END

acknowledgements

This novel took about seven years from concept to completion, and because of that it would be impossible to name everyone who has supported me during the process. Suffice it to say, if you are a friend, family member, coworker, or passing acquaintance who ever took a moment to listen to my passionate—and most likely, incoherent—ramblings about David and Chloe and their story, I thank you.

This endeavor began when I decided, on a whim, to attempt National Novel Writing Month (or, as the cool kids call it, NaNoWriMo). Thank you to the organizers, the sponsors, and the vibrant, diverse, and unfailingly positive community who make it possible, including the local friends I've met at "write-ins." Without NaNoWriMo, this novel would not exist.

Through West Virginia Writers, I have learned an incredible amount about writing and made many, many good friends. There are far too many of you to name, and I will not risk leaving anyone out. Thanks to all of you for your inspiration, encouragement, and camaraderie.

Thanks to my editor, Debra Burge, who helped me polish my words and patiently responded to my occasionally defensive ranting concerning certain revisions. You were right about pretty much everything, I admit! I'd also like to thank Sheila Redling for recommending Debra and giving me some awesome writing advice related to *Evil Dead 2.*

Thanks to Ginger Brookover and Anna Eplin for being among my first real writing friends. Thank you, Amber Decker, for inspiring me to try my hand at poetry. While there aren't any poems in this novel, the exercise has definitely improved my writing. Thanks to another amazing poet, Mary Lucille DeBerry, for your enthusiastic words of kindness and support. Jo Ann Dadisman, thank you for your superb writing workshops that are always as enlightening as they are fun.

To my early readers, Geoff Fuller, Candace Jordan, Patricia Patteson, and Elizabeth Seckman, thank you for your time, honesty, and guidance. Each of you brought a unique perspective that made the story a lot stronger, and I'm grateful to have such a talented team. Thanks to Martina Fetzer for reading an even earlier draft and filling it with snarky comments that were both hilarious and helpful.

Thank you, Mom, for raising me to believe I could do anything and pushing me to work hard at everything. Thanks to Paige and Tyler for being the best younger siblings a guy could ask for. You're always there when I need you, and I'm blessed to have such a close and loving family.

Finally, thank you to my amazing wife, Anna. You were there when this crazy idea took shape and gave your unwavering support as I ventured into the world of writing. Thanks for all your love, patience, advice, criticism, inspiration, and the beautiful cover for this book. In short, thank you for being my someone.

about the author

Joshua S. Robinson holds a Master's degree from West Virginia University and works full-time as a systems engineer. He recently rediscovered a love of writing, and was first published in the anthology *Fed From the Blade*. He is a native West Virginian and still lives there with his wife, Anna. This is his first novel.